"Beth? Will you not look at me, my love?" she heard in accents so unlike the duke's usual tones that she looked up startled. He was very close to her, and her eyes widened at what she saw in his dark face. For a long moment he searched her face, and then he bent his head and kissed her.

Whatever she had imagined an embrace to be, she was completely unprepared for the tide of emotion that welled up in her breast. His mouth was warm and insistent on hers, and she kissed him back eagerly. After a long moment he raised his head and smiled at her.

"My love!" he said huskily, and then he gave her a little shake. "You will marry me, do you understand?"

Beth laughed unevenly as his hands tightened possessively on her shoulders. "If you continue to hold me so tightly, I do not see how I will be able to do so!"

Fawcett Crest Books
by Barbara Hazard:

BETH
KATHLEEN

BETH

Barbara Hazard

FAWCETT CREST • NEW YORK

A Fawcett Crest Book
Published by Ballantine Books
Copyright © 1980 by Barbara Hazard

Selection of the Doubleday Romance Library

ISBN 0-449-21397-8

Manufactured in the United States of America

First Fawcett Coventry Printing: August 1980
First Ballantine Books Edition: July 1987

For Linda . . . who believed first

CHAPTER I

The sun could not have been said to rise that cold January morning in 1813; rather, the sky slowly lightened and somewhat sullenly illuminated the landscape. It looked remarkably like more snow before evening, to add to that which already lay thick on the ground, for there had been several falls through December and a blizzard of major proportions on Boxing Day. The inn at the crossroads between Wolverton and the village of St. Edmund-in-the-Field was still and quiet as the day began, although a cock crowed some way off and was answered by a farm dog too cold to huddle in his kennel any longer. Jed Hopkins shivered as he stepped out a side door and paused to check the weather. Best get that lazy stableboy up and fetching wood, he thought, for they would need it today!

There were no guests at the inn at the moment, for it was somewhat off the beaten path, the main post road being some miles to the east. It was a rambling structure with a thatch roof, set low to the ground and

7

not unattractive in spite of the numerous additions that had been attached to it over the years. It was certainly unpretentious with its unevenly set windows and small yard, but it looked comfortable. It had had a reputation as a way station for smugglers in years past, but now relied mainly on local custom and an ale considered superior to that of the other taproom, located in the village proper. Jed had settled down here happily after a musket ball had stiffened his left arm and the Royal Navy had decided he was of no more use to them. He had served during the first American war and was glad now the ball had found its mark, with England again at war with the Americans. He didn't care if he ever saw the sea again, and when he found his older sister and her husband, Henry Griffen, had bought the Bird and Bottle and could use an extra hand, he put away his sea bag and served as waiter, ostler, or bartender with every sign of contentment and quite a bit of competency. The Royal Navy had a way of making a man competent. As he did every morning, he checked the brightly painted sign that creaked on its chains in the wind. The pheasant and the bottle were his work, and he was proud of the results. Jed rubbed his arms in the chill with gnarled hands which showed the marks of his years at sea; the fingers curled as if they still hauled a line or handled a marlinespike. He was of average height, with a grizzled head of graying hair, eyes permanently wrinkled from staring into the sun, and a wide mouth. He was still as lean as he had been when he was a sailor. Shivering again, he hastened to the stables.

A thin plume of smoke curled upward from the kitchen chimney as Bessie began breakfast preparations. Soon Jed carried in a load of wood for her and returned to get some more. Willy, the stableboy, yawning and stretching, also picked up an armload and took it to the taproom, and then he hurried to the kitchen before Henry could appear and give him another chore. Bessie served him a steaming bowl of porridge and passed him the milk pitcher as Jed came in, stamping the snow from his clogs. "Lor, shut the door, do, Jed!" his sister exclaimed. "'Tis a cold morning, and no mistake! Fair goes right through a body!"

Jed grinned at her. "Not so cold it won't snow, m'dear! I expect this will be quite a storm before evening. 'Ow are we set for provisions? If you're short of anything, best fetch it this morning."

Abby, the kitchen maid, and her sister, Jill, brought their bowls to the scrubbed deal table as Henry bustled in.

"Provisions?" he asked. "Why, do you think it will be a big 'un, Jed?" The inhabitants of the inn were used to attending to Jed's weather predictions, for as an ex-sailor he was often right about storms or a spell of fair weather.

"Aye, I think 'twill be bigger than the storm we had on Boxing Day, and last longer as well."

Abby sighed and nudged her sister. They had been promised a day to visit their family on the morrow, but if they were snowed in it would have to be postponed. Henry sat down with a steaming cup of coffee. He was not above medium height, but he was a heavy man, with a red cheerful face and a kindly manner, and Bessie was as stout and as plain as her husband. Together they made a comfortable pair, and no one who worked at the Bird and Bottle had any cause to complain of ill treatment, so it was a companionable group who gathered to eat breakfast.

Henry set down his coffee cup. "As for supplies, we should be fine," he said, considering the situation. "Even if the rooms were full, which I don't hardly expect! Well, we shall have a nice quiet time of it, no doubt, and although it's 'ardly good for custom, I don't regret it."

Neither did Willy, to whom guests meant more work than usual, or the good-natured Bessie, and Jed cared not a whit one way or the other, but as it turned out, a quiet time was not to be. Even now the actors in the play

9

were assembling and setting out on their various journeys that would lead them all to the little inn.

The snow began sometime before noon. At first, only a few fat lazy flakes fell, but in a very short time the snow was falling in earnest, covering the mud of the stableyard, the manure pile behind the barn, and all the paths with a fresh clean coating of white. In an hour the wind rose and began howling around the eaves. Abby and Jill gave up looking out the windows and resigned themselves to the delay of their visit, and Jed set Willy to clearing the paths. Willy saw no sense in keeping the paths open, and would have waited for the storm to pass before worrying about them, but both Jed and Henry knew how quickly their isolation could end and wanted to be ready, just in case; so it was Willy alone, reluctantly wielding his broom, who saw the strange procession that struggled up to the inn through the storm. He stopped work gladly and gaped.

Coming from the direction of the main post road, three bundled-up figures appeared, leaning forward against the wind and the snow. The largest by far was a middle-aged lady of surprising girth, who, besides wearing a voluminous purple traveling cloak trimmed lavishly with fur, appeared to wrapped in a blanket. She was supported on one side by a footman in gold livery, and on the other by a slight young girl also richly dressed, but none too warmly, to judge by her shivers. The footman's face was blue with cold, and his thin-gloved hands shook. Willy shut his mouth to hide a grin as the large lady slipped a bit and nearly took her two attendants down with her. They managed to steady her, however, and as they stopped to catch their breath, the lady looked up and saw the inn and Willy leaning on his broom.

"At last! You, boy! What are you gaping at? Come here this instant and help us!" the older woman commanded, in a piercing voice. Willy hastened to her side and took the place of the young girl. The large

10

lady, who had not stopped talking the while, ordered her to the inn.

"Go ahead, Letty, and tell them to prepare a private parlor, and a hot drink. I swear we shall perish with the cold if we do not get out of these wet clothes! We shall need the best private rooms, and someone must ride instantly to the coach to fetch our baggage. You, James!" she addressed the shivering footman. "You shall have to borrow some clothes, for you are no good to us at all dead, and dead you certainly will be if you do not get dry. However, the baggage must be fetched first; see to it! I do not know how I was ever persuaded to drive on this morning; any fool could tell this was going to be a major storm, and as for Captain Alwin's coach! I shall have something to say to that gentleman when next we meet. . . ."

She continued to scold as Letty ran ahead to the inn door, where she collided with Jed, coming out to see if Willy had finished the paths.

"Why, miss," he exclaimed, assisting her inside, and catching sight of the group that followed. "Why, here's a to-do! Come here near the fire and warm yourself." He helped her to a rough settle in the taproom and hastened away to call Henry and Bessie. Letty tried to relay her instructions, but he was gone in an instant. Gratefully, she held out her gloved hands to the fire, too cold to even remove her stylish bonnet and cloak, now somewhat the worse from the storm. A moment later, she heard her mother's loud voice and hastily rose to go and help her. As she gained the door, she saw this would not be possible, for the hall was full of people. The footman leaned exhausted against the wall, Willy stood cravenly still under the large lady's gloved hand, Bessie tried to remove the blanket wound about her, and Henry rubbed his hands and tried to get a word in edgewise. Jed took one look from the back of the hall and hurried away to start some water heating and send the two maids scurrying upstairs to prepare some rooms and start the fires. The lady finally stopped

11

of necessity, to take a breath, and Henry managed to speak.

"Ma'am! Please let me help you in here, before the fire. You must be frozen!"

"Frozen! Just about, landlord, I do assure you. I have struggled through this storm for what seems like hours, and for one in my precarious health, it may well be *the end*. You, James! Make yourself useful, man! Take away this horse blanket at once!"

The footman pushed himself away from the wall just as Bessie untied the knot holding the blanket around the lady, and managed to extricate her from it. She dropped the wet blanket to the floor and escorted the lady to the taproom door, where Letty was waiting.

"Not here, if you please, my good woman! I demanded a private parlor, not a common taproom!" The lady seemed to swell with indignation, from her sodden purple plumes to her damp half-boots.

"Oh, Mama," wailed Letty, ineffectually trying to remove the lady's cloak. "What difference does it make? There is a good fire burning here, and it's warm! Do come in and be comfortable."

Her mother looked at her aghast. "Can it be possible that you have so far forgotten your station as to imagine that either one of us would ever be caught dead in such a place? The Orvis-Ryders have always known their worth, my girl, and don't you forget it! A common taproom indeed!" She turned majestically to Bessie. "A private parlor at once!"

Bessie straightened up from the fire and bobbed a curtsy. "I will 'ave a fire lit immediately, ma'am, but in the meantime, perhaps you would condescend to sit here before the hearth? No one else will come in, I promise, and you should get warm as soon as possible."

The lady bristled and seemed about to continue her demands, but the sight of the glowing flames and crackling logs sending out such delicious streamers of warmth was too much for her. She strode into the

12

room and collapsed on the settle, saying in a suddenly weakened voice, "My salts, Letty! I fear I am about to have one of *my spells!*"

Letty hastened to her side, loosening the cloak and taking a large reticule from her nerveless hands. As she was searching this for the desired salts and all the other potions her mother habitually carried in case of emergency, Bessie hurried from the room in search of her husband and Jed. How she was going to provide the large lady with a private parlor when the inn boasted no such thing, she didn't know. Perhaps they could put them in the coffeeroom, and use the taproom for any other unlucky travelers who appeared. She found Jed, who told her that the maids were preparing the two front bedrooms, and asked him to build up the fire in the coffeeroom. "Jed, I can see there is going to be trouble about it! Perhaps if we make it as comfortable as possible she won't notice—maybe the large armchair from our room—and I truly don't expect any more guests now that the storm is gettin' so bad," she added, in a disjointed way.

Jed grinned at her. "Aye, she's like a ship of the line, ain't she? Blazin' into battle! You're right, my dear, and she hasn't run out the heavy guns yet, not by a long shot!"

He took himself off to the coffeeroom as a distressed Bessie hastened to the kitchens. Perhaps a hot drink of tea would pacify the lady. She found the footman in front of the fire with a mug of mulled cider, wrapped in the despised horse blanket. He already looked more cheerful as Henry questioned him.

"You say you were on the way to Luton when the axle on the coach broke? How far away did this happen? And what happened to the coachman and the horses?"

The footman took a gulp of his cider. "John Coachman took the team on to the nearest town. There was nothing to be done for the coach, and he knew he could get help there as soon as the storm let up. He

13

also knew, bein' the captain's man, about this inn, and since it was nearer suggested the ladies come here. 'Tis not above two miles from the accident, in spite o' *her* claiming to have walked for hours! Old behemoth!" he snorted, and then added darkly, "Wish I'd gone with the horses! They'd be less trouble than her majesty!"

Bessie began to prepare a tray as she listened. "Henry, we'd best send Willy or Jed for their baggage, before the storm gets any worse. 'Twill be the next thing she wants!" She told him about the lady's demands for a private parlor, and what she had decided to do about it.

The footman chuckled. "Aye, she would want a private parlor, but don't be misled by her royal ways. There's none too much money there, in spite o' her being an Orvis-Ryder, and what there is she squeezes every ounce from! She and Miss Letty were on their way to relatives the old lady hoped to talk into sponsoring the girl in London. To save the expense of an inn, they broke their journey at the captain's; that's why they were traveling in his coach. He was an old friend of her husband's—dead now, poor man, though he is. She probably talked him to death, I always say! Anyway, the captain stood her as long as he could before he hurried her on her way by lending her his town coach. You notice there's no lady's maid with either of them? She's too tight with a farthing to bring a maid along when she can use one where she's staying. I'm just along to give her consequence, as she puts it, and be her dogsbody whenever there's dirty work to do."

He held out his mug to Henry. "That was good, I thank you! Wish I could get into some dry clothes, though."

Bessie left them discussing whose clothes would fit him best, and hurried to the taproom with her tray. She knocked on the door and was bidden to enter. She found the lady divested of her outer clothing, half

14

reclining on the settle, a cushion behind her head. The girl, Letty, had also removed her cloak and bonnet and was hovering around her mother. The afflicted lady was seen to be of surprising weight, even without her cloak. She wore a traveling gown of purple wool, trimmed with heavy lace and adorned with an ornate brooch. Bessie thought to herself that if she would lose some of her weight, the savings in material needed for her gowns would be substantial. She did not look at all unwell; her round face was glowing red as the fire warmed it, and her black eyes snapped as she saw the tea tray.

"Come here, my good woman! Perhaps a hot drink will help me recover from my ordeal, although I have had to wait so long for it to be prepared I began to think you had forgotten my order!"

"Oh, Mama, how can you!" exclaimed Letty.

Bessie stole a glance at the girl and gasped. Never in her born days had she seen such a lovely face! Surely it was unusual that she hadn't noticed it before, but with the fat one making such a fuss . . .

Letty sank down on a footstool near the fire with her tea. Her hair caught the light of the blaze, which turned its delicate golden color to copper. She had a flawless complexion which glowed from the exercise of escorting her mother to the inn, and her features were perfect, from the straight little nose to the rosebud mouth. She was unusual in that her brows and eyes were dark, a startling contrast to her delicate complexion and golden hair, and much more arresting than the usual limpid blue eyes generally found in blondes. She was dressed in the first mode of fashion, in a gown of soft green trimmed with satin ribbons, to match her fur-lined cloak and smart traveling bonnet, which she had laid carefully across the back of the settle. She waved a little hand at her mother and said, "Oh, Mama! Isn't it good to be warm again? And the tea is lovely." She smiled shyly at Bessie in gratitude. Bessie thought that only by her dark eyes would you

15

know her to be related to the other lady. Surely she was as slim as her mother was fat! She turned her attention reluctantly back to Mrs. Orvis-Ryder.

"Your rooms are being prepared, ma'am, and the private parlor, although to be truthful, 'tis no parlor at all!" Bessie had decided to get this over with promptly. Before the lady had time to open an indignant mouth, she hurried on. "We *have* no private parlors, but I have arranged for the coffeeroom to be reserved for your use. I don't expect anyone else in this weather, so you will be quite private. As soon as you have finished your tea, perhaps I might show you to your rooms? Oh, and your baggage will be fetched by the stableboy shortly." She stopped, feeling she had covered all areas that might cause dispute. The lady rose majestically.

"This," she said in quelling tones, "is not at all what we are used to. Let me tell you that *I* am Adelaide Orvis-Ryder, and this is my daughter Leticia. *The* Orvis-Ryders of Durham," she added importantly, as Bessie stood politely unimpressed. Bessie didn't care, and wouldn't know if they were the Orvis-Ryders of *any* county, but she bobbed a curtsy respectfully.

Mrs. Orvis-Ryder moved slowly to the door. "Come, Letty! The sooner we quit these squalid surroundings, the better! I am sure your sainted father would never have imagined that his wife and precious child should ever be reduced to a common taproom! One can only be thankful he has been spared the knowledge of such an indignity. Come, we might as well investigate our lodgings and find out the worst!"

She swept out the door, leaving Letty and Bessie to gather up the cloaks, bonnets, and reticules, with Letty turning a deeper shade of rose, and murmuring, "Oh, Mama!"

Bessie wondered if she ever said anything else, or got a chance to for that matter, as she led both ladies up the steep narrow stairs to her best front bedchambers.

Mrs. Orvis-Ryder sniffed, but made no other comment than to question the dampness of the sheets as she inspected the rooms, so Bessie imagined she must be content, if not overwhelmed by the accommodations, unless she was still out of breath from climbing the stairs. The rooms did look welcoming with their blazing fires and freshly made beds, on which Jill and Abby had spread colorful quilts. The maids appeared with pitchers of hot water and warmed towels for the ladies to wash with, and Bessie hastened away to watch for the baggage before she was given another peremptory order.

Outside, the storm was growing worse, but Jed had no trouble finding the captain's coach when he drove up in the gig, although it lay on its side in a ditch and was fast being covered with snow. There was quite a crowd assembled; Jed could see one man searching the interior, while another man held the bridles of two saddle horses. A little distance away another man and a woman stood at the heads of two horses hitched to a traveling chaise. Jed pulled up his horse just as the man inside stuck his head out the coach door and exclaimed, "No one here, Tony! Yoicks! Gone away! We'll have to try a tantivy!"

"Quiet, Dolph, you idiot!" said the other young man as his companion scrambled agilely from the coach, and then catching sight of Jed, he asked, "Would you know anything about this, my man? No trace of horses, coachman, or travelers—only a prodigious amount of baggage on the roof."

Jed touched his forelock as he got down from the gig and tied the horse to a convenient sapling.

"Aye, sir," he replied. "There were two ladies in the coach, but they are now safe and unhurt at the inn—the Bird and Bottle that would be, about two miles back down this road. The coachman took the horses on to town, and I don't expect we'll see him till this storm is over."

The woman near the chaise dropped the bridle she

was holding and came closer, exclaiming, "Thank heavens no one was hurt! It seemed to be such a serious accident. Did you hear, Father? Everyone is all right!"

Jed peered through the snow and saw that the man left in sole charge of the chaise was somewhat elderly; a slight man dressed in clerical orders, who beamed at the news. Jed turned to Tony and explained, "I've come for the baggage, sir."

"Let me help you," Dolph said, and scrambled back onto the roof of the coach, causing it to sway precariously before it settled deeper on its side in the ditch. Soon he began to hand down various bandboxes, trunks, and parcels to Jed and Tony, who stowed them in the gig. As they worked, Dolph kept up an inane and aimless chatter.

In the meantime, the parson and his daughter were engaged in serious conversation. As Jed secured the last box, he looked down to see the lady shyly smiling up at him. She was warmly covered in a gray cloak and hood and appeared to be past girlhood by several years, although not yet, Jed surmised, at her last prayers. She had a lovely, unself conscious smile.

"Would there be room for us at this inn you mentioned? My father and I are bound for Oxford, and fear we may not make it through the storm."

Jed chuckled. "Not to Oxford, you won't, miss! Aye, there's room and plenty, and ye'd be wise to break your journey till this storm is over. 'Twill be a mighty blizzard afore it's done, or I miss my guess!"

Dolph stopped dusting off his greatcoat and said to Tony, "What say we break our jouney, too, brother? At least until we've had a bite to eat and some warmed ale! 'Pon rep, a carter's job has made me hungry!"

Tony stepped up to his brother, and Jed saw they were twins; as alike as two peas in a pod, he thought, from their fashionably combed blond hair to their high complexions and bright blue eyes. Although not above average height and of slim build, they were a handsome pair, he thought, and young enough to be full of high spirits, no doubt.

Tony frowned and appeared to be thinking. "Well, just for a bit, Dolph. No storm can stop us, and you know we must be on our way shortly. We'll win through, never fear!"

Jed doubted this very much, for the wind if anything was blowing more strongly now, and whipping the snow into high drifts. The breath steamed from the horses' nostrils, and it seemed to be growing colder. The snow, instead of showing signs of stopping, appeared to be gathering strength as the day wore on. It was almost impossible to see the road, for the snow and the wind had obliterated Jed's tracks, and when the little procession started out for the inn shortly thereafter, they were glad to have Jed leading the way. The woman in the chaise put her hand on her father's arm. "I am so glad we decided to stop! I am sure the bishop will understand, Father."

The parson clucked to the horse, and then sighed, "I hope so, Beth, I hope so. But I agree with you; I was getting nervous about the state of the road long before the two young gentlemen caught us up. Perhaps we can continue tomorrow, if the skies clear."

They were almost upon the inn before they saw it through the blowing snow. Jed helped the lady down and told her to go into the inn and get warm, and then he led the others to the stable, calling for Willy as he went.

Beth stood uncertainly for a moment in the hall, shaking the snow from her cloak and putting back her hood. She was of above medium height, with soft brown hair twisted severely into a coil low on her neck. A few tendrils had escaped to curl about her forehead, but somehow one knew that this was not generally allowed. Her face, glowing from the cold, was in no way remarkable. She had a straight nose, a determined little chin, and a mouth too generous for beauty. Her large blue-gray eyes were her best feature.

The severity of her dress and style, and a certain air of competence, made her appear older than her twenty-four years.

Hearing voices, she moved toward a doorway, and seeing it was a coffeeroom stepped over the threshold, looking about her calmly. Letty and her mother were seated in comfortable chairs before the fire, awaiting the arrival of the baggage. Letty gazed into the fire while Mrs. Orvis-Ryder conducted a lengthy monologue, in her overpowering voice. Catching sight of Beth, she stopped abruptly and rose to her full height.

"And what do you want, my good girl?" she asked awfully.

Beth approached the fire and smiled at Letty. "Why, to get warm, to be sure!" she said lightly, beginning to remove her cloak, all unaware that Mrs. Orvis-Ryder had mistaken her for a servant. An indrawn hiss stayed her hands, and she turned to the indignant lady inquiringly.

"Not in here, you won't, miss! This is a private room! The very idea of brazenly coming into our personal parlor!"

Beth looked around the coffeeroom in bewilderment. At the door, Tony stopped his brother with a hand and listened.

"Why, my apologies, ma'am," Beth said, as Letty wailed, "Oh, mama!" in the background. "It appears to be an ordinary coffeeroom to me, open to the public."

Mrs. Orvis-Ryder turned to her daughter furiously. "There, you see, Letty! I knew it would not answer! And after that woman assured us it would be private! And now we are to be subjected to every riffraff who chooses to walk in the door!"

Beth stiffened as Tony decided it was time to intervene. He moved forward, followed closely by Dolph, and bowed to the ladies. Dolph caught sight of Letty, and forgot to make his bow as he stared at her.

"Well, here's more riffraff for you, ma'am," Tony

explained to the indignant Mrs. Orvis-Ryder. "But perhaps it might be more accurate to say 'refugees of the storm'? I am sure you will agree with me. Neither my brother nor I—or this lady—have ever considered ourselves riffraff!" He bowed courteously to Beth, and then continued, "Perhaps an introduction would reassure you? I am Anthony Allensworth, and this is my brother Adolphus." He turned to Beth in inquiry, missing the sudden look of chagrin on Mrs. Orvis-Ryder's face as she learned their names.

"I am sorry, ma'am. I did not catch your name or your father's when we all stopped by this lady's coach to try to assist her." He smiled warmly at Beth, and she smiled back. He *was* an engaging young man, she thought.

After a slight hesitation, she said, "My name is Elizabeth Cummings, sir, and my father is the Reverend Edward Cummings."

Tony bowed again, and poked Dolph, still mesmerized by the lovely Letty, now blushing prettily at his unswerving attention.

"Oh, just so, pleased to make your acquaintance, ma'am," Dolph stammered, dragging his eyes away from Letty and making a hasty but elegant bow. Beth forgot her anger, and a deep dimple quivered for a moment beside her mouth as she tried to keep from laughing. Her gray eyes, stormy a moment before, now twinkled with suppressed laughter. There was an answering twinkle in Tony's eyes as he turned back to a suddenly cordial Mrs. Orvis-Ryder, now smiling warmly at him. Not for nothing had she studied her peerage, and the London papers that carried the smart social news.

"You must forgive me, m'lord," she said. "I had no idea! But ladies traveling alone must be very careful; especially ladies of *our* degree, for I am Mrs. Orvis-Ryder, you know, and this is my daughter, Leticia." She turned ponderously and indicated her daughter, who rose and curtsied.

Tony bowed again to Mrs. Orvis-Ryder, and turning, bowed also to Leticia. His eyebrows rose as he inspected her. Now the fat was in the fire! He'd never be able to drag Dolph away from such startling perfection of face and form, especially into a raging blizzard. He sighed, resigning himself to an indefinite and uncomfortable stay.

Bessie appeared in the doorway, her homely face showing her worry. Mrs. Orvis-Ryder chose to be gracious.

"It is quite all right, my good woman. As his lordship explained to me, we are all refugees from the blizzard. I am sure I have no objection to sharing our private room with members of the nobility, and other . . . er . . . genteel persons." The smallest and stiffest of bows to Beth accompanied this last statement.

"Well, 'tis a good thing, I'm sure, ma'am," Bessie replied in a flustered way, "for where I was to put them otherwise, I didn't know! Oh, your baggage has been fetched, and is in your rooms."

Mrs. Orvis-Ryder beckoned majestically. "Come, m'love," she said to Letty. "We must waste no time in changing these damp garments. I only hope irremediable damage has not already been done." As she swept by Tony and Dolph, she added, "*my health,* you know, *so precarious!*"

As she left the room, shepherding Letty before her, the Allensworths and Miss Cummings were careful not to look at each other or speak, so they heard her quite plainly in the hall, telling Bessie that she expected her bill to be lower since she did not have a private parlor. Beth gurgled and put her hands to her mouth to stop the laughter.

"Wouldn't the duke be amazed to hear us stigmatized as 'riffraff,' Dolph?" Tony asked.

Dolph seemed puzzled. "Don't know why, Tony! He's called us worse than that, himself!"

Tony laughed. "But surely that is different from one of the family, twin!"

22

Beth meanwhile was removing her damp cloak and warming her hands at the fire. She smiled at both young men. "This riffraff thanks you sincerely, m'lords! I must admit it is a new sobriquet for me, too!"

Tony strolled to the fire and looked at her intently. "I am sure it is! You must never mind what the ill-mannered say of you, Miss Cummings, even if they *are* one of the Orvis-Ryders!" Dolph joined them in front of the hearth, his amiable handsome face puckered with thought.

"Yes, but Tony ... should we *know* the Orvis-Ryders? Who are they? Never heard of 'em, myself!"

"Neither have I, dear boy, neither have I! But obviously *quite* important, don't you think? We may count ourselves fortunate to be marooned in such exalted company!"

Tony raised a surprised eyebrow at Beth's hastily suppressed chortle, which caused them both to break into laughter. A few moments later, Dolph joined in. It was a joke!

The Reverend Mr. Commings, having bespoke two rooms for himself and his daughter, followed the sound of the laughter to the coffeeroom, where Beth lost no time in presenting the twins to him. He liked the look of them, so handsome and pleasant, and obviously of high degree although perfectly easy in their manners. It wasn't many minutes, however, before he perceived that although they might be identical in looks, the Lord had come down heavily in favor of Anthony when he divided the brains between them.

The landlord bustled in with mugs of ale and announced that some food would be served shortly. Tony and Dolph assured him there would be no problem about sharing his last bedchamber after Tony tried in vain to get his twin to ride on immediately before the storm got any worse. He knew it would be to no avail with the lovely Leticia snowbound here, but he gave it a valiant try. Mr. Cummings and Beth left to change their clothes while the argument was still in progress, but neither had any doubts of the outcome either, especially since Beth described the other two guests to her father. In a few succinct phrases she painted a vivid picture of the obese, overpowering Mrs. Orvis-Ryder and her beautiful daughter. Mr. Cummings said, "Dear, dear!" And then he added solemnly, "Colossians 4, verse 5, Beth!"

She twinkled at him. "Yes, my dear father, to be sure!"

When everyone was again assembled in the coffee-room, a long afternoon ensued. Tony challenged Dolph to a hand or two of piquet, Mr. Cummings opened a book and heard not a word thereafter, and Beth politely tried to engage the lovely Leticia in conversation, while her mother busied herself with some needle-work and answered all Beth's questions for her daughter. This was perhaps just as well, for it did not take Beth long to realize that Letty's conversation was extremely limited, even had she been given a free hand. Her few remarks were trite, and she seemed to have no interests beyond her clothes, the coming London season, and her beaux. Mrs. Orvis-Ryder informed Beth, or rather all the occupants of the room, since she did not chose to lower her voice, that they were on their way to visit Letty's paternal aunt, Lady Rogers, and from there to travel to London for the season. She told Beth about her home in Durham, and all her more exalted relatives, no matter how distant the connec-tion, but as Beth was well aware that she was merely being used as a means to get this information to Tony and Dolph, she was not overwhelmed by the conde-scension of Mrs. Orvis-Ryder's addressing her in such a friendly manner. Volunteering no information about herself, and interjecting only an occasional murmer of agreement, she was soon heartily bored, and wished she had had the forethought to arm herself with a book too.

Presently she rose and wandered to the windows overlooking the front of the inn. The storm had not diminished its fury; indeed, it appeared to be snowing more heavily than ever, so there was very little to see. Jed's brightly painted sign was covered with snow, and the path that Willy had swept had almost disappeared again. She did not think that she and her father would be able to travel on the morrow, and resigned herself to a period of tedium.

The Reverend Mr. Cummings was a very learned cleric, and left with the upbringing of a baby girl at the untimely death of his wife, had educated her himself, with no regard to convention. This meant that Beth, although she was fluent in Greek, Latin, and French, and had studied history and the sciences as well as the current political scene, had no notion of water-color painting, the latest dance steps, or how to knot a fringe, and if she had been called on to perform at a smart musical evening would have laughed heartily at the very idea. She would, however, have been happy to tell you what she thought of Lord Liverpool's administration, especially Earl Bathurst, secretary for war and the colonies. She found no fault with her upbringing, since she had a highly intelligent mind and had enjoyed her studies very much.

Willy appeared every now and then to attend to the fire, bowing low to Mrs. Orvis-Ryder each time. She was his idea of high society—coo, as good as a queen her were, he thought, with her peremptory commands; not those two 'dentical gentlemen, who were too free and easy for his taste. Tony had actually thrown his boot at him when he answered a summons from their room.

"Here, boy! Polish these boots, and mind you watch your large thumbs when you do it!" was Tony's cheerful order, not at all like a lord.

Mrs. Orvis-Ryder tried valiantly to find out which twin had actually entered the world first, thereby earning succession to the title, but Tony chose to ignore her heavy hints, and Dolph was seemingly oblivious to anything but Lettie, when he could steal a

25

glance from his cards. Finally the lady realized that only a direct assault would do.

"M'lord!" She smiled archly at Tony. "I fear I have forgotten the exact line of succession in your family, and it has been bothering me exceedingly, like trying to remember a name that you know well, but escapes your memory. Pray refresh my recollection! Is it Anthony or Adolphus who is the heir?"

Beth turned slightly from the window, amusement deepening the dimple by the side of her mouth. How would the adroit Tony handle a direct question? she wondered.

The gentleman looked up lazily from his cards and smiled sweetly. "*Puer primus cum pater nōn est*, ma'am. Yes, Dolph?" He turned to his brother as Dolph giggled.

"Lord, ma'am, good thing the old 'un ain't here to hear you!" Dolph said in mock terror. "He only has fifty years in his dish, and if I know anything about it, intends to live fifty more!"

"And poor Mama!" added Tony wickedly. "I do assure you, ma'am, no one is less suited to being a dowager duchess than my mother! How it would distress her! Why, she would feel she had to give up all her mad escapades—hunting with the Quorn, gambling till dawn, all her . . . ahem . . . amusements! Let us change the subject! There is no question of anyone succeeding to the title for many years. We never think of it, do we, Dolph?"

Mrs. Orvis-Ryder was flustered. Having no knowledge of Latin, she could not translate the answer and did not wish to reveal her ignorance, so she was no better off than before.

"Why, to be sure, m'lord," she replied, busying herself in searching for her handkerchief, "I am sure we all wish your dear parents a long and happy life."

Beth turned hastily back to the window to hide her amusement as Tony rose and stretched his legs. Suddenly she heard his voice speaking softly behind her.

"Do you think Mrs. Orvis-Ryder could translate my schoolboy Latin, miss? I was afraid she might know French!"

"*Misera* Mrs. Orvis-Ryder, *et miser pater!* How he must miss you both, *primus et secundus!* No, I am sure she could not understand, not that it would have done her much good when you merely told her that the heir was not with his father!"

Tony raised an eyebrow as he stared down at her. So, the lady knew Latin, did she? As she smiled again, he decided he had seldom seen such an expressive pair of eyes, fringed as they were in their dark lashes. Suddenly he leaned forward and peered through the window. He thought he had caught some motion outside, even through the storm. It was getting darker now, and he couldn't be sure. . . .

Beth followed his gaze and exclaimed, "M'lord! Isn't that a team and phaeton, there by the gate?"

Tony peered in the direction she indicated, but the snow swirled around the pane, and the brief image was gone. "I thought I saw something a moment ago, Miss Cummings," he said. "Perhaps we should tell the landlord or the estimable Jed."

Just then the outer door flew open with a crash, and an angry voice called out. "Landlord! Landlord! Where the devil *is* the man?"

Henry hurried by the coffeeroom door, followed by Bessie and Jed, as the room's occupants strained their ears to hear more. Even the Reverend Mr. Cummings put down his book to listen. For a moment, all was confusion with Bessie, Henry, and Jed all exclaiming at once. How had the traveler found his way to the inn through the storm? Were there any more in his party? (This from Bessie, who had no more rooms, for the gentry anyway.) Was his horse in the stable? Had he been traveling long?

"Enough!" the loud commanding voice expostulated angrily. "Here I am, half dead with cold and damp, and you keep me standing in this draughty hall! How

27

I found my way here I cannot tell. I had hoped to gain the inn at Wolverton on the turnpike road, but it is obvious I lost my way. My manservant is with me, naturally; he is even now taking the horses to the stables. And now," with awful sarcasm, "perhaps you would be so kind as to show me to a room with a large fire, and prepare rooms for me? I also need a hot toddy immediately, and dry clothes as soon as it can be arranged. If, that is, I have answered all your questions! I would hate not to completely satisfy your curiosity!"

Tony had gone to the door, and in the sudden silence that fell before this sarcastic remark, he spoke up.

"The only large fire is in here, sir. Won't you join the rest of us, all like you breaking our journey because of the storm?"

He stepped back as a large dominant figure appeared in the doorway. His eyes raked the other occupants of the room, and then he made his bow to Tony, and carelessly to the rest. He strode in and went immediately to the fire. Beth had the sudden notion, from her position by the window, that they had all been waiting somehow for his appearance. The gentleman held his hands to the fire and spoke over his shoulder.

"By the way, I'm Barrington," he said casually, as if that brief pronouncement was all that was necessary to inform everyone of his estate. Mrs. Orvis-Ryder, for once speechless, widened her eyes. Mr. Cummings fussed with his book, Letty looked a little frightened, and the twins frowned at his abruptness. Only Beth appeared unmoved, her head tilted slightly to one side as she studied the newcomer. He was well above average height, with an almost swarthy complexion. His dark hair was caught back with a plain dark ribbon, and he wore his well-fitting riding clothes just as carelessly. He would never need two footmen to ease him into his coat, wide though his shoulders were, and although his buckskin breeches clung fashionably

28

to his powerful muscular legs, they were not in the popular primrose or dove gray shades the twins sported, but were a medium brown. His boots were obviously handmade, but had no tassles or other adornments. He looked tired, and he frowned as he glanced sardonically around the room.

"Well, have I wandered into a society of mutes?"

Mr. Cummings spoke, startling everyone but Beth, for the rest had quite forgotten his existence. "Forgive us, your grace!" he said, laying aside his book and rising to bow to Barrington. "We thought our party was quite complete, and no one else could get through the storm. I am the Reverend Edward Cummings," he said gently, bowing again. "And this is my daughter, Elizabeth."

Beth curtsied to the gentleman, eyes demurely lowered, as her father continued.

"May I also present Mrs. Adelaide Orvis-Ryder, and her daughter, Miss Leticia?" The ladies mentioned bowed slightly. "And these two gentlemen are Lord Anthony and Lord Adolphus Allensworth."

"At your service, your grace," murmured Tony, with Dolph rising hastily to make an elegant leg.

"Quite an assembly, for such a backward inn," Barrington said. He turned to the twins. "I know your father, of course, m'lords, and your mother too."

"Everyone knows our mother, sir!" Dolph said brightly.

"One sincerely hopes not, my dear boy," Barrington murmured.

Tony opened his mouth to speak, but just then Henry appeared with a tray and a steaming mug, which he hastened to present to Barrington. Bessie followed, and dropped the company a hasty curtsy.

"Pardon me, sir," she said, twisting her apron in a flustered way. "I don't rightly know where we are to put you! I have no private rooms left, what with Mrs. Orvis-Ryder and her daughter in the two big front rooms, and the reverend and his daughter in two more—as it

is, these gentlemen are sharing the last bedroom!"
She stopped, confused by the gentleman's frown, which
brought his dark brows together above a hawklike
nose.

"Well, that is easily solved, my good woman," he
said, turning to the large lady in the most comfortable
chair and waving a careless hand in her direction.

"Perhaps Mrs. ... um ... Orvis-Ryder, was it not?
Yes, quite so. Perhaps Mrs. Orvis-Ryder and her daughter would not object to sharing a room, since they
have the two largest in the house."

Beth held her breath in anticipation, as Mrs.
Orvis-Ryder stiffened.

"But I would object, your grace!" she said in her
piercing voice. "I object strenuously! I am not in the
habit of sharing a room with anyone!"

Barrington narrowed his eyes and purred, "That is
obvious, madam." He paused inquiringly, as Mrs.
Orvis-Ryder gasped, and then continued, "But perhaps,
under the circumstances, you might be persuaded to
relax your ... um ... standards?"

"But, but," the outraged lady exclaimed, "why should
I give up my room, or my daughter either? It is not at
all what we are accustomed to, I do assure you! Why,
the Orvis-Ryders are—"

"Yes, yes, of course, it will no doubt be a novel
experience for you," Barrington interposed. "But after
all, you did at one time share a room with your daughter, did you not?"

"Never!" said Mrs. Orvis-Ryder indignantly.

"Oh, surely, ma'am, I think you are in error. There
was a period of some nine months ... she is your
natural daughter, is she not?"

Mrs. Orvis-Ryder gasped again, and her color changed
alarmingly. Beth choked down her laughter and moved
forward, since all the rest of the company did appear
to be mute now. What would the man say next? Mrs.
Orvis-Ryder appeared on the verge of apoplexy.

"Perhaps Miss Orvis-Ryder could share my room,

ma'am?" she asked, with only the slightest quiver to her voice. "It is perfectly ample for the two of us, and you no doubt will be more comfortable."

Letty threw her a glance brimming with gratitude, and before her mother could speak, Barrington took charge again.

"A perfect solution, to be sure! My thanks, Miss Cummings!" For the first time he looked at Beth observantly, a grin lighting up his dark, forbidding face before he turned to Bessie.

"You! Yes, you! See that the young lady's belongings are transferred without delay. And landlord," to Henry, standing nervously by, "a simple dinner will be all that I require, and since you have no private rooms, I prefer it served to me abovestairs." He turned to the company. "If you will excuse me? It has been a fatiguing day."

He swept them a careless bow, and with one last speculative look at Beth, he was gone. The room was very still, and it was not until a log snapped in the fireplace that the spell was broken.

"*Well!*" said Mrs. Orvis-Ryder, bosom swelling ominously. "*Well!* I have never seen the like of it! Such discourtesy! Such manners! It is not at all what *I* am used to, let me tell you! The Orvis-Ryders have never been treated in such a way! Letty, my vinaigrette! I definitely feel a *spasm* coming on!" She pressed a fat and much bejeweled hand to her heaving breast before she was able to continue. "And to think not one of you gentlemen thought to intervene on my behalf. *Well!*"

"Oh, Mama," Letty said weakly, handing her the vinaigrette. "I am sure it is no great matter. I shall not mind sharing Miss Cummings' room. And the gentleman must sleep somewhere!"

Mrs. Orvis-Ryder snorted as she rose to leave.

"*Well!* It is not at all the thing, even if he is a duke! Such highhandedness! I feel distinctly unwell and must retire. Attend me, Letty, if you please!"

She moved heavily to the door, which Dolph opened hastily, smiling at Letty as he did so. Only when the sounds of the ladies' footsteps had receded did Beth dare to look directly at Tony. That gentleman smiled at her and murmured, "Yes, I think he found the perfect solution. Surely Miss Letty will be more comfortable with you, Miss Cummings!"

Beth looked inquiringly at him.

"So much more room, for one thing," he explained wickedly, and Beth choked down her laughter, remembering Mrs. Orvis-Ryder's ample girth.

Shortly thereafter, they all retired to change for dinner, and as the early dusk closed down and the storm continued, the wind now keening fiercely around the shutters and rattling the panes, the Bird and Bottle settled down for the evening. The actors were all assembled, and the play was about to begin.

Chapter II

In the kitchen, Bessie was busy with the final dinner preparations, assisted by Jill, while Abby and Jed set the table in the coffeeroom. James had been summoned by Mrs. Orvis-Ryder some time ago, and Henry was conferring with Barrington on the choices available for his solitary meal. Bessie had stepped into the pantry for more flour for one of her sauces, leaving Jill to stir the various pots, when suddenly the back door opened and Willy stumbled in, his face white and frightened. He opened his mouth, but no words came.

" 'Ere! What's the matter with you, Willy?" Jill asked crossly, wiping her brow, which was perspiring from the heat of the fire and the steam from the pots.

Still Willy could not manage a word, although he pointed a trembling hand in the direction of the stables. Jill stared at him perplexed.

"Shut your mouth, do, Willy! You look like a dead fish!" she snapped, just as a tall imposing figure filled the doorway. Although dressed soberly in the dark livery of a servant, he was unlike anyone Jill had ever seen, with his copper skin, forbidding features, and long black hair secured with a headband of colored beads and adorned with a white feather tipped in scarlet. Jill took one incredulous look, dropped the spoon in the pot, screamed as loud as she could, and fainted dead away. Fortunately, she fell away from the fire, since Willy was incapable of helping her, cowering against the wall as far from the door as he could get. It had been quite a shock when he came down the ladder from the hayloft after an illicit nap to encounter such a figure, and he had run to the inn as soon as the stranger had turned his back to curry the horses.

In response to Jill's scream, Jed arrived in the kitchen just as Bessie did. Catching sight of the stranger and seeing Jill in a heap on the floor, she dropped the bowl of flour and stood stock still, her heart pounding.

"Good evening," the stranger said, slowly and stiffly.

Jed took control at once. "Good evening! You must be the duke's man, right? My name is Jed." He advanced to the tall Indian, who stood impassively with his arms folded against his chest, and then saw Jill and exclaimed, " 'Ere, Willy! Help me lift her to a chair! Come on! Don't be such a silly gudgeon! 'Tis only an Indian from the Americas; I've seen 'em often before."

Bessie moved forward at these reassuring words and tried to smile at the tall dangerous-looking man. Henry bustled in then, and although he was startled, he had been prepared for "Albert" by the duke, so he was in control of himself. Barrington had told him that Albert would be no trouble, since he stayed mostly with the horses, not trusting the English arrangement of houses separate from the stables, and outside of simple meals would be seen but rarely. Henry greeted him cordially; Albert inclined his head and then moved

34

forward to the fireplace where he sat down on a low stool to one side.

"Does he . . . does he speak English?" whispered Bessie, waving some burned feathers under Jill's nose.

"Aye, he understands us, but will say little. Don't be afeared, m'dear; the duke assures me he is harmless, unless the duke himself should be threatened."

Jill was soon restored and reassured, and Jed hurried back to the coffeeroom to prepare Abby, who, spared the initial encounter, was all agog to see a "real savage." Coo, wait till I tell 'em at 'ome, she thought peeping around the kitchen door at Albert in his place by the fire, ignoring everyone. She was soon set to sweeping up the flour and the broken bowl, and order was again restored to the kitchen, although Willy told Jed in a slightly hysterical whisper that no amount of money in the world would induce him to sleep in the stable with the Indian, and he intended to roll up in a blanket before the kitchen fire as long as Albert was in residence.

Albert remained oblivious, stirring only when Abby timidly brought him a bowl of stew and some bread for his supper. He ignored the bread, but ate two helpings of the stew, using a spoon like a Christian, Bessie was pleased to see. The others ate around the table, trying to be casual and not stare too obviously. When the Indian was finished, he rose silently, bowed to Bessie and Henry, and strode out the door. Willy drew a deep breath and began to eat his stew with more appetite than he had shown previously.

Unaware of the commotion in the kitchen, Beth went to her father's room abovestairs before she began to change for dinner. As she had suspected, he was deep in his book again. Laughing, she took it away from him and reminded him that dinner would be served shortly.

"You know, Father," she said more seriously, "I don't think the inn is prepared to serve more than one dinner, and it would be very upsetting to the good landlord and his wife if you were not there when they were ready to begin. Besides, they already have to serve the dark and devilish Barrington separately."

Mr. Cummings was much struck by this and rose with alacrity. "You are right, my dear, as always! Romans 12, verse 16! I promise you I will be down shortly!" Then, with a twinkle reminiscent of his daughter, he added, "I think our hosts have enough to worry about with this ill-assorted group of travelers; heaven knows what will occur if the storm continues much longer!"

Beth agreed, although privately she thought it was going to be more amusing than she had first imagined, and quite looked forward to it. As she hurried to her room she met Jill, who had come to unpack the prodigious amount of baggage that belonged to Letty; she sent the girl back to the kitchen for hot water while she found her portmanteau and took out a dress of dark green. It was not in the first height of fashion, but it was warm, with its long tight sleeves and demure neckline. She shook it briskly, hoping it had not become too wrinkled. As she was brushing her hair, a breathless Letty arrived. Her mother had kept her until she herself had changed, vowing that the maids at the inn were worthless incompetents; indeed, she had already sent Abby scurrying away in tears from the scolding she had administered when the girl dropped a jewelry case while unpacking. Abby could not agree with Willy that Mrs. Orvis-Ryder was as good as a queen. Instead she was forcefully reminded of her old aunt; sharp as a tack, impatient, and always short-tempered.

Mrs. Orvis-Ryder gave Letty implicit instructions on what she was to wear, for although she had been foiled in finding out which twin was the heir, *one* of them was, and now that Barrington had arrived, she had other fish to fry as well. Really, the blizzard now appeared positively providential! She hoped it would snow for a week!

Looking into the mirror at her lovely daughter trying to arrange her hair to her mother's satisfaction, she determined to make the most of this opportunity, for there was no depending on her sister-in-law's agreeing to sponsor Letty in London. Mrs. Orvis-Ryder had quarreled with Lady Rogers too many times over the years to be sure of her assenting to the scheme, although to be just, that lady was also at fault, for she had made no secret of the fact that she considered her brother had married beneath him. Indeed, it had only been with extreme reluctance that she had agreed to this visit, but Mrs. Orvis-Ryder hoped that having no daughters of her own, Lady Rogers would be overcome by Letty's beauty and enjoy presenting her to society.

However, now Barrington was here, surely there was a good chance she might snare him for Letty. She knew how beautiful her daughter was; she did not see how any man, given proximity and opportunity, could fail to fall in love with her. She realized that Letty was not one of your clever sorts, but what gentleman wanted intelligent conversation when he could gaze into a pair of sparkling black eyes? It was disappointing that the duke was not dining with them, but perhaps he would come down after dinner, and the vision of Letty in a clinging shell-pink muslin gown, with its tiny puffed sleeves and lowcut bodice showing off her young breasts, would be ready if he did. She knew all about Alistair St. Clare, Duke of Barrington, Marquess of Rotheringham and Barton, and lord of this and that as well. He was in his middle thirties, and he had never married. Well, more than one bachelor had fallen into a parson's mousetrap just when all the matchmaking mamas had given him up! She knew of several beauties who had snared members of the nobility with nothing but a pretty face; Letty, of course, had the added distinction of being an Orvis-Ryder! She disregarded the duke's abominable manners airily. She felt a duke had every right to be as rude as he liked, and having no manners herself, she did not feel this detrimental.

Letty summoned Jill, and was soon attired in the designated pink muslin. The dress clung to her girlish figure tightly, and as she wore little underneath, she could not control an occasional shiver as Jill did her hair. Beth watched in some amusement.

"My dear Miss Orvis-Ryder," she said, "wouldn't you be more comfortable in a warmer gown? With this north wind blowing so fiercely, even the fires don't seem to keep the drafts at bay!" She chose a soft warm shawl for herself as she spoke. Letty looked at her in alarm.

"Why, I cannot!" she exclaimed. "I mean . . . Mama especially desired me to wear this gown. And I cannot . . . I mean, I would not wish to disappoint her, Miss Cummings."

Beth smiled at her kindly. It was not her fault her mother was putting her on display. "Oh, please call me Beth. Since we are to share a room, let us not stand on ceremony."

"Too kind," murmured Letty shyly. "Thank you, and you will call me Letty, won't you? It will almost be like having a sister for a few days!" She halted in some confusion, feeling she had gone too far, but Beth merely questioned her about her family and the aunt she was going to visit to put her at her ease. After finding out that Letty was an only child too, she realized that the conversation was distressing the girl for some reason, so she soon stopped and suggested they repair to the coffeeroom. Letty begged her to go ahead, and went to escort her mama down the narrow stairs, and also to pass inspection, if the truth be told, since James, the footman, now dressed again in his dry livery, was also in attendance.

As Beth neared the coffeeroom, she heard the voices of the twins and her father. Dolph stood before the fire, anxiously patting his elaborate cravat as he peered into the dim mirror over the mantelpiece, but Tony and the Reverend Cummings were conversing amiably. They rose as she entered, and she gave them all her bright smile. Tony hastened to draw up a chair for her, just as Mrs. Orvis-Ryder sailed into the room, closely followed by her daughter and her footman. She moved forward and aggressively took the seat Tony was holding. Dolph was mesmerized by Letty to the point of neglecting his handsome image, and even Tony appeared much struck by the vision of Letty, who did look fetching, although much too elaborately dressed for a simple inn, in the pink dress. Beth thought the goose bumps on her arms rather spoiled the picture she presented, but only suggested that she draw nearer the fire. James helped her tenderly to a seat, and Beth exchanged a quick glance with her father, who was observing Tony and Dolph in some amusement.

In a few moments, Jed hastened in with the first course and called them to dinner. Mrs. Orvis-Ryder rose, and waving in the general direction of the twins, said positively, "You must take the head, m'lord!"

"No, no, ma'am!" both young men replied as one.

Tony laughed, and continued, "No, ma'am, indeed we must have Mr. Cummings at the head!"

"Quite right," chimed in Dolph. "And your place is definitely at the foot, ma'am."

Mrs. Orvis-Ryder bristled as Tony explained gently, "My brother means you to have the place of next importance, ma'am."

Dolph looked blank for a moment, then recovered himself with a muttered, "Of course, of course! Didn't I just say so?"

As Tony escorted the lady to her seat, Dolph hastened to Letty's side and placed her to Mr. Cummings' left, taking the seat next to her, and quite forgetting Beth in his hurry to be next to the vision in pink. Tony frowned at him as he helped Beth to the place at her father's right, but Dolph was not attending. The Reverend Mr. Cummings stood indecisively at the head of the table, and then, shrugging gently, he took his seat.

Mrs. Orvis-Ryder recovered her poise and asked him to say grace, "for," she said, "I quite miss my dear chaplain, generally always in attendance." Letty stole a quick startled glance at her mama, but James, poised behind Mrs. Orvis-Ryder's chair, stared stolidly into space. His unmoved expression was worth all his ten pounds per annum at that moment.

Mr. Cummings gave a short grace, thanking the Lord for His goodness in allowing them to escape the storm, and begging His protection for all traveling this wild night. He spoke almost casually, as if he and the Lord were continuing an earlier conversation.

There was a short silence after the amen, and then Beth raised her head, and shaking out her napkin said, "My, that soup smells good! I am more hungry than I thought."

Jed began to ladle out the soup, and as James brought the first bowl to Mrs. Orvis-Ryder, she looked at it suspiciously through her jeweled lorgnette.

"It is to be hoped that the woman is a good cook," she said repressively. "I do not believe women generally are, and of course I only employ a *chef de cuisine* myself. *We* are accustomed to the best, and with my *delicate constitution* I must be extremely careful what I eat."

"And eat . . . and eat . . . and eat!" whispered Tony to Beth, eyeing Mrs. Orvis-Ryder's several chins. Beth turned to her father, afraid her expression would betray her.

The soup was good, as was the game pie which followed, accompanied by braised onions and carrots, and removed with broiled chickens and some veal scallops in a Spanish sauce. Conversation was fairly general, although Dolph gave Letty his undivided attention until Tony kicked him under the table. Mrs. Orvis-Ryder favored the company with such positive statements as she felt moved to deliver, but since none of these seemed to require comment or ask anyone's opinion, Dolph soon went back to devouring Letty with his eyes as he devoured his dinner, and Tony and Beth chatted with Mr. Cummings. Beth glanced down the table as a bowl of winter apples was presented to the lady and waved imperiously away. She did, however, accept a large serving of the custard which followed and pronounced it quite acceptable. Beth felt sorry for her suddenly, and spoke to her kindly.

"It was a good dinner, wasn't it, ma'am? I am sure we are lucky in our choice of havens from the storm!" She smiled at Jed as he placed a dish of comfits by her elbow. Mrs. Orvis-Ryder inclined her head distantly. She had no interest in the parson or his daughter, and did not intend to waste any time on them. Instead, she tapped Dolph's sleeve to get his attention.

"M'lord!" she said commandingly, as Dolph dragged his eyes from Letty's lovely face. "I do not believe that you or your brother told us why you were traveling on such a day as this. Pray enlighten us!"

Dolph stared at her uneasily. "Why, why, ma'am, I don't believe Mr. Cummings told us his destination either," he stammered, looking desperately to Tony. Tony laughed and came to his rescue.

"Why, ma'am, we are for London eventually, like yourselves. Perhaps we may meet during the season if you continue to the metropolis. I am not acquainted with your sister-in-law Lady Rogers, but I am sure she will see you have the entré to all the best parties. As for our immediate destination, shall we merely say that we were executing a commission for our father?" He turned to the Reverend Mr. Cummings. "And you sir, can you satisfy the lady's curiosity?"

Mrs. Orvis-Ryder bristled, as Mr. Cummings replied mildly, "Why, m'lord, let me say that I too was about my Father's business."

"Well said, Father!" commended Beth.

Mrs. Orvis-Ryder rose, in no good humor, as James

hastened to assist her. Changing the subject, she said,
"I fear we will be unable to leave you gentlemen to
your port. However, we will withdraw to the fire." She
summoned Letty to her side and stared haughtily at
Beth, who rose reluctantly. She was anxious to continue the discussion with Tony and her father about
Brook's campaign in upper Canada this past summer,
which Mrs. Orvis-Ryder had interrupted, but she
resigned herself to banishment.

Tony said knowingly, as he helped her with her
chair, "We won't continue until we join you." Beth
smiled and retreated as Jed put the decanter in
front of her father. She moved to the fire, which Letty
was positively hugging, adjusting her shawl as she did
so.

"So coming! Most brazen indeed!" She heard Mrs.
Orvis-Ryder say, but she did not ask to be enlightened,
but merely took a seat and folded her hands with
composure.

Letty said weakly, "Oh, Mama," and surreptitiously
rubbed her arms. Unfortunately her mother noticed
and took her to task in a harsh whisper.

"Stop that immediately, my girl! You know that
ladies of fashion are ever lightly clad and must never
appear to feel the cold, no matter how flimsy their
wraps. *You* will never drape yourself in shawls, m'love!"
This last statement was accompanied by a venomous
stare at Beth, who looked back at her in bewilderment.
Little did she suspect that she had aroused Mrs.
Orvis-Ryder's wrath by conversing so easily with Tony,
thereby drawing his attention away from Leticia.

However, she merely said, "But surely, ma'am, while
we are snowbound at a country inn, it must be considered proper. I fear Letty might become ill if she does
not take care."

Mrs. Orvis-Ryder shook her turbaned head repressively. "*I* know what is best for my daughter. Indeed, Miss Cummings, if I may say so, I am sure

that in matters of society and fashion, I am surely more experienced than a parson's daughter!"

Even Letty gasped at the rudeness of this statement, and Jed, bringing in more wood for the fire, thought to himself, Aha! The old gentry-mort! Drawn up the order of battle now, she has!

Beth's eyes grew stormy and seemed to darken with anger, but she controlled herself. There was no point in arguing with the woman, although she had never been treated in such a way in her life. She wondered what her grandmother, the dowager duchess of Woltan, would have had to say to such impertinence.

Dolph was fidgeting at the table, eyeing Letty with longing, and soon Tony and Mr. Cummings put him out of his exile by rising and joining the ladies by the fire. Tony settled Mr. Cummings in a comfortable chair, and turning to Beth, said, "Miss Cummings! Let us continue our discussion of Brook's campaign. I had not heard the details before. Is it true then that General Hall was driven back from Toronto?"

Beth turned to him thankfully. "Yes, m'lord, and forced to surrender his entire force as well."

Mr. Cummings added, "Some 2,500 men that would be. A great victory."

Dolph appeared to have caught some of the conversation, for he said suddenly, "Have you heard about Barrington's manservant? He is a native American. What we call an Indian, you know," he explained to the ladies. Letty turned quite pale, and Mrs. Orvis-Ryder gasped.

"Do I understand you correctly, m'lord?" she managed to say. "We are staying in the same place as a *savage?*"

Tony took up the tale. "Yes, the stableboy told us before dinner. It caused quite a commotion in the kitchen, I can tell you. One of the maids fainted, and there was much alarm until everyone was reassured that he was not in the least dangerous."

43

"Not dangerous?" Letty said in an anguished whisper. "Oh, Mama, I am so frightened! Why, we may all be murdered as we sleep!"

"Nonsense, Letty!" Beth said briskly. "I, for one, am most anxious to see him, and surely the duke would not introduce a hostile savage in our midst. How exciting, Father!"

Her father nodded as she continued, "I wonder what part of the Americas he is from? You know, it is strange how little attention has been paid to this latest conflict with the Americans. Everyone seems much more concerned with Napoleon still."

"Perhaps, my dear," her father said, "it is because we have been at war with Napoleon for so long. And of course, he is the nearer threat."

Tony nodded. "I agree, sir. But perhaps that might be resolved ere long. With Wellington prepared to advance in the Peninsula, and Napoleon retreating from that disastrous Russian campaign . . ."

Dolph looked up in interest and said brightly, "Now that is a bad man, old Boney!"

The conversation became more general, and it was not long before the tea tray was brought in by Bessie. Mrs. Orvis-Ryder poured, asking Letty to present the cups, although by right of precedence Beth should have performed the task. As she thanked Letty, who prettily handed her a cup, she was unaware that she had been snubbed again.

Bessie hovered about to be sure her guests had everything they needed, until Mr. Cummings asked her kindly about the progress of the storm. She beamed at him and said it showed no signs of letting up.

"Indeed, sir," she continued, " 'tis something fierce out there this night! And Jed says we're in for a regular blizzard!" She stopped in confusion as Mrs. Orvis-Ryder fixed her with a glacial stare for her audacity in contributing to the conversation, and poor Bessie would have fled in confusion if Beth had not stopped her and thanked her for the delicious dinner.

44

As the good woman left, she muttered to herself, "Aye, a sweet lady she is, and her father a good man too. As for Mrs. High-and-Mighty, even if she *is* someone, I'd sooner not have 'er in my house!"

The ladies soon took their candles and made their ways to bed. Dolph managed to press Letty's hand meaningfully as he gave her her candle. Tony frowned slightly and resolved to talk to his twin before they went to sleep. He knew Dolph and his amorous adventures, and while Dolph might consider it a harmless flirtation to while away the time, as he had in so many cases before, Tony wanted no part of the Orvis-Ryders.

Beth was soon in bed, and fast asleep before Mrs. Orvis-Ryder had released Letty from helping her undress. Beth's last thought before dropping off to sleep was to wonder if Barrington had spent a pleasant evening, alone in his room.

Belowstairs, Mr. Cummings soon excused himself, but the twins called for another bottle and settled down by the fire. It was considerably later before they decided to retire, and although Tony spent quite a bit of time remonstrating with his brother, he did not feel his eloquence had been enough to deter Dolph from his pursuit of Miss Orvis-Ryder, and he determined to keep a close eye on him on the morrow, and insist they ride on just as soon as there was any break in the weather.

Beth woke early when Abby came in softly to make up the fire, although Letty still slumbered on at her side. She rose, and pulling on a warm morning gown and hastily washing and brushing her hair, hurried to the coffeeroom. There was no one there, and she went to the front window to check the weather. It was still snowing, although the wind did seem to be less violent this morning. she shivered and moved back to the fire, wondering how she was to get a cup of coffee. As she pondered seeking out the kitchen, Jed appeared.

"Good morning, miss," he said cheerfully.

"Good morning, Jed," she answered. "Or is it a good morning? It seems to be snowing as hard as ever!"

"Aye, ma'am, that it do! I suspect 'twill snow until tomorrow at least. A proper blizzard we got 'ere, and no mistake. Must be at least a foot of new snow already on the ground." Then he added kindly, "Now you sit here by the fire and be comfortable. I'll be back in a bit with some coffee and breakfast for you."

Beth took a seat, wondering when the rest of the company would appear. She certainly had never expected the duke to be the first, but before Jed could return, she heard heavily booted feet on the stairs, and a moment later he stood on the threshold.

"Gawd!" she thought she heard him mutter, causing her eyebrows to rise, and then he shouted, "Landlord! *If* you please!"

Advancing into the room, he stood frowning in front of the fire, his mind on other matters than morning courtesies. Beth took out her book and composedly began to read. She was thoroughly enjoying the new Jane Austen. A moment later, Henry bustled in with a heavy tray.

"Here you are, miss," he said, and then, spotting the duke, he asked, "Was you wanting your breakfast, sir? Won't take a minute!"

As Beth took her place at the table, Barrington recalled himself.

"Yes, immediately! Some ham, or sirloin, a dish of eggs, and plenty of coffee!"

Henry bowed and withdrew, and Barrington strolled to the table. Beth was buttering a roll, but she looked up when she felt his eyes on her.

"Good morning, Miss Cummings," he said, since Beth made no move to speak first. Beth inclined her head gravely and continued to eat her roll.

"What, are you not speaking this morning?" he inquired.

"Your grace." Beth acknowledged his greeting briefly, pouring herself some coffee at the same time.

46

"Aha!" the duke said, pointing a finger at her. "You have decided it is not at all correct to have breakfast alone with a strange man. I would instantly go away, except there is no place to go away *to*, if I want my breakfast!"

Beth looked at him steadily. "Pray sit down, sir," she said. "I assure you such was not my intent, having outgrown the girlhood proprieties many years ago."

Barrington took a seat and snorted, "Yes, I can see you have faded into spinsterhood by dozens of years! Don't be foolish! I'm sure that large person—what was her name—I'm sure she would tell you it is not at all the thing!"

"Mrs. Orvis-Ryder, do you mean?" asked Beth.

"Yes, her! The ill-bred 'un with the gorgeous girl in tow. Wouldn't catch her letting her Letty dine with a stranger unchaperoned!"

"Not even a duke, your grace?" Beth couldn't resist asking. As he laughed, she hurriedly continued, "Of course, the situation is quite different. Miss Orvis-Ryder is barely eighteen, while I am four and twenty! Then too, I travel with my father. If you should feel amorous, I have only to scream for his assistance."

She looked at him curiously as he began to laugh in earnest, and continued demurely, "However, I feel quite safe. In my experience, gentlemen do not tend toward romance before breakfast."

"Quite right, miss," Barrington managed. "And I wonder how you know that?"

Beth blushed, and was glad when Henry came in with Barrington's breakfast. As usual she had let her tongue run away with her!

Barrington served himself a large plateful and began to eat with relish, and Beth returned to her book. Several moments, later, he glanced across at her.

"Do you find the printed word preferable to the usual social intercourse, Miss Cummings?" he asked mockingly.

Beth looked up from her book. "Why no, sir, not

47

at all. I merely perceived, from your reaction on finding the coffeeroom occupied when you entered the
room, that you preferred not to chat. I believe many
gentlemen feel the same," she added kindly. "Allow
me to pour you some more coffee."

Barrington frowned, trying to remember what she
was talking about, but before he could challenge her,
Mr. Cummings entered the room and bent to kiss his
daughter.

"Good morning, my dear!" he said, and then with a
bow to Barrington, "Your grace!"

Barrington waved him to a seat and took a huge
forkful of ham. "Join us, Mr. Cummings! I cannot tell
you how relieved your daughter is to see you here,
thus sparing her blushes at being alone with me."

Mr. Cummings looked puzzled. "Beth?" he asked.
"Beth is not so missish, sir!"

"I believe the duke is funning, Father," Beth said
with dignity. "Do sit down and let me serve you a
plate. The ham is quite good; at least it appears that
way," she added, looking at Barrington's heavily laden
plate.

"*Touché,* m'lady, that takes the trick!" the gentleman said airily. "I recommend it, sir."

Beth sat back to enjoy her coffee, and let her father
converse with the duke. Several moments later, Letty
appeared in the doorway and hesitated until she spied
Beth.

"Good morning," she said, advancing a bit nervously,
eyeing the large Barrington apprehensively and glancing quickly around the room in case the "savage" was
in attendance. Barrington cocked an eyebrow at her,
but as he had his mouth full of the delicious ham,
made no comment.

Mr. Cummings rose and held out a chair for the
girl, smiling at her kindly. "Do sit down, my dear
Miss Orvis-Ryder," he said. "Shall I procure breakfast
for you? And your mother? Is she too coming to join
us?"

"Thank you, sir," Letty said. "No, Mama never rises before noon."

"Although she probably starts trying to rise an hour before, I'm sure," Barrington breathed in an aside to Beth, having disposed of the ham. Beth frowned at him over the napkin she hurriedly raised to cover her answering smile.

"Is it still snowing?" asked Letty, to make conversation as Mr. Cummings went to summon Henry.

"Obviously, miss," said Barrington, "as you can see if you but had the wits to look!" He waved a large hand at the window, and Letty looked at Beth, very distressed, with tears starting in her eyes.

"That will do, your grace!" Beth said sternly. "There is no need for such sarcasm! Let the girl have her breakfast in peace, if you please!"

Barrington stared at Beth, his eyebrows drawing together in a mighty frown. It was doubtful he was used to being brought to task by anyone, Beth thought, and she waited a bit breathlessly for his reply, although her gaze did not falter from his. He hesitated, and then bowed ironically to her, and to a cowering Letty.

"Your pardon, ladies! Perhaps you are right, Miss Cummings, and man is not meant to converse so early in the morning."

With this handsome apology Beth had to be content, and she was careful to stay at the table while Letty ate her breakfast, chatting lightly until the girl had recovered herself.

When Willy came in with a load of wood, Barrington stopped him and said, "You, boy! Fetch my man to me, if you please!"

Willy backed out of the door, nodding his head, determined to send Jed on the errand. He planned to have as little as possible to do with the duke and his Indian servant. He was still a little stiff from spending the night on the kitchen floor, but what was a little discomfort when it saved him from a night spent in close proximity to a savage?

49

When Albert made his appearance, Letty gasped audibly, but Beth studied him carefully over her coffee cup. She thought him magnificent, and as he stood with the duke she was struck by the similarity between the two men—both so tall, with hawklike features and black hair. If it were not for his complexion, Albert could easily be mistaken for the duke's brother, although he stood a great deal straighter.

Barrington questioned the Indian about the horses, in a mixture of English, some tongue Beth did not know, and sign language. Albert replied briefly, the same way, and then the two of them left for the stables. It seemed one of Barrington's matched pair of chestnuts had developed a slight limp yesterday, and he was anxious to see to it.

Mr. Cummings, who had also been fascinated by the Indian, recalled himself as they left, and asked to be excused, for, as he said to his daughter, "It appears it will be impossible to travel today, and I must get on with my work. I will be in my room if you need me, m'dear." Beth kissed him lightly, and he hurried away to his beloved books.

Letty took a chair by the fire with a small workbasket, and Beth reluctantly took an adjoining chair and opened her book again. She did not have any great hopes of being allowed to read in peace, and it was not many more moments before she quietly closed it, in the face of Letty's artless conversation. Released from her mother's domination, Letty became quite a chatterer, although she was no more interesting than her few comments had been the day before.

She first asked Beth what she thought of Albert and the duke, adding with a shiver, "I do not know which one of them frightens me more! What a harsh cruel face the savage has! And Barrington! Perhaps he is not what he seems; he appears so sinister, he may be taking the place of the real duke, with the savage as his henchman!"

"Having murdered him in some foul way?" Beth

suggested, confirmed in her opinion that Letty's reading tended toward the more frightful gothic tales. Letty's eyes widened.

"Oh, do you think so indeed?" she whispered, turning quite pale. "Oh, I shall never sleep soundly until we leave here!"

"Of course I don't think so, you silly girl!" Beth said sharply. Really, that was all it needed, Letty spreading tales about Barrington, to bring the pot to a boil. Then she added more calmly, "I am sure he is the real duke, although he has not been seen much in the past few years. If he acquired the Indian in the Americas, that would explain his absence. We can ask my father; he knows the family, I believe."

Letty did not question why a country parson would have this knowledge, she merely repeated that she wished fate had not brought such a frightening pair to the inn, a sentiment Beth could not agree with, although she made no further comment. After taking a few careful stitches, Letty asked, keeping her face bent over her work, "Do you find the twins handsome, Beth?"

"Assuredly!" replied Beth cheerfully. "Top of the trees Corinthians, and up to every deviltry they can find!"

Letty colored up prettily. "I am sure it is impossible to tell them apart, so alike they are!"

Beth privately thought you merely had to wait till one of them opened his mouth, but she made no comment, merely rising and shaking out her skirts, before she said, "You must excuse me, Letty. I wish to see my father; there may be some work he wishes me to do."

She went out of the room and up the stairs, and although she knocked at her father's door, she knew it was only an excuse to escape a morning's chatter so she could read her book. The bedroom fire was dying down, so she threw on a couple of pieces of wood from the basket by the hearth, and pulling up a comfortable wing chair, settled down comfortably. Between Letty and Miss Austen there was no comparison as to which was the more enjoyable companion.

Left to her own devices, Letty pouted a little, went and stared out the window at the falling snow, and then settled down again with her needlework. Jill peeked in and then went away, and a moment later Letty heard a sharp squeal, hastily repressed. The maid giggled, as Letty looked up expectantly at the sound of footsteps approaching the coffeeroom. She was not disappointed to see one of the twins in the doorway. That young gentleman came in beaming, and bowed to her.

"Good morning, Miss Letty! I may call you Miss Letty?"

Letty fluttered her eyelashes at him and nodded. The twin took a seat across from her and said eagerly, "Now this I had not hoped for!"

"Hoped for, m'lord?"

"I mean I had not hoped to have the good fortune to find you here . . . and alone!"

Letty looked around apprehensively. "Perhaps I should not be here," she said quickly, "Mama may not approve—"

The gentleman waved his hand airily. "Surely she cannot object! Heard her say m'self she didn't mind sharing the coffeeroom with members of the nobility. And it is just by chance—by a very lucky chance"—he bowed slightly—"that I wandered in here and found you. Not like an assignation, you know! And now we may have a comfortable coz without other people interrupting."

Letty smiled coyly at him. "There is only one thing, m'lord . . ."

He leaned forward eagerly. "Anything!" he breathed reverently.

"Well, how can we have a comfortable coz when I don't know which Allensworth you are?"

Dolph laughed and rose to sweep her his most elegant bow.

"Adolphus Eugene Allensworth, at your service!" he intoned. Moving to her side and sitting down next to her, he continued, "See why you were confused. Lord, the stories I could tell of mixups when people thought I was Tony or he me! There was one time . . ." He stopped and thought for a moment. "No, best not tell you that one! Not suitable for a lady's ears! Such a beautiful lady, too!" He edged slightly closer, causing Letty to look fearfully toward the door, but as she had been in situations like this many times before, she was not as nervous as she pretended.

In fact, the reason her mother was taking her to London was that she had found Letty and the squire's son exchanging kisses in the conservatory. Mrs. Orvis-Ryder's plans did not include a farmer's son for her daughter, and she had realized that unless she removed Letty from the neighborhood, she would soon be swamped with offers from the most ineligible young men for twenty miles around. She did not credit Letty with much sense, and knew she would think herself in love with the tinker, if he was young and handsome. Letty, however, did have the sense to realize that her mama would not be at all displeased to find her alone with Lord Adolphus, and so she set out to captivate the young man with her artless chatter. When she dropped a spool of thread, Dolph went to his knees to fetch it as it threatened to roll across the room, and still in this position presented it to her gallantly, just as Barrington put his head in the door.

"Edifying, I'm sure!" he said tartly, causing Letty to press her hands to her heart in shocked surprise, and Dolph to spring to his feet, his color rising. He held up the thread and said, "Just fetchin' Miss Letty's spool, your grace!"

"Lord, it's nothing to me, madcap, but Mrs. Orvis-Ryder is coming down the stairs now. You wouldn't want to raise the lady's hopes too soon, would you?"

Dolph moved away from the sofa hurriedly, and nodded his thanks as he took out his handkerchief to dust his knees. Barrington snorted and turned away. A moment later, Mrs. Orvis-Ryder's piercing tones were heard plainly.

"Your grace! Good morning—or is it afternoon? I trust you spent a pleasant night?"

"Not really, I was alone," Barrington replied, outrageously. "The word I would use is 'restful.' And was your solitary state to your liking, ma'am?"

Mrs. Orvis-Ryder spent several minutes relating the problems of a hard bed, a too soft pillow, and a smoking fire.

"Why, I swear I hardly closed my eyes at all!"

"How unfortunate," Barrington said. "And I could have sworn I heard your sn—slumbers, right through the wall!"

Mrs. Orvis-Ryder tapped his hand lightly with her reticule. "Naughty man!" she said, determined to be pleasant. Barrington took an abrupt leave of her, and she entered the coffeeroom. Letty sat demurely sewing, and Dolph stood staring out at the snow, but although her eyes narrowed slightly, she said nothing other than a pleasant good morning as she seated herself at the table. Bessie soon appeared and was ordered to bring a fresh pot of coffee and some dry toast.

"For," Mrs. Orvis-Ryder confided to Dolph, "I do not believe in eating at this hour. *My health* will not allow it." Neither Letty nor Dolph replied to this conversational gambit, so she continued with what she assumed to be a winning smile, "How is the storm, m'lord? Does it appear to be abating?"

Dolph turned from the window reluctantly, wishing Tony would come in.

"No, ma'am," he said. "Must resign ourselves to a lengthy stay. Wind is blowin' as hard as ever, and the snow is still fallin' heavily."

54

Mrs. Orvis-Ryder was not displeased. She settled herself more comfortably and prepared to do battle. She was well aware that Dolph was the weak chink in the twins' armor, and now that she had him alone was determined to find out which Allensworth was worthy of cultivation. Before she could begin, however, there was an interruption in the large person of Bessie, hurrying in with the coffee pot.

She fussed around the table, beamed at Letty and Dolph, and went to stir up the fire. Mrs. Orvis-Ryder sipped her coffee and waited. Finally, Bessie curtsied her way out, and she turned to a suddenly uneasy Dolph and smiled in her most ingratiating way. It did nothing to relieve his mind.

"M'lord!" she began. "Do tell us about your home! Letty and I are most interested in Allensworth Park— we have heard of its antiquity and beauty, even in Durham County! Is it true it has been in the family since William the Conqueror?"

Dolph stole a look at Letty, who looked up from her work, blushed slightly, and smiled at him encouragingly. Somehow he felt better, and smoothing his already faultless locks, strolled to the table and bowed to Mrs. Orvis-Ryder.

"As to that, ma'am," he said brightly, "you had better ask m'brother. He has all that old history down pat. Anyway, Allensworth Park is just like any other place I've seen." He paused, and then feeling that perhaps this had not been completely satisfactory, added with a grin, "My mother says it's a drafty old pile and won't spend a moment longer there than she has to!" Observing Mrs. Orvis-Ryder's frown at these artless words, he added hastily, "Ah . . . good huntin' country, of course! Tony and I try to get up during the season!"

"Surely you are too modest, m'lord," Mrs. Orvis-Ryder pursued. "So many guidebooks mention the Venetian ballroom, the water gradens, the Queen's rooms . . . it must be beautiful! I must tell you that Letty is quite an enthusiast on old buildings. How she would love to see it!" She paused expectantly, but Dolph appeared completely absorbed in smoothing a wrinkle he had just discovered in his puce sleeve. Mrs. Orvis-Ryder swallowed another frown and turned to Letty.

"Is that not so, my love?" she asked.

"If . . . if you say so, mama," Letty managed to get out, but before Mrs. Orvis-Ryder could remonstrate with her for this hardly enthusiastic reply, they were joined by the Reverend Mr. Cummings. He greeted the company absently, and went at once to the small table where he had left a book. Flicking over the pages until he found the reference he sought, he was soon unaware of the others, but Dolph drew a relieved breath, Letty's blush died down, and Mrs. Orvis-Ryder seethed inwardly.

Shortly thereafter, Tony made an appearance, and called his brother to go with him to check their horses, and also to find out what if anything he had said to Mrs. Orvis-Ryder. They were gone some time, and as Barrington did not reappear, Mrs. Orvis-Ryder gave up for the moment and commanded Letty to accompany her upstairs. Mr. Cummings looked up absent-mindedly.

"Do not let me disturb you, ma'am," he said mildly, as that lady twitched her skirts in frustration. It was all very well to be snowbound with her quarry, but if the quarry avoided her, she must seek other means. She sniffed, and eyed him haughtily.

"*That* would be quite beyond your powers, Mr. Cummings!" she said.

"Oh, Mama!" Letty said, quite shocked.

Mr. Cummings looked at her gravely, and feeling she had gone too far, she added, "I must rest. I fear that yesterday was too much for one in my *delicate state*. And of course, I must have my daughter with me, for one cannot be too careful with the present state of affairs; consider the savage! Two ladies traveling alone, you know, must be extremely careful of their reputation," she added. "My dear Mr. Orvis-Ryder would be horrified if he knew to what we have been subjected!"

Mr. Cummings looked amused. He could not answer for Albert, but surely she did not suspect him of cherishing designs on her daughter's virtue? Before he could reassure her, however, she bowed slightly, and sweeping Letty before her, left the room.

Jed came in to tend the fire and inquire if there was anything the gentleman wanted, and on being reassured that there was not, stayed to chat for a moment. On learning of his service in the Royal Navy, Mr. Cummings asked many questions, and quite forgot his book. Jed, assuming correctly that the good parson would not be shocked by his tales in spite of his orders, soon relaxed and answered all the queries about impressment, living conditions, discipline, and the battles he had seen. When Beth came downstairs she found them deep in conversation, but her presence put an end to the confidences and recalled Jed to his duties.

She strolled to the window and exclaimed, "Why look! The snow has stopped falling!"

Jed came to the winow and looked out pessimistically.

"Aye, miss, for a bit only, I'm sure. You'll see 'twill soon begin to blow hard again!"

"Jed, you are a spoilsport!" Beth retorted. "Well, I, for one, am going to get a breath of fresh air before it does." She quickly left the room and was soon back, dressed in her warm cloak and hood. Peeping in the door, she asked her father if he cared to join her.

"I think not, my dear, and since I have a very good opinion of Jed and his weather predictions, I beg you to stay close to the inn."

"Never fear, Father!" Beth replied gaily, drawing on her warm mitts. "I will be gone only a little while, for I fear the drifts will be too high for more than a short stroll."

She let herself out the door and was delighted to see

the changes in the landscape. Every gatepost wore a high hat of snow, and drifts had formed in the most unlikely places. At the corner of the inn, a drift reached almost to the second story, where the wind-driven snow had swirled from the stableyard beyond. A weak sun was trying valiantly to brighten the day, and showed every tree and bush bowed down by a heavy blanket of white. The path to the gate was only dimly visible, and the inn's sign was completely covered with snow. Beth picked up a handful of snow and made a snowball, which she tossed rather inexpertly at the gatepost. She missed it by several feet, but managed to hit a tree nearby. Tony and Dolph, coming back from the stables, applauded her efforts.

"I say! Good shot!" Dolph exclaimed, eyeing the snow and wondering if it was beneath his dignity to try.

Beth laughed. "Yes, if I had been aiming for the tree! Unfortunately I was trying to hit the gatepost!"

That decided Dolph, who hurriedly made a snowball and heaved it, knocking off the snow with an expert toss. Beth commended him, and invited Tony to try for the other gatepost. Before long, the three of them were pelting every reachable object with a great deal of merriment, and making remarks about each other's ability, or lack of it. When they had cleared the sign of snow, they walked to the road, or what they could find of it.

"Tony!" Dolph exclaimed. "Let us make a snowman as we did when we were boys!"

Tony laughed at him. "Why, Dolph, and how would we explain it in town? Two Corinthians like us! 'And what did you do in the great blizzard, m'lord?' 'Why, sir, we made a snowman!' Lord, they'd laugh us out of White's!"

Dolph looked crestfallen, but Beth said in a rallying tone, "I think it would be great fun! Perhaps we could have a competition and ask some of the others to be judges. It would be better than being cooped up in the inn all day!"

Much struck by this, Tony agreed. Anything to keep Dolph away from luscious Letty and her managing mama! As they began discussing possible sites for their artistic endeavors, the sky darkened and snow again began to fall. Beth and Tony persuaded Dolph that tomorrow would be time enough to start, and hurried back to shelter.

As they gained the inn door, two pairs of curtains twitched back into place at the windows of the two best front bedrooms on the second floor. Barrington was smiling faintly, as he had been ever since he had spied the threesome playing in the snow, but Mrs. Orvis-Ryder had an awful frown on her face as she rejoined Letty by the fire. So, Miss Parson was entering the lists, was she! Well, we will see about that, she thought, settling herself to a period of reflection. No country miss, well past girlhood, was going to be allowed to upset her plans!

Chapter III

When Beth appeared in the coffeeroom that evening, she was pleased to see that Barrington had decided to grace the company. He stood before the fire with the twins and Mr. Cummings, and swept her a bow as she approached. Beth was attired in the same dark-green gown she had worn the night before, and Tony and the duke were still in morning dress, but Dolph was resplendent in fawn-colored pantaloons and a dark evening coat, with his cravat tied even more elaborately than usual. He sported several rings and fobs, and clutched an ornate snuffbox in one hand, complete with a large lace handkerchief as a finishing touch. He did not take his eyes from the door, and Barrington smiled sardonically, but before he could make one of his withering comments, the door opened and Mrs. Orvis-Ryder appeared, attended by the faithful James and a blushing Letty.

This evening, Letty was breathtaking in primrose muslin, cut in a deceptively simple style. The low-cut neckline was banded with satin ribbons which crossed under her breasts and then flowed freely to the floor. Dolph bowed to her reverently as Barrington lazily raised his quizzing glass in observation, none of which escaped the young lady's mother.

Turning to Beth standing near him, Barrington said in an undertone, "Definitely dampened her petticoats! The gal is sure to catch cold!"

Beth looked at him haughtily as he added, still whispering, "Although on looking more closely I doubt she is wearing any!" Then in a louder voice to include the rest, he quoted.

" 'Like Mother Eve our maids may stray unblam'd
    For they are naked . . . and are not ashamed.' "

Beth looked shocked, Mrs. Orvis-Ryder gasped, and Letty's delicate blush turned to carmine, and he added in a kindly tone, "I was quoting Byron, m'lady."

"Lord Byron is not a favorite of mine, I fear, your grace," Beth said repressively.

"Nor mine either, I admit. The couplet does have the advantage of an uncharacteristic moral tone though. So unlike him!"

Reverend Cummings was heard to murmur "Matthew six: verses twenty eight, twenty nine," and when everyone looked at him, explained, " 'Consider the lilies of the field,' you know!" This gave Mrs. Orvis-Ryder a chance to recover and she was all complaisance.

"Oh, Lord Byron, divine author! How Letty and I enjoyed his 'Bride of Abydous'!"

"Naturally you would," Barrington said smoothly. "And did you also enjoy 'The Corsair,' Mrs. Orvis-Ryder?"

"That has not come my way, your grace," said the lady. "But if *you* recommend it, I shall certainly procure a copy as soon as we reach London."

Barrington turned to Beth. "And you, Miss Cummings," he asked, "even if you are not a devotée of Byron, surely you must have read it!"

"Certainly I began it. However, I found it so ridiculously romantic I did not finish it."

"You are not romantic?" he asked with a wicked grin lighting up his swarthy features. "No wonder you are still enjoying single blessedness at the advanced age of . . . what was it . . . twenty four? You must cultivate a more feminine attitude! All our ladies adore romance, and the so romantic George Byron of course!"

Mrs. Orvis-Ryder looked triumphantly at Beth, who gave Barrington a flashing glance of scorn before turning away to her father.

Jed and Jill carried in large trays and dinner was announced. There was a moment of awkwardness, since Barrington made an uneven number at the table. Bessie had put three places on one side and two on the other, and Mrs. Orvis-Ryder bustled around telling everyone where to sit. The twins were busily trying to satisfy their own wishes—Dolph determined to be next to Letty, and Tony trying hard to keep them apart, Mr. Cummings patiently awaiting the outcome, and Beth standing to one side looking amused at the various strategies being employed. How long the game might have gone on no one was to know, for suddenly Barrington took a hand.

"Enough!" he said in a commanding voice. "I for one am too hungry for all these niceties. Mr. Cummings, take the head, sir! Mrs. Orvis-Ryder, sit on his right, if you please! Miss Letty and the Allensworths can sort themselves out on the other side, and Miss Cummings shall sit opposite her father. I shall take this chair next to Mrs. Orvis-Ryder. Ma'am!" And suiting his actions to his words, he handed the speechless lady into the designated chair and went to seat Beth.

"Masterful, your grace!" she breathed over her shoulder. "Are you always so abrupt when you are hungry?"

"But of course!" he replied. "Otherwise we would be waltzing around this table playing musical chairs forever, and dinner would be cold!"

Beth looked at him teasingly. "And that would never do, would it? Perhaps I should have asked, are you always so hungry? Every time I see you, you are eating!"

Barrington took his seat and shook out his napkin. "Well, there is a great deal of me to keep up, as you can see." And turning to Mrs. Orvis-Ryder he added, "I am sure *you* will agree with me, ma'am, that missing a meal is a serious thing!"

Mrs. Orvis-Ryder nodded distantly, at a loss for a reply, while Letty was seated between the twins. Tony found himself next to Beth, and poor Mr. Cummings had to make do with Dolph and Mrs. Orvis-Ryder. He hoped the food would be good at least, for the conversation was sure to be tedious.

Bessie had outdone herself, and everyone made a good meal. As the turkey roast and the ham fritters were removed, Tony announced to the company that if the weather abated tomorrow, he and Beth and Dolph were going to have a snow-sculpture party, and asked the others to be judges.

Mrs. Orvis-Ryder quickly exclaimed, "What a good idea, m'lord! I am sure Letty would be delighted to join you!"

"I say!" Dolph chimed in, much struck by the promised addition to their party. "Perhaps Miss Letty and I could compete against m'brother and Miss Cummings! What do you say, Miss Letty? Shall we challenge them?"

Tony did not appear pleased with this, but Dolph airily ignored him, as Letty smiled and agreed. Barrington turned to Beth and murmured, "See she puts something on, will you? Otherwise she will become part of the sculpture, frozen stiff!"

Beth eyed him, the dimple appearing as she smiled. "But surely they would win in that case, your grace—she is so beautiful!"

Barrington raised his quizzing glass and inspected Letty carefully, which fortunately she did not notice.

At length he turned again to Beth and said seriously, "Perhaps not. I do not think she would be beautiful . . . *blue!*"

Beth choked a little over the wine she was sipping, and turned to Tony. Really, one should definitely not encourage the man! One never knew what outrageous thing he would say next!

"What is to be our subject, m'lord? Do you have any ideas?"

Tony smiled at her. "Not a one," he said. "What would you suggest?"

Beth thought for a moment and then replied lightly, "Anything you wish, as long as you do not insist on a faithful reproduction of the battle of Queenstown, m'lord!"

Tony laughed, and Barrington looked keenly at Beth, his forkful of soufflé forgotten.

"And what do you know of that, Miss Cummings?" he asked sharply.

Beth was surprised. "Why," she replied, "only that General Wadsworth surrendered near there with nine hundred men this past summer. I wish I knew more of the details!"

Tony broke in. "I do not think we have time to make nine hundred soldiers, but at least that would be preferable to attempting the twenty-five hundred that Hall surrendered!"

"You are also well informed!" Barrington said abruptly.

Tony raised an eyebrow at his tone. "I have my information from Miss Cummings and her father, sir. We were discussing it last night."

"They are correct," Barrington agreed, more easily. "It was a successful summer's campaigning for our forces." He turned to Beth. "I am impressed!"

"Impressed?" she asked in bewilderment.

He made her a sardonic bow. "Most ladies would not only not know, but would not consider it of any interest. I see you are something quite out of the common way!"

65

"Besides being uninterested in romance, your grace?" Beth asked innocently.

Barrington laughed. "Of course! Or the latest fashions, gossip, or scandal. How refreshing to find a woman with a brain who is not ashamed to use it!"

Beth considered the compliment and decided magnanimously to ignore the indirect reference to her green gown.

"I have been very well brought up, your grace, by a father who considers women to be just as intelligent as men." She sent a fond look down the table at her father as she spoke.

"Heresy, m'lady!" Tony said gaily. "Any *man* can tell you women are generally known to be unequal to men in every way; you have only to ask one of them!"

"Anyone *can*," Barrington added, "but perhaps they had much better not! I do not think Miss Cummings would take it kindly, and from what I have observed, would be glad to take up the argument without hesitation. I would not bet on the outcome, either," he mused.

Mrs. Orvis-Ryder decided the conversation had turned on that lady quite long enough. So coming! She was not accustomed to gentlemen ignoring her beautiful Leticia for even a moment. Clearing her throat and sending Beth a baleful glance, she took command.

"Surely any truly feminine woman acknowledges the superiority of men," she said. "Why, Letty would never consider herself equal in any way, nor do I. We are happy to bow to men's superior judgment! Surely a woman raised in a genteel way would never force her ideas or arguments on any man!"

Beth opened her mouth and then shut it firmly. Tony gave her a commiserating glance as Barrington said to Mrs. Orvis-Ryder, "You are in error, ma'am. It is one of her most appealing traits."

Mrs. Orvis-Ryder shrugged and changed the subject. "M'lord! Letty! Have you decided what your sculpture is to be?"

66

The two young people, who had not heard a word of the conversation, were startled. Letty looked helplessly at Dolph, who tried to appear as if he had been giving the matter much thought.

"I think," he said finally, "we will keep it a secret. Yes! That is what we must do, don't you agree, Miss Letty?"

Letty nodded assent eagerly, having no idea what to make except the snowmen she had always seen. Barrington raised his glass to Beth and Tony.

"I do not think you will have much difficulty capturing the prize. Are you artistic, Miss Cummings, as well as intelligent?"

Beth answered stiffly, still deeply angry at Mrs. Orvis-Ryder. "I do not know, your grace. It has been many years since I made a snowman, but perhaps if we keep it simple, we may win out."

"May I suggest Lord Byron as a subject?" Barrington went on. "In one of his romantic poses, clutching his wild locks?"

Beth ignored the sally and said to Tony, "If our competitors are keeping their design a secret, I think we might follow their lead, do you not agree, sir?"

Tony not only agreed, he promised to bend all his thoughts to a suitable subject, and then he turned abruptly to Letty on his other side, determined to wrest her attention from Dolph, which pleased Mrs. Orvis-Ryder so much she was moved to bestow a few pleasantries on the Reverend Mr. Cummings. Beth was surprised, but in no way discomforted by being abandoned so suddenly, and she continued to eat her dinner with composure.

Talk became more general, although when Mrs. Orvis-Ryder bemoaned the weather for the third time, Barrington appeared to become restive, and as soon as Jed had brought in the decanter of port, made haste to rise and help Mrs. Orvis-Ryder from her seat. Although by right she should have given the signal to retire to the ladies, she made the best of it, for she was determined to get him talking to Letty sometime that evening.

Once again, the three ladies found themselves before the fire, the gentlemen still at the table with their port. Mrs. Orvis-Ryder ignored Beth, who smiled inwardly. She was beginning to realize that Mrs. Orvis-Ryder was jealous of the attentions paid to her instead of her daughter; that young lady, in all innocence, chatted gaily to Beth and only occasionally sent a glance in the twins' direction. When the gentlemen finally rose and approached the fire, Mrs. Orvis-Ryder began her campaign.

"Your grace," she said to the duke, "won't you sit next to Letty and tell us all the latest *on dits* of the London scene? Letty is so looking forward to visiting the capital!"

Letty merely looked alarmed at this strategy, but Barrington grinned and took the seat indicated, causing the girl to shrink to one side of the settle in fright. He turned to her and asked in his abrupt way, "Well, are you, Miss Orvis-Ryder?"

"Am . . . am I what, your grace?" whispered Letty.

"Looking forward to your first London season, girl!" Barrington exclaimed. Letty swallowed and nodded her head mutely, and when he saw she was not going to speak, he went on.

"Although I am not the one to tell you of the London scene, for I have not been there during the season for the past two years. You should apply to the Allensworths for that! I have not been away so long, however, that I cannot foresee what a brilliant season you will have, Miss Letty." He paused and she looked at him inquiringly.

"I mean you will be fired off early as an Incomparable," he explained, and then he added in a kindly way, "Although I would suggest that you curb your impulse to chatter on any and every subject. It is very confusing not to be able to get a word in edgewise when conversing with you!"

Letty looked confused as Dolph said, coming to her defense, "But I say, duke! She wasn't! Barely said a word, 'pon rep, I do declare. Must be mistaken!"

He looked as confused as Letty when Barrington began to laugh, and was soon joined by Tony and Beth, but Letty gave him a grateful smile. Mrs. Orvis-Ryder decided to take a hand.

"Do tell us about your servant, duke. So ... so unusual to have a savage in attendance!"

Barrington stared at her. "I must object to the word 'savage,' and I know Albert would object to being called a servant. He is my blood brother, you know, and considers he is looking out for me."

He would have left it at that, but Mr. Cummings asked eagerly for more information, so he continued.

"You should see him dressed in his ceremonial robes—he is magnificent and rivals royalty! Well, he is royal, for he is the son of a chief of one of the Ohio tribes loyal to the king. His real name is practically unpronounceable, although it means "Wolf-Who-Runs-with-the-Moon." I had dealings with his father while on a journey in America, and the chief insisted I take Albert along, to learn the English ways and language. A farseeing man, the chief. He knows the Indians must learn to live with the whites or they will not survive. You would be amazed, Mrs. Orvis-Ryder," turning slightly to this lady and surprising her in a tiny yawn, "how quickly he learns—for a 'savage,' that is! And how wise he is in ways that we have forgotten!"

Mrs. Orvis-Ryder took another comfit and said, "How interesting!" in a way that did little to hide her supreme boredom.

Barrington did not take offense but merely grinned at her and said, "But enough of that; I fear I am boring the company, although I would be glad to chat with you, Mr. Cummings, some other time." He turned to the twins. "What do you think of the new Regent

Street, m'lords? I have not seen it of course, but I understand Nash has outdone himself."

Tony agreed, "Yes, it is quite well done, and most unusual with its crescents and terraces. I understand he has also completed a garden suburb in Regent's Park."

Beth said eagerly, "Oh, I have heard so much about it, I am so looking forward to seeing it!"

"I think you would like it, Miss Cummings." Tony smiled at her. "Especially the grass and trees that have been incorporated in the design. Do you plan a stay in London in the near future? I would be glad to escort you to the site."

"Our plans are uncertain at this time," Beth said, glancing at her father. "I hope to see it—I have been told so much of the charming curve of the street, and the extensive use of Ionic pillars."

Mrs. Orvis-Ryder broke in. "What a shame we will be there before you," she said in her positive way. "Although I am sure only bluestockings have much interest in architecture," she added, completely forgetting her avowal to Dolph that morning of Letty's supposed passion of old buildings. Letty gasped, and Barrington frowned and appeared to be about to speak, when she continued on, "I suppose you also visit monuments and museums?"

Beth nodded, her eyes dark with anger. "Of course, ma'am."

Barrington rose abruptly and stretched. "I wonder if there are any cards at hand? I would challenge you two young ones to a game!"

Tony eagerly produced the rather elderly pack, and the awkward moment brought about by Mrs. Orvis-Ryder's scorn was soon forgotten, although Mr. Cummings bent over Beth when he rose to fetch his book and whispered, "Luke six, verse thirty five!" Beth smiled at him and rose and strolled away from the fire as the three men placed their chairs around a small table and rearranged the candles. She did not feel she

70

would be able to control her temper if she was forced to converse with Mrs. Orvis-Ryder any longer, for surely it was a very hard thing to do, to love such an enemy!

Mrs. Orvis-Ryder was not quite ready to relinquish the gentlemen.

"It is too bad we are not spending the evening at home, m'love," she said loudly to Letty, and then turning to Barrington, she added coyly, "There would be no need for you to play cards there, your grace! I must tell you that Letty is a talented musician!"

Letty squirmed and appeared to be delighted with her present location, but Barrington sent an amused glance at Beth as he replied, "Do not tell me! I am sure I can guess her instrument!" He thought for a moment, and then said, "Of course! She plays the harp, I am sure. It could only be the harp!"

Mrs. Orvis-Ryder gasped and pressed her fat little hands together in applause. "How did you guess, your grace? Yes, she plays the harp, and very creditably too."

Barrington bowed ironically and murmured, "Anything *less* than the harp would not be just." He then took his seat and proceeded to ignore any and all conversational sallies even though Mrs. Orvis-Ryder continued to expound on Letty's musicianship; not only her expertise on the harp, but her singularly sweet singing voice.

The evening passed slowly, and long before the tea tray was brought in, Beth was heartily bored. She resolved to arm herself with a book from now on, no matter how rude it appeared, and it was with a profound sense of relief that she finally rose as the party broke up after the tea had been drunk and made her way thankfully to bed.

In the kitchen, the servants were assembled when Henry brought back the tea tray and settled in his chair by the fire with a tired sigh. Abby and Jill waited to be summoned by the ladies for assistance in getting ready for bed, and James to help Mrs. Orvis-Ryder up the steep stairs. Only Albert was missing; he had sat quietly before the fire for a long time, gazing into the flames, and then, before anyone was quite aware of it, he was gone. Jed was the only one who was easy with him; Willy still watched him carefully whenever he had to be near him. He had had another fright that afternoon when Albert had grabbed him and pointed to the careless job he had done polishing a bridle. Without a word, Willy had gone back to work with a vengeance. It was a shame that the duke and his man would soon be gone, for the quality of work done in the stables would then speedily return to its former state. At the moment, brass twinkled, leather gleamed, and the stalls were mucked out twice a day.

Everyone was more relaxed when the Indian left, and Bessie rocked placidly, her hands folded over her apron, as James reported on the scenes at dinner. Jed looked up from the piece of wood he was whittling.

"Aye, your mistress was close hauled tonight! Why is she so against Miss Cummings? Nearly took 'er 'ead off a couple o' times, and if looks could kill, the girl would be stretched out lifeless on the coffeeroom floor!"

James shrugged his shoulders. "Who knows? She's a strange 'un!"

Henry said slowly, pondering the matter, "Appears to me she don't like the lady drawing off m'lords and the duke. Miss Cummings has a deal to say, and all Miss Letty does is blush and look 'andsome."

"And say, 'Oh, Mama,' " added Bessie.

Jill said archly, smiling at James, "Ever so 'andsome those twins are, ain't they, Abby?"

Abby agreed, and then, rubbing her bottom thoughtfully, added, "A girl always knows who's who though, for all they look the same! That Dolph with 'is wandering 'ands! M'lord Tony don't bother me, but surely I 'ate to meet 'is twin in the hall!"

Jill giggled and nodded agreement. "You'd think

'e'd enough on 'is mind with Miss Leticia!" she said. "Coo! Never saw such beautiful clothes! It's a pleasure to 'elp 'er dress! What I wouldn't do for just one of her dresses!" She gazed absently into the fire, her work-roughened hands restless in her lap as she dreamed of the picture she'd make in the primrose muslin Letty had worn that evening.

"Get along with you, girl!" Bessie said, breaking into her revery. "Them dresses ain't 'alf decent, to my mind! It's plain to see what 'er mother 'as in mind, pushing 'er forward, half-clothed as it were! I feel sorry for her, poor young lady! I'm sure I would never be caught dead in such immodest dresses!"

There was a short silence as everyone contemplated Bessie so attired, and then she laughed heartily and added, "Can't you just picture it? Good as a raree-show!" Everyone laughed with her, and she got up to bank the fire as the bells rang, summoning the servants upstairs.

By two o'clock, the inn was quiet, with everyone peacefully sleeping. Suddenly a piercing scream rent the air, and woke the guests most abruptly. Beth sat bolt upright in bed, her heart pounding, and Letty began to wail.

"Oh, oh! What is it? We will be murdered in our beds! Oh dear!"

Beth slid from under the covers and hastily donned her dressing gown and slippers.

"Hush, Letty! I will find out what's happening!"

"Oh, do not open that door, Miss Cummings, I beg you! I am sure it is that savage! He will then be able to get in and scalp us both!"

Beth paid no attention to this cowardly statement, and grasping the poker, threw open the door to the landing. Mr. Cummings was standing there looking puzzled, his nightcap askew over one eye, and Tony suddenly appeared, drawing on his dressing gown, as the screams continued from the direction of Mrs. Orvis-Ryder's room.

"What's to do?" Tony demanded.

Beth moved forward and said, "I think we should check on Mrs. Orvis-Ryder; she appears to be in much distress."

They all turned to that lady's door, when suddenly it opened, and a sheepish Dolph came hastily out, followed by even more hysterical screaming. By this time, Henry and Jed, the latter still trying to pull on his breeches while holding a brace of pistols, had appeared on the scene. Henry strode forward, and raising his lantern, took command.

" 'Ere! What's all this? Is there a robber in the house?"

Dolph leaned against the wall and closed his eyes. He swallowed several times, but no sounds came from his trembling lips. Tony put his arm around his twin.

"Oh no, Dolph! You didn't!"

"Didn't what?" a lazy voice behind them inquired. Beth whirled to see Barrington leaning casually against his doorjamb, resplendent in a brocade dressing gown. Everyone was silent as he continued, "Can no one quiet that infernal woman? I do not admire your taste, sir," he added, bowing to Dolph ironically, "but perhaps you did not make the lady aware that you had such a *tendresse* for her? I am sure we have all been misled by your assiduous attentions to quite another lady!"

Dolph shook his head, but still no explanation came.

Tony said sternly, "Your jest is in bad taste, sir. Mr brother has the misfortune to be subject to sleepwalking."

"One can only deplore his destination, then," Barrington replied, as Beth moved forward impatiently.

"Oh, do stop this!" she said, waving her poker. "Let me through! Someone must see to Mrs. Orvis-Ryder!"

"By all means, Miss Cummings," Barrington agreed promptly. "And do feel free to use your—hmm—weapon, if you cannot quiet her screams in any other way!"

Beth paid no attention to this sally, but hastened

toward the door Dolph had quitted so precipitously, followed by Bessie, who had just arrived on the scene. Within moments, the noise from within had died down to a few moans and gasps, and Beth reappeared at the door.

"I think you might all return to bed, gentlemen, and let Bessie and me handle this. Mrs. Orvis-Ryder will soon be calm."

Barrington bowed to her. "I make you my compliments. Surely that is turning the other cheek! And where is the dutiful daughter all this time?"

"Hiding under the covers," Beth retorted, "afraid of being murdered in her bed!" She was about to add that Albert was the supposed murderer when she caught sight of him on the stairs, and thought better of it.

"Ah, sharper than a serpent's tooth, etc., eh, Mr. Cummings?" Barrington confided to Beth's parent, who, with Tony, was trying to soothe Dolph in the meantime. The young man appeared to have had at least as great a shock as Mrs. Orvis-Ryder.

"It's all right, twin! It's all right!" Tony said. "Whatever set you off this time, I wonder? You haven't had a sleepwalking episode for such a long time!"

Barrington eyed them sardonically. "I really think we can eliminate the possibility that the lady's charms so intrigued him that he was helpless in her spell, m'boy. But stay! How is his sense of direction when he does this? Perhaps he arrived at the wrong door? And had quite another objective in mind?"

Tony flashed him a warning look, as Dolph merely looked at him helplessly. Barrington continued smoothly, "However, if my supposition is correct, perhaps you had better keep the poker handy, Miss Cummings."

"Nonsense!" Beth said briskly. "Do you take him downstairs and give him a glass of brandy, Tony! He will be better in the morning, I'm sure!"

Tony smiled at her gratefully. "I'll take care of him, never fear. He never has two spells close together."

"Thank heavens!" murmured Barrington, depositing a wicked-looking dueling pistol in the pocket of his robe. Jed eyed it respectfully. There was a sound from the stairs, and Barrington turned and saw Albert, holding a knife that was every bit as lethal-looking as his pistol. He spoke briefly to his man, and Albert disappeared soundlessly.

"Perhaps we can all get back to our interrupted rest now," Barrington continued. "Oh, Miss Cummings, perhaps I should go and reassure Miss Orvis-Ryder that her mother has not been vilely raped? I should be glad to help, you know!"

"Yes, thereby assuring another screaming session!" Beth snapped in exasperation. "I will inform Miss Orvis-Ryder myself, thank you very much!"

Barrington smiled at her lazily. She looked quite lovely with her expressive eyes flashing, and her soft brown hair free of its braid and streaming down her back. She still clutched the poker in one small white hand. Something in his expression made her aware of her disheveled state, and she put up her free hand to her throat, closing more securely the neck of her dressing gown. Barrington smiled again, and with an intent look, bowed to her.

"My compliments again, Miss Cummings," he said seriously.

Beth turned away in confusion and returned to Mrs. Orvis-Ryder's room, as Tony and Henry helped Dolph to the stairs, and Mr. Cummings prepared to retire. He bid Barrington goodnight, for, as he said earnestly, "I do not think either of us can be anything but frightfully in the way, your grace. I do not believe that Mrs. Orvis-Ryder wants counseling in any spiritual way, do you think?" There was a distinct twinkle in his eye.

"I definitely agree with you, sir," Barrington replied. "Probably the most exciting thing that has happened to her in years! Perhaps she might even feel the need to keep to her room tomorrow, nursing a *spell*."

76

"Aye, it's an ill wind that doesn't blow good for somebody!" Jed muttered, and then recalling himself as both gentlemen laughed out loud, hastily removed himself from the scene.

Beth deplored the laughter which she heard plainly from within Mrs. Orvis-Ryder's room, but fortunately that lady was unaware of it, for she was indeed having one of her *spells,* and for good reason. Sure that the Indian had invaded her room, complete with tomahawk, she had become so distraught that Beth left her in Bessie's capable hands while she went and fetched Letty to assist them. She looked speculatively at Barrington's closed door as she passed it, wondering again why she had felt such a strange feeling of delight when he smiled at her a moment ago. There had been something in his expression . . . She shook her head sternly, and putting it firmly from her mind, went and implored Letty for help in calming her mother. That young lady, once she was reassured that no Indians, robbers, murderers, or worse were within the inn, hastened to her mother's side, and it was not much longer before the Bird and Bottle was again quiet for the remainder of the night.

Chapter IV

The following morning, everyone slept late as a result of the alarms of the night before. When Beth finally awoke, she went to the window, stifling a yawn with one hand as she drew back the curtains with the other. The snow had stopped, but the prospect below her was not cheering. The sky was still a leaden gray even though the hour was well advanced. Nothing stirred; even the wind had stopped. The yard looked cold and forlorn under its heavy blanket of snow. The whole scene gave Beth the distinct feeling of being truly marooned. She shivered, and turned as a sound from the big bed caught her attention. Letty sat up, an engaging lace-trimmed nightcap hiding all but a few of her golden curls. She yawned and stretched, and then smiled shyly at Beth.

"Good morning, Miss ... uh ... Beth!" she said. "Has it stopped snowing yet?"

"Thank heavens, yes! But it's a dull gray day for all of that, and cold-looking, too!"

"Oh, that doesn't signify," Letty said airily. "We will be able to have our sculpture party after all!"

If Beth thought this unconcerned pronouncement a bit heartless when the young lady's mother was lying distraught and possibly ill a few feet away, she made no comment, merely ringing the bell for Jill. Letty chatted gaily about the coming activities as she sipped her chocolate. As the girls were dressing, Beth pointed out to Letty the advantage of warm clothing when a morning in the cold air was in store, and Letty agreed, putting on a warm black dress and then ruining this practicality by selecting a matching cloak trimmed with ermine, which Beth realized would be ravishing with her black eyes and blond hair. She spent a considerable amount of time deciding which of two bonnets became her best, until Beth suggested a warm hood or scarf might be more appropriate, no matter how fetching the shiny black crown hat with its matching satin tassels might be. Fortunately, Letty remembered her ermine hood before Beth quite lost patience with her, and they went down to the coffee-room together in perfect amity.

Beth had asked Letty if she wished to see her mother before breakfast, but the young lady merely widened her big dark eyes and declared she would never dare to disturb her mama before she awoke and had called for her chocolate. Then she colored slightly, and smoothing her fur hood abstractly, added, "Miss . . . I mean, Beth! I hope you will not be offended at the things Mama says. . . . She has had so much to contend with in her life . . . and her health, you know . . . well, sometimes she gets a little mifty!" She paused, and then confided, "The family, too, has quarreled with her repeatedly, and it is never Mama's fault, of course! But she does have this nervous habit of insulting people! I pray you, do not take it seriously!" Letty stopped in confusion, and Beth patted her hand and assured her she would not be offended again, although privately she did not blame Mrs. Orvis-Ryder's family for any of the quarrels, and decided that "mifty" was not quite the word she would have chosen to describe the lady.

As they entered the lower hall, they met Bessie coming from the coffeeroom, who assured them she would bring their breakfast shortly. Barrington had not made an appearance, and Beth was annoyed with herself when she realized how much she was disappointed, but Tony and Dolph were seated at the table over cups of coffee. The used plates and empty serving dishes showed they had already eaten, and the inroads made on a huge sirloin made it clear it had been no light snack they had consumed. Mr. Cummings was seated before the fire, already reading, which was no surprise to his daugher, who greeted him fondly, as Tony and Dolph rose and offered the ladies a seat at the table.

"Well, the snow has stopped, Miss Cummings!" Tony said cheerfully. "So there will be no impediment to our sculpture attempts!"

Beth announced she would be ready to begin as soon as she had had her breakfast, and asked if he had chosen a subject.

Tony's eyes sparkled, and he looked very devilish as he admitted he had not one, but three designs in mind, but would leave the final choice to her.

"I will not mention them now, while our competition is so near . . . that is, if Miss Orvis-Ryder is still going to join us?" He glanced across the table, and seeing his brother sitting much too close to the lady, frowned.

Letty looked up in surprise. "Why, of course I am going to be there! Why should you think I would fail?"

"Well, Miss Orvis-Ryder," Tony replied, "I did think you might feel you should be with your mother, after her fright of last night."

Letty looked amazed and made no answer, and Dolph, blushing, looked first at her and then at Beth as he stammered, "Must forgive me, ladies . . . humble apologies and all that ... I ... I am so sorry to have disturbed you all last night. Don't know why it happened? Haven't had a toddle at night for ages!"

Beth kindly inquired if he was quite recovered, and made light of the episode until Dolph was reassured. In fact he felt so much better he made a light jest about how glad he was he had not encountered Albert in the hall while sleepwalking.

"What an incongrous name that is," Beth said, changing the subject. "Anyone less like an 'Albert' I have yet to see!"

Dolph and Letty looked at her blankly, but Tony agreed with a laugh. "We must ask the duke why he chose that name! There must be a story there!"

They were finishing their breakfast when Jill came in to announce that Mrs. Orvis-Ryder was calling for her daughter. Letty's face fell ludicrously, but she rose obediently and went upstairs, with Dolph assuring her they would wait for her return before they got started.

In the best bedroom, Mrs. Orvis-Ryder was awake, and made no objections when Letty said they were all ready to begin the sculpture.

"For, m'love," she said weakly, "I shall be forced to stay in bed all day. This has been a *terrible shock* to my *system*. You know how *delicate* my *sensibilities* are!" Letty hastily agreed, and after asking if there was anything she could do for her mama, made haste to escape.

"One moment!" that lady said, in stronger tones. Letty paused by the door. "What are you wearing?" Letty told her about the black velvet cloak and ermine hood.

"Very well thought-on, m'dear. And Letty!" as that young lady once again grasped the door handle, "I rely on you ... I think you know what I mean!" Letty did not appear to be confused by this obscure direction, and made good her escape.

A few moments later, all four young people were outside. It was still very cold, but as Beth had noted earlier, there was no wind. Tony fetched a shovel from the stable, and he and Beth decided to make their entry right by the gate. Letty and Dolph disappeared around the side of the inn, causing Tony again to look thoughtful. Dolph explained, carefully nonchalant, "Mustn't let you see what we're doin', you know!"

"That's what I'm afraid of, bro," Tony mumbled, causing Beth to turn away so he couldn't see the laughter in her eyes.

"Besides," Letty added, "it will be warmer there, out of the wind!"

On these sensible words they left, and Beth innocently asked Tony if he thought they would be uncomfortable where they were, in such a gale, causing him to grin at her in understanding.

When he told her his three ideas, she burst into laughter.

"No, no, m'lord! How can you?" she said of the first. "It is sure to cause offense, as well you know!"

"How can you say so?" Tony retorted. "Surely if we make it a faithful reproduction, the lady can only be flattered!"

"M'lord," Beth said between chuckles, "if we faithfully depict Mrs. Orvis-Ryder, she cannot help but be offended! And think of all the snow we would need! We would be here for days!"

Tony put his head back and shouted his laughter, and a window on the second floor opened. Barrington's tousled head appeared and he exclaimed angrily, "What is all this insane cackling? Oh, your pardon, Miss Cummings," he said sarcastically as he saw Beth by the gate, and Tony clutching his shovel for support. "I had forgot! The sculpture competition! Well, do not let the thought that others may be sleeping deter you from your merriment!"

He made to withdraw his head, as Beth looked up at him and replied, "Pooh!"

"I beg your pardon?" he said awfully.

"I said 'Pooh' ", Beth answered cheerfully. "It surely must be time for your next meal, there being such a lot of you to keep up, as you yourself admitted! I recommend the sirloin—not that the Allensworths left you much!"

"Oh, I say!" Tony protested.

Barrington started to speak, thought better of it, and withdrew his head, merely sending Beth a mighty frown as she stood there, smiling up at him in her warm gray cloak and hood, her eyes sparkling with amusement and the cold air bringing color to her cheeks.

She turned back to Tony, and after a short discussion, they were agreed that the second idea of his was worthy of merit. His third suggestion was that Albert would make a noble subject, clutching a tomahawk and looking ferocious, but when Beth said he might be offended, Tony willingly gave up the idea. Beth pointed out that some primitive people felt their souls were lost if they were represented in any way, a premise Tony had never heard. He was interested, and questioned her carefully until she reminded him of their task. Tony hastened away to get some sturdy branches.

"We will need something to brace the arms and legs if we are going to do a good job, Miss Cummings!"

Beth noticed he went searching for the wood in Dolph's direction. Coming around the corner of the inn, he surprised them virtuously rolling large snowballs, at some distance from each other. Dolph cheerfully banished him from the site.

"We've no intention of spying on your efforts, twin," he said. "In fact, if Miss Letty gets cold, we'll pop into the inn through the kitchen door, so off you go!" Tony was forced to retreat.

For some time there was much busy activity in the yard. Willy escaped from the stable, and Albert's critical eye, supposedly to sweep the walks, but really because he was curious. Neither effort at the moment repaid him for his trouble, and when he asked them what they were making, Beth and Tony only said it was a secret, while Dolph just pointed a shovel at him and told him to "git!"

Albert appeared silently, causing Tony to drop his shovel in surprise as he inadvertently backed into him, stepping back to get a perspective. Albert grunted and retrieved the shovel, as Beth said, with her warm smile, "Good morning, Albert. Thank you!" The Indian nodded silently and soon disappeared as quietly as he had appeared.

Beth and Tony had decided to do as faithful a facsimile as they could of Jed, leaning on the gate in his navy bell-bottoms and tunic, complete with the flat hat, tarred pigtail, and seabag of his former profession. They had not originally planned to have him leaning, but after several of their efforts tumbled in the snow, in spite of the braces, they realized it was necessary. When they were half done, Beth began to feel the cold, and Tony insisted she retire to the inn for a hot drink and a spell by the fire.

The coffeeroom was empty except for Barrington, who was seated in front of the fire with several official-looking papers spread out before him. She wondered why her heart suddenly seemed to skip a beat as she came in and moved slowly toward the hearth.

Barrington nodded brusquely, but made no motion to rise, merely collecting his papers into a neat pile and covering them with a leather case—just as if, Beth thought indignantly, she had been going to try to read them! Her voice was stiff as she said, holding out her hands to the blaze, "I will not disturb you, sir. It was unnecessary to stop what you are doing. I just wanted to get warm and have a hot drink before returning to the yard."

Barrington looked at her thoughtfully. "I wonder if you have any idea," he said softly, "how much you are beginning to disturb me, without even trying!"

He rose suddenly and started toward her, as Beth stood very still, looking confused and a little frightened.

"My dear girl," he said, stretching out his hands, while she wondered if she should take umbrage at such an informal address. She realized that all she really wanted to do was to put her hands in his, but before she could move, there was a knock on the door, closely followed by the appearance of Bessie, beaming at them both and bearing a hot mug of cocoa for Beth, who did not know whether to be glad or sorry for the interruption.

Barrington dropped his hands and turned abruptly away, as Bessie said, "Here you are, miss! This will warm you up in a thrice! And was you and the young gentleman wantin' a luncheon?"

Beth asked the time, and composing herself, said they would be in shortly, just as Mr. Cummings came in to inquire on the progress of the morning's work. Beth drank her cocoa and told him they would need a little more time, and when she turned around, she saw that Barrington had left the room. She did not know whether she felt disappointed or reprieved by his defection.

Shortly thereafter, she took leave of her father and went thoughtfully out into the yard. What had Barrington meant? Surely she had imagined the fond look and those disturbing words? She tried to put it from her mind as she reached the gate and saw the great progress Tony had made. The figure was almost done, but the head needed work still, for although he had finished the heavy work, the features were not perfect yet.

"You see," he explained, "I have left the face for you. My artistic talents fail me there!"

Beth complimented him on his progress and they began to work again. In the silence, she heard Letty giggle, and there was a suddenly hushed protest. Tony looked up from the shoes he was trying to fashion and frowned.

"Dolph!" he called, "I say, Dolph!"

After a moment, a flustered voice replied.

"Finish up for a while, and we will all share a luncheon," Tony commanded. "The ladies must be tired and cold, and I know Miss Orvis-Ryder is anxious to check on her mother!"

Dolph agreed, and they all went back in the inn, one couple through the front, and one through the kitchen door, meeting again in the coffeeroom. Beth carried a flushed Letty away with her to remove their cloaks. Her color was high, but after all, it was a cold day.

Tony began to speak furiously as soon as the door closed.

"For heavens sakes, bro," he said, "will you think? What will be the end of all this? I warn you most strongly that the old man ain't about to welcome the likes of the Orvis-Ryders into the family!"

Dolph looked at his twin from his favorite position in front of the mirror, where he was repairing the damage done by the exertions of the morning to his exquisite hair. He colored slightly at the reprimand but airily dismissed it.

"You refine on it too much, my dear Tony," he said. "There is no thought of marriage, for that young lady is not as innocent as she looks, and if she welcomes my . . . ahem . . . attentions, where's the harm?"

Tony pointed a stern finger at his twin.

"The harm, as you put it, is very large, very ill-bred, and, I'm sure, very positive that she is going to snare one of us, if she can't get Barrington for her daughter. We may not know the Orvis-Ryders, but be assured marriage is what's wanted, not the honor of being your next mistress! Lord, Dolph! This is no

87

cypriar, but a *bourgeoise!* You know how Pa always warned us about them! 'Keep to your own class,' he said, 'where they understand such things.' You'll land in the soup for sure if you're not careful!"

Dolph seemed much struck by these words, especially when he remembered Letty's mama. He promised to be more circumspect, and in truth really intended to withdraw slightly, but his good resolutions lasted only until Letty and Beth reappeared in the coffeeroom. She was so beautiful! He had had many flirts in his young life and he was sure he could handle any situation, but he remembered Tony was watching him, so he went to Beth and made much of handing her into a seat and then sat beside her as Jill brought in a tray, chatting lightly about the morning's activities and asking her if she felt chilled or tired. Tony seated a pouting Letty, and as they were about to begin their repast, Mr. Cummings appeared.

"Well, my children," he said, smiling at them, "and how is the sculpture coming? You look better for your morning in the air, at least, even if you have not accomplished works of art!"

"Father!" Beth scolded him. "Our sculpture is almost finished, and I am sure you will be surprised at it! Is yours done, Letty?" she asked, leaning across the table. "How are you two getting on?"

Letty tossed her head. "We are finished!"

"No, no, Miss Letty!" Dolph protested. "Surely you remember we have those few final touches that we discussed? It will take us a little while longer yet!"

Tony broke in before Letty could reply, to say that he and Beth also had some work yet to do. Mr. Cummings took out his watch and agreed that the judging should be held at three that afternoon, "If I can get the duke to help me judge at that time. I fear Mrs. Orvis-Ryder will be unable to assist us. How is your mother, my dear?" he asked Letty.

"She is still resting, and I am quite worried about

88

her," Letty said. "Last night was such a shock to her system! Why, she did not want any luncheon at all, when I went to inquire!" There was silence, as all at the table contemplated the large lady's actually missing a meal. Dolph colored slightly and bent his head more industriously over his dish of baked eggs.

"I am most sorry to hear it, dear child," Mr. Cummings said finally, "but perhaps a good rest will make her feel more the thing."

"Father, maybe Henry and Bessie could also be judges," Beth said, changing the subject, to Dolph's relief. "I think they would be pleased to be asked, and the more judges, the better!"

Mr. Cummings agreed to ask them, and after finishing their repast, the two couples dressed warmly again and went out to complete their sculptures. Tony was more lighthearted than he had been in the morning, but as Beth was thinking about Barrington, she did not notice his relief that Dolph had drawn off from Miss Orvis-Ryder. Suddenly he took her hand as they approached the gate, and squeezed it warmly.

"Miss Cummings!" he said, looking fondly at her. "Thank you for being so kind and understanding, always! I know you realize how much I worry about Dolph, and for good reason, I am sure you will agree. Lord, he thinks he's up to the nines, alert on every suit, but he's a mere Banbury babe when it comes to women! Sometimes I wish I weren't his twin, but he would quickly come to grief if I weren't there to help him out of his scrapes."

He looked so serious and disconsolate that Beth squeezed his hand back and smiled warmly at him, which caused the occupant of the second-best bedroom to drop the curtain with an oath of annoyance. How dare that young puppy hold her hand! And what had he been saying to bring that warm look to her eyes? Barrington determined to do something about it as soon as may be.

Meanwhile, Letty was still pouting as Dolph helped her out the back door. To be ignored was a novel experience for her. Dolph eyed her anxiously and gave her arm a hug before he released it. She looked at him haughtily. "M'lord?"

"Lord, Letty, what's amiss?" a bewildered Dolph asked, remembering her flirting of the morning.

"Why, nothing, I'm sure! What can you mean?" Letty asked, flouncing off toward their snowmen. He caught up with her, and putting one arm around her waist, drew her close.

"Now Letty, little love, something's wrong! Why so cold? When just this morning you were all smiles for me!"

Letty put up two little hands and tried to push him away, which just made him hold her tighter. He looked down into her stormy black eyes, and then, tipping up her chin, he kissed her. Letty tried ineffectively to get away, but was soon kissing him back. He was so handsome! When she was finally released, she leaned back in the circle of his arms, her mouth making a small oooh of contentment, which just caused Dolph to bend and kiss her again.

"Now, tell me!" he demanded, when they had both caught their breaths.

"Well, it was not very kind of you to ignore me at luncheon," sniffed Letty. "Hovering all over Miss Cummings the way you did!"

"Oh, that!" said Dolph, relieved that that was all it was. "Must tell you, m'brother don't like our . . . ahem . . . friendship! Nasty moment in there while you were upstairs! I promised him I'd not be so close in my attentions!"

"Well!" bridled an indignant Letty. "And may I ask why he doesn't approve? Can it be possible he doesn't approve of *me*?"

Dolph squirmed, and tried to think what he could say that wasn't too close to the truth. It would hardly help his cause if he announced that no matter how important the Orvis-Ryders might be in Durham, they were not suitable *partis* for the Allensworth family. Desperately he cast his mind about for an answer, as Letty waited, hands on hips.

"Jealous!" he got out, as inspiration struck. "That's it! Jealous! He sees that you prefer me, and he is trying to keep us apart, so he can have a chance with you!"

Letty was much struck by this. As she was not clever, she forgot that she had welcomed Tony's advances as much as Dolph's, and since she had never known anything but devotion and admiration from any young man who had ever been in her orbit, she was very content with the logic of what Dolph had told her. Of course! It was all clear to her!

She smiled at Dolph, determined now to bring the envious Tony into her court too.

"Perhaps, m'lord," she ventured shyly. "we should be more distant in public."

Dolph seized her again. "Yes, that's the ticket! Just as long as we can be as close as this in private!"

Letty laughed and evaded him. "And now, sir, shall we finish our snowmen?"

They both looked at the three slightly lopsided figures they had made—a father, mother, and small child. They were not very good, but perhaps that was the result of a morning spent in flirtation instead of attending to the matter at hand.

"Don't know what it is," Dolph said, studying them carefully. "Don't look quite right, somehow! What have we forgotten?"

Letty pondered the matter, and then, clapping her hands, said, "They need hats! And a cane for the father, and a shawl for the mother!"

The cane was soon produced from a tree branch, and Letty persuaded Dolph to try his own hat on the male figure. This he was very loath to do, for it was new

91

and had been made for him by the leading haberdashery in London only a short time before. When she saw his hesitation, Letty stamped her foot.

"Surely you don't mind lending it for a little while? I will get one of my shawls for the lady, and we can put them on just before the judging." Dolph agreed reluctantly, still smoothing the brim of his curly beaver.

In the meantime, Beth and Tony, admiring Jed, were also aware that they were in trouble, for the right arm kept slipping. They had tried to place the arm so that it appeared Jed was tugging his forelock, in that now familiar gesture. The hand would not stay on the brow, however.

"I know!" said Tony. "Perhaps if we had a telescope, we could prop the arm up on that!"

"Yes, but we don't have one," said Beth, ever practical.

"I know, but surely we could make one! How about a piece of stiff paper? If we rolled it into shape and then dampened it, it would freeze solid, and then we could use it as a brace."

"Good idea, m'lord!" Beth agreed. "I'll go in and see if the good landlord has any paper."

She hurried into the inn, but on her way back to the kitchen, thought perhaps her father might be a better source, so she turned aside and went into the coffeeroom. There was no one there, and as she turned to leave, she dropped one of her mittens. Stooping to pick it up, she spied a paper under the settle. It was just the right size, so she went over, and picking it up, rolled it into a cylinder. Perfect! She made her way back to the kitchen, where Bessie gave her some string to tie the roll in place and some water to wet it with. She carried it outside, and packing a thin layer of wet snow around it, laid it carefully down to freeze. Tony, meanwhile, had been putting the finishing touches on the sea bag.

At last they were ready, the telescope in place, looking just as if Jed were leaning on the gate and peering through his glass down the road, in search of other guests. They were well pleased with their efforts. As they returned to the inn and the warm fire, Tony pressed her hand again and said admiringly, "Barrington was right! You *are* something out of the common way!"

Laughing lightly, Beth withdrew her hand and swept him a mock curtsy. Dolph was before the fire in the coffeeroom, but Letty was nowhere in sight, having gone up to see her mother and report on the latest development. Dolph helped Beth remove her cloak and shake it free of snow, as Tony called for some mulled wine.

At three o'clock, Mr. Cummings came in with a silent Barrington as well as Bessie and Henry. Bessie was wrapping a warm shawl around her head and beamed as if delighted to be included in the judging. Beth thought Barrington looked rather stern and pale, and wondered why. They all trooped out into the snow, following Letty and Dolph, who had pleaded for a few moments for their final preparations. Letty put her shawl and one of her best bonnets on the lady, while Dolph reluctantly set his hat at a jaunty angle on the largest figure.

Bessie was much struck by their efforts, although Barrington did not appear to be overwhelmed by it. He eyed Dolph sardonically, after spying the rakish beaver. The young man's golden hair was blowing in the breeze, as he tried desperately to smooth it down.

"Surely that is the utmost sacrifice to your art, m'lord," he murmured. "Do you know that it is entirely possible that that beaver was trapped by an American Indian, as well as the ermine on Miss Letty's cloak? Why, it might even have been Albert!"

Letty shivered and looked distastefully at her soft

furs, as Mr. Cummings walked slowly around the three figures.

"Very creditable, very creditable indeed!" he said.

"But wait till you see ours, sir!" enthused Tony, drawing the group around the corner of the inn while Dolph hastily retrieved his precious misused hat. Bessie gasped when she saw Jed in snow, at the gate.

"My lands!" she exclaimed. "It's the spit of 'im, so it is! Oh, I must fetch 'im, and the girls too! Wait till they see this!"

She hurried to the door, calling her brother, while the others admired the sculpture.

"That's won the prize, twin!" Dolph said cheerfully. "Lord, ours ain't even in the running!"

"I fear you have the right of it, sir," Mr. Cummings said. "Do you agree, your grace? And Henry?"

Barrington was smiling. "Yes, it is very like. You are definitely the winners, if our good host agrees." As Henry assured him he did, Barrington turned to Beth for the first time since they had quitted the inn.

"So you are artistic, Miss Cummings! What other talents and delights do you possess, I wonder?" He spoke softly, with a lazy intimate smile, and Beth was hard put to answer him lightly.

"As to that, sir, you must remember that Tony did most of the work," she said, feeling slightly breathless with his dark intent eyes holding her glance.

Jed appeared, followed by Willy and the maids, who all exclaimed over the snow figure. Jed was flattered to be their subject, but declared he was glad he wasn't in uniform during weather like this. "Oh!" said Abby softly. "But what a shame!"

Henry asked her what she meant. "What a shame that it must melt, I mean!" Everyone laughed, causing her to turn pink with embarrassment.

"Much as I would dislike to see all your work disappear too quickly, my dear," the Reverend Mr. Cummings confided to Beth as they all returned to the inn, "I wish it would happen soon! Then we could be on our way again. One does not like to try the bishop's patience too far!"

Beth agreed, but secretly she hoped it would remain inclement awhile longer, although she put firmly from her mind the reason why she felt this to be desirable.

The ladies went up to rest and change, and Letty hurried in to see her mother and sit with that lady while Mrs. Orvis-Ryder questioned her about the day's activities and planned her evening attire. Beth sat before the bedroom fire, thinking confusing thoughts that all intertwined with piercing, intent dark eyes, a sardonic white grin, and a pair of powerful shoulders.

Was it possible that the duke was indulging in a flirtation? He did not seem the type for it, and must certainly be aware that she would not welcome such a diversion. It was all so confusing! She wondered why she was reacting to his attentions as she did. She had had a few suitors during her first season in London, and with her grandmother's help had been a moderate success, but when she compared Barrington to Mr. Horace Billingsley or Lord Fraser, or her feelings for them, it was not at all the same. She knew she was not beautiful; in considering her assets she could think of nothing that would attract him, except possibly her outspokenness and wit. She shook her head briskly. Surely she was making too much of the gentleman's boredom at being cooped up in a small country inn with such an ill-assorted group of travelers. If he did not prefer the beautiful Leticia—and she could see clearly why such a pea goose would not attract him—then, perforce, there was only one lady left. She remembered Mrs. Orvis-Ryder, and immediately dismissed her from consideration. That was all it was, she told herself sternly, even as she mentally went over her wardrobe to see if there was not some more becoming gown to wear that evening. She remembered a pale-gray moire taffeta, and wondered if it would be remarked on if she wore it. She had brought it in case she and her father were asked to dine with the bishop, and even as she dismissed the idea as vanity, was on her feet, taking it from the clothespress and shaking it free of wrinkles.

By the time she was dressed for dinner in the gray gown with her mother's pearls gracing its modest neckline, she knew it made no difference what she wore as long as Letty was in the same room. No, not even fixing her hair in a more informal arrangement had helped. She sighed and picked up a soft white shawl, as she watched Jill dress Letty's hair in artless curls. Who would look at a gray dove when there was a swan at hand?

Letty had on yet another gown this evening—a deep-brown one shot through with golden lights that seemed to match her eyes. The dark color made her skin—and there was a lot of it showing—turn even more creamy. The low-cut neckline revealed quite half her breasts, and she had put on a topaz necklace and brooch set that were perfect for her outfit. Beth wished drearily that she had paid more attention when her grandmother had spoken to her about clothes. Letty had a becoming flush to her face, but this was not due to any artifice with paint or powder, but rather the result of a stolen kiss from Dolph, whom she had encountered on leaving her mother's room.

Beth felt quite shy as both girls entered the coffee-room and the assembled gentlemen rose to greet them. Mr. Cummings thought his daughter looked quite well this evening, without even realizing why, and Beth was relieved he did not mention her gown. Barrington bowed to her formally without speaking.

As Mrs. Orvis-Ryder kept to her room, it was a more lighthearted group that sat down to Bessie's excellent dinner, served by Jed and the footman, James. Dolph was careful to pay no more attention to Letty than he did to Beth, and as Tony kept her busy with his chatter, Barrington had competition in the conversation, which caused him to raise his eyebrows sharply at both twins. Tony was delighted that his warnings had had some effect, and was also assiduous in his attentions to Letty, pleasing her very much. She would have a good report for her mama this evening, she thought, fluttering her eyelashes at Tony, and since she and Dolph had had their talk in the yard, she was not upset by his attention to Beth.

There was some conversation about the possibility of travel on the morrow, but since no carriage or rider had passed the inn all day, it was felt that the roads were still generally impassable. Mr. Cummings sighed, and wondered how much longer he would be delayed, but none of the others seemed to be concerned. As Dolph turned to answer a query from Mr. Cummings, Barrington said to Beth, "I must compliment you again, Miss Cummings, on your excellent sculpture. The subject was well thought of, too."

Remembering the other subjects that Tony had proposed caused Beth to smile. "We did have a discussion about that, your grace. I must tell you that Lord Anthony had two other persons in mind, but I persuaded him they would not do." Barrington looked as if he were about to ask who they were, and she added hastily, "No, no, sir! It was not Lord Byron! I cannot tell you!"

The dimple was pronounced, and her eyes flashed warningly at an unrepentant Tony, sitting across from her. "And you shall not mention it either, sir!"

"My lips are sealed!" vowed Tony, with a quick sidelong glance at Letty. Letty and Dolph both insisted he tell them.

Under cover of the other's conversation, Barrington leaned toward her and said softly, "I have another

97

quote for you from Byron. This one is much more appropriate. Perhaps it will change your mind about him.

> 'She walks in beauty, like the night
> Of cloudless climes and starry skies;
> And all that's best of dark and bright
> Meet in her aspect and her eyes.'

You are looking very handsome this evening, my girl! I like that gray gown; it matches your eyes."

Beth looked up at him. What she saw caused those same gray eyes to widen, at his soft intimate tones, and she drew in her breath sharply. This was no casual flirtation! There was an intent look in Barrington's dark eyes that shocked her. He smiled steadily at her as her color rose, and the gray gown rose and fell over her suddenly agitated breast.

She searched her mind desperately for a light reply, feeling quite short of breath, but before one occurred to her, Barrington added, rallyingly, "What? At a loss for words? I find it hard to believe, for I am sure you have received numerous compliments before this. However, for your instruction, your reply should be, 'Thank you, your grace,' said as demurely as possible, with lowered eyes. What a pity you do not have a fan. In my experience, fans are a great aid in situations like this!"

Beth had recovered by the time he finished, and although she thought the nonsense had been his way of giving her time to do so, she did not appear grateful.

"You are frivolous, sir!" she said in dismissal, and hurriedly turned her attention to Dolph. Barrington's eyebrows rose again, but he made no further comment.

After dinner, he sat with Mr. Cummings before the fire in a conversation that, although he found it interesting, he wished he could have curtailed. Mr. Cummings was fascinated by his experiences in the

Americas and wished to have as much information on the Indian tribes as Barrington could tell him. This evening he made no move to pick up a book and read, but instead plied the duke with one eager question after another.

Beth would have liked to have joined them, but Letty and Dolph proposed some games, and soon all four young people were seated around the table, playing all the nursery games they could remember. Tony tried to introduce charades, but that could not be said to be a success, since neither Letty nor Dolph were very good at it, although Beth and Tony were very quick. Soon Tony proposed a hand of whist. Beth had never played, and she wondered if she should, but it seemed unkind to back out when four players were needed. She stole a glance at Barrington every so often, glad he was safely with her father on the one hand, and then wishing he were seated beside her on the other. She shook her head and firmly dismissed these ideas as she tried to concentrate on her hand. If she had known how often that gentleman's eyes strayed to the figure in the gray gown, she would have been disconcerted.

At one point, Barrington went and called Henry to bring the ingredients for a bowl of punch. As he explained to Mr. Cummings, "I flatter myself that I have quite a hand with a punch bowl, and as the young people seem so festive, I felt it might be appropriate. Unless you have some objection, sir?"

Mr. Cummings agreed a glass of punch would be very well, for his throat was dry from his long talk with the duke. It was quite the most interesting conversation he had had in days, and he was feeling quite mellow with all the new information he had absorbed about a truly fascinating subject.

By the time the punch was prepared, the whist game had grown very lighthearted, and Beth rose from the table to discover she had won an impossibly large amount of fictitious pounds. She thanked her partner for it, declaring he had made her rich, and only hoping she would not discover she had a fated attraction for gambling. Tony grinned at her and then hastened to get Letty a glass of punch, leaving Beth and Dolph to gather up the cards and the matchsticks they had used for counters.

Beth wondered why Barrington did not approach her, but he made no move to seek her out again. He knew he had upset her at the table, and determined to go more slowly. She was such an innocent, he thought fondly, in spite of her assurance that she was a woman of experience. He did not want to distress her, but he had every intention of formally remedying the situation as soon as might be. He frowned when he remembered his errand in London; that had to come first, but as soon as he had delivered his report to the Secretary for War and the Colonies, he intended to seek Miss Cummings out without delay. To this end, he had been plying her father with questions and was content that he would have no trouble locating her in the future. Mr. Cummings had mentioned his interview with the bishop, after which he had it in mind to visit his mother, the Dowager Duchess of Woltan, and his brother, the present duke, at the family estate in Hertfordshire. Barrington, pleasantly surprised to discover that the modest cleric was a younger son of his own father's friend Woltan, mentally reviewed his acquaintances, for he was determined he would soon be visiting in that locality too.

Since Dolph slept soundly that night, everyone, including Mrs. Orvis-Ryder, had a good night's rest. That lady had been very pleased with Letty's report that she had both young Allensworths dangling on her leading strings, eager to do her bidding, and Mrs. Orvis-Ryder could hardly wait to make an appearance on the morrow to see for herself. She had not given up on the duke either, and felt that if a push was needed in that direction she would be happy to supply it. She went to sleep with a faint smile on her fat face, imagining her sister-in-law's amazement if she could announce that Letty was to be Her Grace the Duchess of Barrington or Lord Anthony's or Adolphus's bride.

The only person who was still awake as the clock struck midnight was Beth, but the day's exertions finally conquered her tumbling thoughts and questions, and she was soon dreaming too. And if her dreams were disturbed by Barrington's image and soft ardent voice, and if she seemed to hear herself saying, "And all that's best of dark and bright/Meet in his aspect and his eyes," only she was aware of it, for the night kept her secret.

Chapter V

There was a return of warmer air during the night, and the inhabitants of the inn woke to the sound of dripping water from the eaves. Beth and Mr. Cummings were the first down that morning, meeting in the coffeeroom and sitting down to enjoy their breakfast together. He was very jovial, for he was pleased with the turn of the weather and sure that by the next day they could again be on their way.

"Not, my dear," he said to Beth, "that it has not been very interesting. I was sure we would be bored, but Barrington has such a well-informed mind, and such a wealth of information about the Americas, I have been quite fascinated. It was providential that he joined us in our exile!"

Beth nodded her head demurely, but she did not point out that she was sure she found him even more fascinating than her father did, for quite different reasons.

They were still discussing the weather when Jed

came in to see if there was anything else they required. He shook his head when he heard that Mr. Cummings was planning an early start in the morning, and made so bold as to interrupt him.

"Aye, it's meltin' now, reverend sir, but it will come on to a hard freeze again before dark, mark my words!"

Beth looked up from her coffee cup. "Why, Jed, I do believe you just don't want our snow-Jed to melt too soon, you are so pessimistic!"

Jed grinned at her, but assured her he had not taken that into consideration at all.

"Many is the time I've seen it, miss, just like this! You wait and see!"

As it turned out, he was right. Around noon, the temperature dropped sharply, and Beth and her father, who had gone out for a stroll and some fresh air, hastened back to the inn. A cold wind rose, causing Mr. Cummings to hold onto his hat firmly and Beth to clutch her suddenly rebellious skirts. Mr. Cummings was dismayed.

"There will be no traveling on icy roads, I fear, Beth!" he said with a worried frown as they stamped the snow from their boots in the hall. On entering the coffeeroom, they saw Mrs. Orvis-Ryder seated before the fire, chatting with Tony and the duke. Beth felt suddenly shy, and turned away to remove her cloak as he smiled at her. She joined her father at the fire as he was greeting Mrs. Orvis-Ryder and asking kindly how she did. The lady deigned to be gracious, and said she felt much recovered.

"Not that I did not have great fears for a while," she elaborated. "It was such a shock to my *system!*"

Tony looked extremely uncomfortable as Barrington said, "Yes, yes! But your *delicate system* seems to have survived!"

Mrs. Orvis-Ryder ignored him and reached over to pat Tony's hand. "Never fear, m'lord," she said. "Irreparable damage has fortunately been averted, and you and your brother have both apologized so nicely, I

104

am sure we should all forget the unfortunate episode!"

This gracious statement was so out of character that everyone looked at the lady in amazement.

Mr. Cummings changed the subject, to Tony's relief, mentioning the drop in temperature and his fears that they would be unable to resume traveling tomorrow. Mrs. Orvis-Ryder appeared quite indifferent to the news, but Barrington frowned, a fact Beth was quick to notice. So, he could hardly wait to get away! Well, she would keep her distance if that was the case, she thought. It had all been a flirtation after all. She felt quite dispirited, and decided firmly that she was probably hungry.

Tony looked around the room and seemed to notice for the first time that the company was not complete.

"Where is Miss Leticia, ma'am?" he asked sharply.

Mrs. Orvis-Ryder heard his tone with satisfaction. Better and better! He must be in love or as near to it as to make no matter if he could not bear to have the girl out of his sight! She smiled at him and replied, "Why, m'lord, I am not sure. Perhaps she is in her room? Have you seen her, Miss Cummings?"

"No, ma'am," said Beth absently, for she was trying to ignore Barrington. "I have been walking with my father this morning and have not seen Letty since before breakfast."

"Well, I am sure there is no cause for alarm, m'lord," Mrs. Orvis-Ryder said, patting his hand again in a reassuring way, which caused that young man to look at her strangely. "Certainly she will soon make an appearance, for it must be almost time for our luncheon."

Little did she suspect, or anyone else, that at that moment a breathless Letty and an ardent Dolph were locked in each other's arms in the deserted taproom, some way down the corridor. They had set up the assignation in a hurried whisper the evening before. Letty thought Dolph quite the superior of the twins. He was kind; he did not confuse her with witticisms or ask questions she had no idea how to answer, as his brother did; and she was so sure he was in love with her, she expected him to be speaking to her mama before evening.

She pressed closer to him, if that were possible, and murmured, "M'lord! How I wish we could be together like this always!"

Dolph looked down on the golden curls resting against his waistcoat in sudden alarm. Surely he had never given her to understand that this was anything but a mild flirtation to pass the time? Or had he? He cast about in his mind, stricken with doubts, and would have moved away except that she raised her head and smiled at him, and when he saw those beautiful dark eyes and that soft rosebud mouth, his good intentions went down to defeat, and he bent to kiss her again.

Before long they were seated on a bench before the empty fireplace, Letty half-reclining in his arms.

"Are you cold, little love?" Dolph asked thickly, one hand caressing her hair.

"Not with you so close, m'lord," she said, innocently provocative, and wondering why he did not ask her to call him Adolphus, since they were soon to be betrothed.

He held her tighter, and moved his hands to her breasts, discreetly covered this morning by a warm gown of beige merino. It was perfectly obvious that she had little on beneath it, however, and Dolph was encouraged by this sign of readiness to move his hand even lower.

"M'lord!" Letty said indignantly. "Whatever are you doing?" She struggled out of his grasp and rose, breathing heavily, although not as heavily as Dolph, who hastened to get to his feet and approach her again.

"Why, love, what we both want, I'm sure! Come here, I know you are only teasing me, you little jade!" he said, grabbing her hand quite roughly and pulling her toward him.

Letty gave a squeak of surprise. All her flirtations had not prepared her for this. A few languid sighs, a hand held a moment longer than necessary, a fervent pleading glance, or an occasional stolen kiss when no one was looking—that was all her experience, and certainly no one had ever dared to touch her like that! She pushed Dolph away, and he, thinking she was just being playful, embraced her again, pinning her arms to her sides and rendering her helpless.

His hot mouth came down on hers, and she felt him pressing himself firmly against her. Letty panicked—this was no adoring lover begging to have the flower from her gown to wear next to his heart. Now his tongue was probing her mouth, and she felt his hard thighs, and good heavens!—something else as well! When he finally raised his head and looked at her triumphantly, Letty screamed.

In the coffeeroom, Jill was just setting down the tray with the luncheon on it, and she dropped it abruptly on the buffet, causing all the dishes to jump, as did everyone in the room. Mrs. Orvis-Ryder rose with as much haste as she could manage, Mr. Cummings hastening to help her. The scream came again, and she exclaimed weakly, "Letty! The savage! My God!"

"No such thing, ma'am," Barrington said sharply, but before he could continue there was the sound of a resounding slap, followed by an indignant outcry, and another scream. Mrs. Orvis-Ryder hurried from the room, attended closely by everyone else except a weeping Jill, who was overcome by the sight of the ruined dishes and spilled food.

Surging down the hall, Mrs. Orvis-Ryder had no trouble tracing the screams to the taproom, and throwing open the door, saw her daughter and Dolph struggling in the middle of the room, Letty still screaming hysterically and trying to push Dolph away while he tried ineffectually to shush her. Even as Mrs. Orvis-Ryder gasped and clutched her massive bosom, he was saying, "Will you be quiet, you little fool! You'll have the pack of them down on us!"

107

Barrington looked over Mrs. Orvis-Ryder's head and smiled sardonically. "The pack has already arrived, dear boy, I'm afraid," he said, strolling into the room as Dolph sprang back and Letty burst into tears.

"Sleepwalking again, m'lord?" Barrington inquired sarcastically, perching on a table, one long leg swinging. And then, turning to Mrs. Orvis-Ryder, he added, "I fear you owe Albert an apology, ma'am! He has infinitely better manners, and Miss Leticia is not at all to his taste!"

Tony pushed past Mrs. Orvis-Ryder, who continued to take up the whole doorway, and sized up the situation in a glance.

"Good Lord, Dolph! After all my warnings! You idiot!"

Mrs. Orvis-Ryder seemed to recover, and she moved forward to gather Letty into her arms.

"Now, now, my dear," she said. "I am sure the gentleman did not mean to alarm you!"

Barrington stared. "What a delicate way of putting it, ma'am! It appears to be at the very least a case of rape, and you treat it so cavalierly as to say he did not mean to 'alarm' her? Fore gad, what a fond parent!"

Mrs. Orvis-Ryder frowned and stiffened. "I am sure, your grace," she said frostily, "that when marriage is their object, such a . . . such a word, is most unnecessary!"

"Marriage?" Dolph stopped patting his brow with his handkerchief and repeated incredulously, "Marriage? No one mentioned *marriage!*"

Letty sobbed harder, Mrs. Orvis-Ryder stiffened even more, and Barrington grinned over their heads to Beth and her father, hovering in the doorway.

"You see, I was right! Obviously a case of rape!"

"No! No such thing, sir!" Dolph disclaimed passionately. "Why . . . why she positively encouraged me to . . . that is . . . she did!"

Mrs. Orvis-Ryder gasped. "An *Orvis-Ryder* encouraged you to think she could be had without *holy matrimony?* You are mistaken, m'lord! Letty knows her worth too well!"

Tony groaned and clutched his head, and Dolph stood speechless, his mouth hanging open in shock, so Barrington got up from the table and took charge.

"Now, my girl," he said firmly to Letty, whose sobs had died away into little hiccups, "think carefully, if you please! Did Lord Adolphus ever mention marriage at any time?"

Letty waved her hands and sobbed. "Why . . . of course I thought . . . oh dear, I am ruined!"

"No you are not!" Mrs. Orvis-Ryder said strongly, thrusting her handkerchief at the distraught girl. "Here, wipe your eyes, and rest assured that if marriage was not mentioned before, it will certainly be mentioned now!" She turned to Dolph, bosom swelling. "Do not think, m'lord, that you can play fast and loose with an Orvis-Ryder! Marriage it will be, for I will see to that! There are all these witnesses—"

Barrington interrupted. "All these witnesses, ma'am, cannot attest to any promises the young man made. It seems obvious to me that Allensworth was merely indulging in a little flirtation, to while away the time."

Mrs. Orvis-Ryder sat down abruptly.

"A 'flirtation,' sir? With an *Orvis-Ryder?*"

"Did you ever ask Miss Leticia to marry you?" Barrington asked Dolph.

"Of course not!" Dolph hastened to answer. "I thought she understood . . . I mean, the Allensworths are much too . . . I mean . . ."

Barrington interrupted this disjointed and potenially dangerous statement. "And how did this meeting come to be this morning? Did you grab the girl and force her into this room?"

"That I did not, your grace!" Dolph said more strongly. "She agreed last night to meet me here!"

"There, ma'am, you see?" Barrington said to Mrs. Orvis-Ryder. "Your daughter is not the little innocent you thought! Surely no well-brought-up young lady

109

makes assignations with hot-blooded young men without being aware of the consequences." He smiled warmly at Beth and continued, "For example, I cannot imagine Miss Cummings ever agreeing to such a scheme."

He turned back to a speechless Mrs. Orvis-Ryder and said more kindly, "I fear you have been misled in your daughter, ma'am. I advise you to watch her more carefully. And you, miss," including Letty, who was softly weeping again, "let this be a lesson to you! Next time you might not be in a crowded inn where help is so swift in coming! And now"—looking to the door where Bessie, Henry, Jed, and Abby were trying to peer over the Cummingses' shoulders—"may I suggest we repair to the coffeeroom for whatever was not spilled of our luncheon? I, for one, have had quite enough of this tiresome farce that is keeping us from our food!"

He helped a mute Mrs. Orvis-Ryder to her feet and called to Beth to assist Letty.

A pale Tony stood resolutely by his twin, and spoke to the company.

"I . . . I must ask your pardons, for my brother's behavior," he said manfully. "He was much at fault, I know."

"There, my boy," the duke said, more kindly than was his wont. "No harm done, you know! Not this time, at least, for all it's such bad *ton*—better not let your father hear of it! And if I may suggest it, you also should keep a better eye on your brother in the future!"

Several minutes later, a serious Mr. Cummings, Beth, and the duke were the only ones to sit down to a delayed repast. Mrs. Orvis-Ryder had swept a subdued Letty upstairs to her room, muttering dire imprecations and threats under her breath, and Tony had taken Dolph off for a walk and a lecture.

Barrington made no more mention of the scene, conversing lightly on a variety of subjects. Beth easily followed his lead, but it was seen that Mr. Cummings

110

was much disturbed, and if Barrington had not casually mentioned his travels in America again, might have brooded about it longer, feeling as he did that as a man of the cloth he should somehow have been able to prevent it. Beth asked the duke about the climate and the terrain, and as he answered, Mr. Cummings brightened considerably, and ventured to ask him, in his turn, what was his opinion of the war. "For," he said seriously, "I feel this whole thing has been most grossly mishandled, beginning with the war of revolution. How could we have been so unforeseeing as to allow such a promising colony to become so discontented that they actually sought their freedom from the crown? And now this latest conflict!" He shook his head sadly as Barrington agreed with him, and as Beth was just as interested they sat for quite a while after the covers were removed. Beth felt warmly grateful to the duke for diverting her father's mind. She knew he was blaming himself, and otherwise would have fallen into a state of melancholy for what he would feel had been his neglect of the situation.

Conversation died, however, when they observed Jed and the Orvis-Ryder footman in their outdoor clothes, leaving the inn.

"Aha!" Barrington observed with satisfaction. "I do not think we will have the company of our dear Mrs. Orvis-Ryder and her lovely Letty much longer. How much will you wager, Miss Cummings, that James is even now on his way to seek a carriage in the nearest town, with Jed to guide him? Perhaps they will leave today! The situation has become so uncomfortable for the lady, I do not feel even icy roads will deter her!"

"I must admit I would be relieved," Beth said absently, "for it could only be unpleasant to have to assemble for dinner again. No, I wouldn't wager a groat, I am sure you are right!"

Mr. Cummings sighed, remembering the scene in the taproom, and said seriously, " 'Brethren, if a man be overtaken in a fault, ye which are spiritual,

111

restore such an one in the spirit of meekness. . . . Bear ye one another's burdens, and so fulfill the law of Christ.' Galatians six, verses one and two," he added mournfully.

Barrington turned to him and said rallyingly, "Now, my dear sir, do not refine on it too much. I assure you there was nothing you could have done to prevent two such . . . er . . . hot blooded young 'uns from their folly. I do not think Adolphus has learned much of a lesson—I pity his poor father and brother!—but I can guarantee that Miss Leticia will be more circumspect in the future!"

As Mr. Cummings still looked grave, he added with a sideways grin for Beth, "Besides, it might have been worse! You might have found yourself performing a marriage out of hand, if Mrs. Orvis-Ryder had had her way! Consider the consequences, my dear sir, of facing their father in such a case! Not to be thought of, I do assure you!"

Mr. Cummings was much struck by this interpretation, and then, observing the time, made haste to get back to his books, leaving Beth with Barrington in the coffeeroom. He looked at her with a smile and said softly, "And now, my dear Miss Cummings . . ."

Beth rose hastily and walked to the door, saying, "I think I must go and see if there is anything I can do for Letty or Mrs. Orvis-Ryder."

The duke strolled with her to the stairs. "How Christian of you, my dear! Or is it that you do not wish to be alone with me, perhaps?"

Beth stopped, one hand on the banister, at a loss for a reply.

Observing he confusion, he said, "Well, I can wait. Perhaps this morning's distasteful scene affected you as well as your father, but I don't think so. I know you have better sense. Remember, dear Beth, all men are not so impetuous, passionate, and pudding-headed— all at the same time! I will wait for a more appropriate occasion."

Observing her still speechless, Barrington laughed softly and, taking possession of her other hand, kissed it lightly. Beth felt it tingle all the way up the stairs, as she fled to the sound of the duke's amused laughter behind her, her head in a whirl.

She did not see Mrs. Orvis-Ryder's door close, or know that that lady had been at the top of the stairs observing them. She was vastly disappointed and angry. Barrington had been right when he said she would wish to quit the inn as soon as possible. There was no more advantage to staying, since Tony would keep Dolph far from Letty—aye, even Dolph would keep away after the scene this morning, and Barrington would never be caught either! Whatever had Letty been thinking of to mishandle the affair so badly? she thought, eyeing her beautiful daughter asleep on her bed, worn out with weeping and the scolding she had received.

She had had some vague idea of asking Barrington's advice, but when she saw him kiss Beth's hand, and heard his soft tones, she knew it was fruitless. Miss Parson had won! Before long she was sure it was all Beth's fault. If she had not been here with her clever conversation and coming ways, Letty's behavior would not have seemed so singular, for there would have been no other young lady to compare her with. And the way she had kept pushing herself forward, in that unbecoming way, carrying on conversations with the gentlemen just as if she knew as much as they did! Well, she was not gone yet! Perhaps there would be a way to do Miss Parson a disservice yet! She paced angrily up and down the room, her fat little hands in fists, as she thought hard.

Jed and the footman returned in the late afternoon. James did not look as if he had had a comfortable trip, but he went at once to report that a chaise had been engaged so that the Orvis-Ryders would be able to travel in the morning, if the roads did not become any worse. Mrs. Orvis-Ryder commanded him to have their dinner served upstairs, and to tell the landlord the hour she appointed for departure in the morning.

James relayed her orders in the kitchen, and Bessie sniffed.

"Aye, she'll want to be off as soon as possible, for it's plain to see 'er grand schemes 'aven't worked out!"

James nodded his agreement. "She's in a fair rage, that I know! I don't envy Miss Letty for the next few days! Or myself," he added, quite downcast at the thought.

Jed chuckled. "Aye, dismasted so she is! She's run down her colors at last, and I for one am glad to see it!" He began to set a tray for the ladies' dinner, and then added, "aye, we'll all be glad to see the back of 'er! Although, we'll be sorry to lose your company, Jim, my boy!"

Abby smiled at the footman, and Bessie patted his arm.

Upstairs, Beth was able to dress for dinner, alone with her thoughts, for Letty had not returned to the room they shared. She put on the dark-green gown again, and then, realizing she was later than usual, hurriedly did her hair, pulling it severely into a tight coil. Miss Austen had been her companion all afternoon, but since she had closed the book at the same page she had opened it to, obviously Miss Austen had not been as amusing as usual.

As she went to the top of the stairs, a door farther along the landing opened softly, but she was unaware that there was anyone else in the hall. Just as she put her foot on the top step, she felt a sudden rush of air, and then felt her hand pulled away from the banister as she tumbled headlong down the stairs, the force of the blow between her shoulders making her unable to save herself.

As she landed in a heap at the bottom, the coffeeroom door opened abruptly, and the duke hurried out and knelt by her side.

"My darling Beth, what has happened?" he asked, as he took her hands.

Beth had not lost consciousness, but she was a good deal shaken, and since the question was unanswerable, feigned a swoon. She felt Barrington's strong but gentle hands feeling for broken bones, and then he lifted her carefully in his arms, just as if she weighed nothing at all, she thought. It was extremely comforting! He turned to the coffeeroom as Tony came out the door.

"What's amiss?" he asked, as Barrington brushed by him. There were exclamations of dismay from Mr. Cummings and Dolph, but the duke, in his forceful way, took care of them.

"She does not appear to have broken anything, Mr. Cummings," he reassured him. "Tony, fetch Mrs. Griffen at once, if you please! You, Dolph, get me a pillow for her head!"

The twins hastened to obey him, and Beth felt herself being lowered to the settle. She felt a stab of regret at leaving those strong arms, and opened her eyes to see her father wringing his hands beside her, and Barrington frowning down at her. He smiled faintly as she looked at him and said, "Good girl! Let me get some brandy, you will soon feel more the thing!"

Her father grasped her hand tightly. "My dear child," he exclaimed, "whatever happened? Are you all right? Should we fetch a physician?"

Beth laughed weakly and attempted to sit up, a plan that was quickly abandoned as Barrington pushed her gently back on the pillow Dolph had fetched.

"Not yet, if you please!" he said. "Here, do not attempt to speak until you have had a sip of brandy."

Beth's head was swimming, and she was glad to obey him. The brandy burned her throat, and she coughed, but she soon felt much better, although from the pain in her right ankle and the throbbing of her head, she realized she was not as fortunate as she had thought.

115

"Thank you," she said, handing the glass back to Barrington and smiling at her father."I may not have broken any bones, but I fear I have acquired some bumps!" She felt her head gingerly, and then her hand was removed as the duke felt softly through her hair. "Ouch!" she exclaimed, when he located it.

The fingers continued to probe gently, and then he said, "Just a small bump, Miss Cummings, and the skin is not broken. You should not have any discomfort there by tomorrow. Where else does it hurt?"

Beth extended her neat kid slipper. "My ankle, your grace. I think I have sprained it."

Her father and Dolph both exclaimed, as Bessie hurried in. Barrington felt the ankle carefully, and sent her back to the kitchen for a basin of hot water and some bandages.

"I think, sir," he said to Mr. Cummings, "it will be more comfortable bound up, but on no condition should she put any weight on it until she can do so without pain."

"I wish you would not talk about me as if I were not here, or as if I were a retarded child!" Beth said in a waspish way. She put both hands to her head, which was aching in earnest now.

"Now, now," the duke said soothingly, just as if she were six years old, she thought indignantly. "Just be calm, you will feel better shortly."

She opened her mouth to give him a blistering retort, but before she could begin, her father spoke to her again.

"But my dear," he asked anxiously, "whatever happened?"

Beth frowned a little and hesitated. She did not see any point in mentioning she had been pushed. It was perfectly obvious that Mrs. Orvis-Ryder had done it, for all the other guests but she and Letty were assembled in the coffeeroom, and she could not see Letty being so vengeful; nor, indeed, any of the inn's staff either. In fact, she could not really imagine why Mrs.

Orvis-Ryder had pushed her! She had had nothing to do with the morning's *contretemps* after all. She recalled everyone was waiting, and tried to smile at them.

"I fear I have been clumsy and tripped on the top step," she explained. "I knew I was late and I was hurrying. I must have caught the hem of my gown."

Mr. Cummings and the twins accepted her words without question, but as she stole a look at the duke, she saw he was frowning at her as if he had some doubts about this interpretation of her fall. Just then Bessie and Jill hurried in with the supplies Barrington had asked for, so he did not press her, but knelt down, and without so much as a by-your-leave, removed her slipper carefully and then her stocking with such an air of unconcern that Beth had no time to consider the impropriety of a man undressing her in public. He helped her to sit up and put her foot in the basin of hot water to soak, and when it began to cool, dried it carefully and then bound it up firmly. It felt better immediately, and she smiled her thanks.

He rested his hand on her tousled hair.

"Do you feel able to sit up to the table for your dinner? We can provide a footstool for support, unless you would like me to carry you upstairs," he asked.

Beth flushed and made light of her injuries. "Of course I can sit up, sir! What a poor creature you must think me! I am afraid, however, that my appearance is such that I should not be seen at the table!"

She felt her hair, which was becoming undone from the severe knot, and attempted to smooth it back into order.

"Nonsense!" Barrington said abruptly. "You look as lovely as ever! Come, let me help you to the table!"

He reached down, and again she felt those strong arms lifting her as she said, somewhat breathlessly, "I am sure I could walk, sir! If I could but lean on someone's arm . . ."

By this time she had been deposited in her chair,

and Tony was putting a cushioned footstool under her injured foot, so her protest went unheeded.

From the top of the stairs, Mrs. Orvis-Ryder returned softly to her room. She felt better, as if all her frustrations in losing a duke, a duke-to-be, and a second son of the nobility had been vented in that single vicious shove. She rejoined Letty at the table and made her customary good dinner, although she did not bother to talk to the girl, letting her see that her anger had not diminished. Letty picked at her food and wished she were dead, or in another country at the very least.

Dolph was also subdued at the table, still somewhat overcome by his relapse into bad ton and narrow escape, but Barrington kept up a gentle flow of chatter with Mr. Cummings, Tony, and Beth. After the joint had been removed and the sweets passed, Beth's head was aching in earnest, and she asked to be excused as soon as the covers were removed. Barrington looked at her searchingly.

"You have the headache, have you not? Yes, I see that you do!" He rose and called for one of the maids, and then said to her father, "With your permission, sir, I will carry Miss Cummings upstairs."

Mr. Cummings nodded and kissed his daughter goodnight, and one more time, Beth was picked up and carried away.

"Masterful, aren't I? You said it yourself, once!" he reminded her, as he maneuvered around the newel post, careful not to jar her ankle. Beth tried to look aloof while wondering what to do with her hands. The easiest thing would be to wrap them around his neck, and although that was what she wanted, it would never do! She folded her arms and tried to appear unconcerned as the duke carried her up the stairs, into her room, and then lowered her gently to her bed. Surely she imagined a soft kiss dropped on her hair!

Jill and Abby bustled in to help her undress, and Barrington prepared to leave. He stopped at the door and said, in a slightly louder than necessary voice, "One of you maids will stay with Miss Cummings tonight, do you understand? I do not wish her to be alone, in case she requires something."

Beth looked surprised, and was about to reply she could manage quite well by herself, when he continued, "Yes, yes, I know you do not wish it so, but Miss Orvis-Ryder can easily stay with her dear mama one night, and we will all feel better to know you have company. That way, it will be unnecessary for you to lock the door!"

Beth looked back at him steadily. "I assume you are not expecting another sleepwalking attempt, your grace?" she asked.

"Not at all—you know what I suspect, I am sure. Your brain and quickness are not the least of your many attractions, you know, and I find it hard to believe your story of the fall, for I have never seen you make an ungraceful move!" Beth blushed as he added, "Sleep well, my dear! You will feel better in the morning!"

With a wave of his hand and a slight bow, he was gone, leaving Beth to be undressed by a chattering Abby as Jill went away to fetch a pallet for herself for the night. The two girls quickly packed Letty's clothes and took them away, and suddenly very tired, Beth made no further protest, although she felt it extremely unlikely that Mrs. Orvis-Ryder would carry her revenge to the point of trying to murder her in her bed.

She fell asleep quickly, ignoring Jill's soft snores and remembering a soft kiss and a voice calling her "darling Beth." It had all become extremely complicated, but she was so tired—she would sort it out tomorrow.

CHAPTER VI

There was a considerable stream of people going in and out of Barrington's room early the following morning. Albert, when he came in to make up the fire and pull the curtains, found the duke already up, clad in his brocade dressing gown, his papers strewn all over the table and a ferocious frown on his face. Some time passed before the Indian silently left the room and fetched the landlord to Barrington. When Henry came out a few minutes later, he was wiping his brow and looking extremely upset, and then, one by one, from Jed and Bessie right down to Jill, Abby, James, and even Willy, summoned hastily from the stables, the servants all made an appearance in the duke's room. The guests of the inn, meanwhile, were still asleep and unaware of the commotion.

Barrington finally dressed, his mouth grim and his eyes narrowed in thought. He made his way to the coffeeroom, which he searched meticulously, having left explicit instructions with Albert, who remained upstairs in the duke's room, the door open so he would be sure to see the other guests when they appeared.

Mr. Cummings was the first, neatly and soberly dressed as always in his clerical garb. Albert moved to intercept him as he made his way to the stairs.

"Sir," he said sternly. "The duke . . . see you . . . downstairs . . . now!" He pointed a commanding finger and looked so ferocious that Mr. Cummings was amazed and a little frightened until a thought occurred to him.

" 'Tis not my daughter, man?" he asked in some agitation.

"No! You go!" Albert gestured again to the stairs, and Mr. Cummings said in some bewilderment, "Well! I will attend his grace at once!"

He hurried down the stairs, and it was not much longer before Tony and Dolph were also sent to Barrington, both looking identically puzzled. On the way down the stairs, Dolph suddenly stopped and grasped Tony's arm.

"I say, twin! You don't think that . . . Miss Letty has done somethin' . . . uh . . . foolish, do you?"

Tony looked even more perplexed as his brother's agitation grew and he turned very pale.

"Miss Letty?" he repeated in confusion.

"Yes! . . . You don't think she . . . she may have . . . er . . . taken her life after yesterday?" Dolph stammered in horrified accents.

Tony's first reaction was to burst out laughing, but when he saw how very upset Dolph was, he realized that this was not the moment to point out that his attractions were not so devastatingly fatal that a girl would kill herself if she were denied them. It was highly more likely that Mrs. Orvis-Ryder had murdered Letty in her frustration! Soothingly he patted the hand clutching his sleeve.

"I am sure that is not it, Dolph! Pull yourself together, bro, and let us find out what's the to-do!"

When they entered the coffeeroom they found a

122

baffled Mr. Cummings toying with his breakfast, and a grim Barrington striding up and down the room. He whirled as they entered and looked hard at them. Tony raised an eyebrow, but Dolph colored and tugged at his cravat. Maybe it was Leticia after all!

"Sit down. I'll have some breakfast sent in," the duke commanded. He left the room abruptly, and they heard him calling for Henry and then Albert.

Tony approached the table. "I say, sir, do you know what this is all about?" he asked Mr. Cummings.

That good man looked up from his half finished plate. "I have no idea, m'lord. The duke would not tell me until everyone is assembled, only that it is a matter of grave national concern."

Tony looked amazed. "National concern, sir? I am all at sea!"

"So am I," Mr. Cummings said dryly, "but I feel we should attend his grace."

Dolph had brightened somewhat, his fears assuaged. Miss Orvis-Ryder was not of national concern, after all, unless she were related to royalty. This seemed highly unlikely, even to Dolph, for if it were so, her mother would have mentioned it within the first few minutes of their arrival. He took a seat at the table feeling a deal better.

Henry came in with a tray of food for the twins, and as he looked very distressed, they did not try to question him. A moment later, Mrs. Orvis-Ryder's strident tones could be heard coming down the stairs.

"I have never heard the like of it! Routed out of bed, hurried into our clothes, and ordered—yes, ordered—to attend the duke in the coffeeroom! This will surely be *the death* of me! An Orvis-Ryder . . . *ordered!*"

"Oh, Mama," Letty broke in weakly as that lady paused for breath, "what can it be? Oh, I wish I did not have to . . ."

Her voice died away, and then both ladies were shepherded into the coffeeroom by Albert. Mrs. Orvis-Ryder declined breakfast with every sign of loathing, gave the other occupants of the room only the smallest and chilliest of bows, and took the best chair. She was dressed for traveling in her purple gown and bonnet, and Letty carried both her own and her mother's cloaks over her arm. As she was putting them down, she raised her eyes briefly and chanced to catch Dolph's eyes, which appeared to overcome her so much she said not a word, but scurried to sit as near her mother as she could get. Dolph's color was high as he tried nonchalantly to continue his breakfast.

There was an uncomfortable silence which no one liked to break, and then Henry, Bessie, and Jed, as well as the maids, James, and even Willy, were ushered into the room by Albert, closely followed by Barrington, who closed the door and nodded brusquely to the Indian. Albert took up his position in front of the door, arms folded, while Mrs. Orvis-Ryder bristled at the presence of the servants.

Barrington strode to the table before the fire and put down a leather case. Mrs. Orvis-Ryder had had enough.

"Will you be so good as to tell me what is the meaning of this?" she asked in an awful tone. "I have never been treated to such discourtesy in my life! An Orvis-Ryder! Well, I shall have something to say about it, let me tell you!"

"Be quiet!" Barrington said forcefully. Mrs. Orvis-Ryder gasped and sank back weakly in her chair. Letty immediately began searching through her mother's reticule for her salts and vinaigrette.

Barrington bowed and said ironically, "I beg your pardon, madam, but this is a serious matter, more serious than the slight inconvenience you have suffered. I am prepared to tell you the whole, but let me also tell you that no one will leave this room until the matter is cleared up."

So saying, he took his pistol from the leather case and laid it ready to hand on the table. Tony frowned, and Dolph started up, only to be pushed back into his seat by Tony, who was staring hard at the duke. There was a murmur from the assembled group, and Letty, paling at the sight of the pistol, dropped Mrs. Orvis-Ryder's salts. Abby and Jill tried to hide behind Jed, who stood stolidly, feet planted wide, as if standing at ease on the deck of one of his majesty's ships. Mr. Cummings glanced at the door and noticed that Albert was also possessed of a pistol.

The duke waited until the room was quiet again and then swept them all with a glance and said, "I am afraid there is a spy in this room."

At once a babble of voices arose, and then Tony jumped up, and in a tone that drowned out the murmurs of wonder said. "I am sure you will explain that, sir! 'Tis a grave charge!" He stood very straight, his young face serious for once, and dark with anger.

"I shall, sir," Barrington promised. "I must begin by telling you that I am late come from the United States, where I was on a mission for His Majesty, George III, and the new Secretary for War and the Colonies, Lord Bathurst. In this case is my report, which I was traveling to deliver. I have worked on it while we were all snowbound here, as many of you know."

Mr. Cummings nodded. "Yes, I have seen you with those papers in this very room, your grace."

"I am sure many of you have seen them," the duke continued. "Last evening, thinking that today I might be able to resume my journey, I went through the papers again and found that the most crucial page was missing—the summary of his majesty's forces in strength and disposition, and the plans for the next campaign."

There was another murmur, and Tony sat down, deep in thought.

Barrington let them wonder among themselves for a moment only; then he rapped the table for attention.

"Attend me please!" he said. "The inn has been searched, in case the missing paper had been mislaid somehow, and it has not been found. Therefore it is only logical that someone has taken it. Since we are the only people who have had access to the papers for the last several days, and since I know I had it two days ago when I added a postscript to the report, we must assume that someone here has stolen it, and that one of you is not what you have represented to us all."

There was a gasp from Mrs. Orvis-Ryder, a moan from Letty, and various whisperings from the others. Tony sat bolt upright in his seat, and Dolph looked distinctly puzzled.

"I say, Tony, what does he mean?" he asked plaintively.

When the room was quiet, Barrington went on, "I am inclined to discount the staff entirely, since they had no way of knowing I would be forced to put up here, and since I find it hard to believe any spy would take up employment in such an out-of-the-way spot hoping for the best. My own man I can vouch for; therefore the field narrows." He looked searchingly at Mr. Cummings, the twins, and the two ladies, as Henry wiped his brow, and Jill and Abby ceased to look as frightened as before.

Tony sprang to his feet and approached Barrington, who took up his pistol calmly.

"Sir! 'Tis to insult us! I will not stand here and be slandered. I—"

"Sit down, m'lord, if so you be," Barrington said with such quiet force that Tony retreated at once. "If any of you are insulted, that is of course unfortunate, but you will see that it is necessary to find out who it is that has taken the report. There are many people in the Americas who would give a great deal to know the contents of it, and there are many sympathizers for the American cause in England. Even the good Jed, after all, does not hold with impressment, which is one of the many reasons for the present conflict, the Americans resenting their ships being stopped and

126

searched on the high seas and their sailors taken bodily to serve the crown."

Jed's eyes narrowed, but he continued to stand stolidly and say nothing.

Dolph spoke for the first time. "Well then, your grace, perhaps it *is* one of the servants! Even if they did not know you would be staying here with the papers ready to hand, if one of them was an American sympathizer they could have seized the moment and—"

Henry and Bessie uttered shocked cries. "No, no, sir," Henry protested. "We are all loyal here! I'd stake my life 'twas not one o' us!"

Barrington nodded his head. "I have no doubt we will find you are right, host, but Lord Adolphus has a good point. Shall we say no one is free of suspicion for the present moment?"

Mr. Cummings spoke up, a bit apologetically. "I can see your dilemma, your grace, and I quite see we are all suspect, but may I point out that if the servants did not know you would be staying here, neither did any of us? You were the last guest to arrive, after all." Tony was much struck by the logic of this, and nodded his head in agreement as Mr. Cummings continued.

"I also do not see how the problem is to be resolved. Surely if there is a spy in our midst, he, or she," bowing slightly to the ladies, "is not about to confess it now, not with the paper in his possession; so how is his identity to be established?"

Barrington frowned. "Your points are well taken, sir. There are several things that can be done, before I have to send Albert for troops to assist me."

"Troops!" whispered Bessie, much shocked, as she twisted her apron.

The duke continued, "We can first find out in detail if everyone is indeed who they say they are. If all appears to be in order there, the baggage must be searched, and if that fails, everyone here must be personally searched."

127

Letty gasped, and Mrs. Orvis-Ryder dropped her vinaigrette.

"Searched?" she exclaimed, in a tone pregnant with disbelief. "Do I hear you correctly, your grace? An *Orvis-Ryder* searched? By whom? Yourself?" She drew herself up in her chair. "I shall never recover from such an indignity to my person, and I shall *take steps* to see that you are severely punished if you lay a hand on me!"

Barrington gave her a withering glance. "Believe me, madam, I shall try every avenue of investigation before I resort to it, for, if you will forgive my frankness, it is not something that has much appeal!"

Then as she bridled indignantly at this cool rejoinder, he turned to the twins.

"Shall we begin with you, m'lords? I know your family fairly well. You!" he said, pointing at Dolph. "What was your mother's maiden name, and where did she grow up?"

Dolph was so flustered at being singled out that he flushed and stammered, and looked so guilty that Albert took a step closer. All coherent thoughts had fled, and it was doubtful he could have given his own name at that moment. Tony made to speak for him, but the duke stopped him with an imperious wave of his hand.

"No, m'lord! I asked *Adolphus* Allensworth, and it is his answer that I require, not yours!"

Dolph stood up and seemed to gather his wits with a visible effort. When he spoke, there was a certain dignity in his stammered tones.

"M'mother's name was . . . was D'aubrey . . . and . . . and she grew up in Scotland."

Barrington nodded and turned to Tony.

"And where was she born, m'lord?"

"Why in Paris, I believe," Tony answered quickly. "She removed to Scotland while still very young."

"And your father, the duke?" Barrington pursued, "Can you tell me the year he ascended to his dukedom?"

Tony thought for a moment. "My grandfather died in . . . let me see . . . 1785 I believe it was."

Barrington snapped another question. "And your father was the heir?"

"Of course!" Tony snapped back, as Dolph grabbed his sleeve.

"No, no, Tony, you've got it wrong! Don't you remember horrible Uncle George? Lord, we've heard Mama castigate him enough!"

Tony nodded. "Of course! I forgot that my father was the second son, and it was only when his brother George was killed in a hunting accident that he succeeded to the title. That would have been in 1792, right, Dolph?" His twin nodded his head in agreement, and Barrington bowed to them both.

"Very well, m'lords. We can now acknowledge that you are who you say you are, and although such family history can easily be learned, I find it hard to believe that two identical spies could be found to impersonate the Allensworths."

Tony and Dolph looked relieved, until he added, "But that is not to say that you could not be sympathizers even so."

Mrs. Orvis-Ryder spoke into the sudden silence.

"Well, I for one think they have behaved in a very suspicious and scaly manner! They have both been extremely secretive about why they were traveling in such weather, and what their destination was, and furthermore . . ."

Her voice died away as Barrington turned and frowned at her, causing Letty to shrink against her mother's substantial frame, looking very white and frightened. The duke bowed ironically. "Well, ladies! It is now your turn. I would like answers to a few questions, if you please!"

Mrs. Orvis-Ryder stared back at him with hatred. "Never, sir! I shall never submit to being questioned! Nor will my daughter tell you a single thing, no matter how you bully and torture us!"

Letty looked as if she would tell him anything he liked, even to admitting she was the spy, at the mention of torture.

"You, madam, are a very silly woman," Barrington said softly. "No one has mentioned torture, and in a matter of grave concern to the nation, a little bullying should not even be considered. Do think! Forget your precious Orvis-Ryder dignity for a moment, and answer me!"

Turning his attention to Letty, he barked, "What is the principal town of Durham?"

"Newcastle-on-Tyne!" gasped Letty, even as her mother was turning to tell her not to reply.

"And it is known principally for what?" Barrington continued relentlessly. Letty faltered, and looked at her mother in confusion.

The duke sighed. "Of course, you would not know unless it was famous for perfume, kid gloves, or a hunt Ball! Mrs. Orvis-Ryder, if you please! Otherwise suspicion will definitely fall on your heads, for it was *your* servant who left the inn yesterday, the only one to do so since the paper was lost."

James was startled into speech. "No, your grace, no! Jed can vouch for me, we were together every minute, I swear! And—"

Barrington motioned him to be quiet and said pensively to Mrs. Orvis-Ryder, "Do you consider the scandal of an Orvis-Ryder being escorted by troops to his majesty's prison for interrogation?"

Much struck by this, the lady demurred no longer. "Newcastle is known for its coal and manufactories. Sir. Principally machinery for the mines."

"Quite right, ma'am! I cannot question you further, since I have never heard of your husband's family in my life and wouldn't know if you were telling me the truth about them or not!"

He turned away, just as Mrs. Orvis-Ryder dropped her salts, gasped, and slipped to the floor in a faint.

Everyone started up, but the duke halted them with a sharp order.

"Stay where you are, all of you! You, James, attend your mistress, and you may assist, Miss Letty. The rest of you stay exactly where you are!"

Mrs. Orvis-Ryder was soon restored to consciousness and hoisted back into her seat. From her disjointed sentences it was discovered that it was not so much being thought a spy and a traitor that had upset her as it was that the duke had never heard of the Orvis-Ryders. She was soon feeling more the thing after a few sips of brandy fetched by an attentive James, but her incredulous stare at Barrington almost sent Tony into whoops of laughter.

As Letty continued to pat her mother's hand in an agitated way, she put down her glass with a snap and blurted out, "And how do we know who *you* are, your grace? Or even if there were any secret papers? And furthermore, if they existed in the first place, it seems to me you have been vastly negligent and careless to have lost one!"

Barrington flushed slightly. "I am well aware of it, madam, and my ignominy makes me even more determined to regain possession without further delay!"

He turned his attention to Reverend Mr. Cummings, still sitting quietly at the table observing the proceedings.

"Sir," he said, "I am afraid I must also question you."

Mr. Cummings inclined his head and said calmly, "Of course, your grace, I quite understand, and I will do anything in my power to help you, but I fear I know nothing about the papers except for seeing you working on them here one day, before the fire."

Barrington nodded. "Yes, that was not well thought-on, I agree. I should have kept them locked up in my room, but . . ." He stopped as he remembered why he had brought them down to the coffeeroom that day,

131

and he looked even more like the Indian as his high cheekbones reddened with embarrassment.

Suddenly Albert spoke in his native tongue, and the duke answered him quickly, causing the Indian to slip out the door. A moment later there was a sound of protest, and then silence until Albert strode through the door with Beth in his arms. He put her gently into a chair and resumed his post before the door. A flustered Beth, her color higher than usual, looked around the crowded room in amazement.

"Why, what is happening?" she asked in confusion.

"I thought I told you to stay off that ankle, Miss Cummings!" Barrington said sharply.

She smiled uncertainly at his stern face.

"Why, and so I would, sir, although it is much better, but I have been ringing and ringing, and no one came. I began to think I was left alone here, and you had all gone; and so I dressed to come downstairs. Indeed, it is almost well." She looked around and saw Albert guarding the door, pistol ready, and gasped. "What is happening? Why are you all here?"

Barrington soon explained the situation, and Beth was so shocked she sank back in her chair speechless.

The duke turned again to her father. "Now, Mr. Cummings, to resume. You and your daughter are on your way to visit the bishop in Oxford, I believe you told us. His name?"

Mr. Cummings replied quietly, and Barrington continued, "But you are something more than a parson, are you not, sir?"

Mr. Cummings made no answer, for he was now as confused as his daughter.

"Why no, sir, I am not."

"But you had another title than "reverend," did you not, at one time?"

Mr. Cummings flushed slightly. "Yes, at one time I was known as Lord Edward Cummings, if that is what you refer to."

"And your brother's name, the present duke?"

"William Everett, your grace. My father's name, you see. There has always been a William, duke of Woltan."

Barrington nodded. "I will give you another test, m'lord! Matthew nineteen, verse twenty three!"

Mr. Cummings frowned in thought, and then said gently, " 'And Jesus said to his disciples, Truly, I say unto you, it will be hard for a rich man to enter into the kingdom of heaven.' "

Barrington nodded slightly. "I congratulate you, sir, you have passed the test!"

Mrs. Orvis-Ryder, who had been seething with a variety of ugly emotions while she absorbed the news of Beth's high connections, spoke up again. "I do not see that either he or his daughter are without suspicion just because he knows his scriptures! Of course anyone in holy orders would! Only consider how much they both know about the war and how many questions they have asked of you! I myself think that if anyone is the spy, they should both be in the forefront of consideration!"

"Oh, Mama!" wailed Letty, horrified by this blunt accusation, as Beth looked daggers at the lady. Mrs. Orvis-Ryder continued in a rush.

"And Miss Cummings! So coming, yes, and so pushing, with her inching ways! Why I—"

Barrington interrupted smoothly. "I do not think, ma'am, it would be wise to continue in this vein. Why, someone might think to question *you* about 'pushing ways.' You take my meaning? Yes, I was sure you would do so!"

Mrs. Orvis-Ryder subsided, her face red with anger and fear and her little black eyes furious.

Barrington sighed audibly and leaned wearily back against the table. His stern face looked worried.

"To continue. We don't seem to have gotten much further, do we? You have all established your identities, there is no question of an impostor. I have already questioned the servants in depth; therefore we

133

must assume that someone in this room has sympathy for the American cause to the extent that he or she would risk death to relay the information to them."

Letty gasped and Beth sat up straighter in her chair. She looked keenly at Barrington and then she said, "Since my father and I are so interested in current events, your grace, perhaps Mrs. Orvis-Ryder is right! No one else has shown the slightest concern about your travels. Furthermore, no member of the church can condone fighting and killing people who were a short while ago our own brothers. Tell me, do you suspect us?"

She stared at the duke, her anger growing that her dear gentle father had to be subjected to this indignity, to say nothing of herself. And just when she had been imagining . . . well! She remembered how she waked that morning with a smile, thinking of his Byron quote and the look in his dark eyes. And now he frowned at her, and thought she might be a spy! She looked around at the other guests. She wished she could suspect Mrs. Orvis-Ryder, but by no stretch of the imagination could she portray her as anything but what she was—a large, vain, venomous middle-aged lady, puffed up with her own importance and consequence. And Letty! She could not see any country, no matter how desperate for secrets, employing Letty in the cause, unless it was a matter of seducing the secrets of a susceptible courier, and even there Letty would fail in spite of her beauty—consider the scene with Dolph in the taproom. She was just too stupid. The twins were more likely. Was Dolph as idiotic as he appeared, or was it an act? Tony had the wits, but . . . She gave herself a mental shake. How could she stoop to such thoughts? She looked again at Barrington. It was all his fault! If he had not lost the paper, none of this would have happened. Her anger at him grew as he slowly replied to her question.

"I must suspect everyone until that paper is returned to me, Miss," he said. Then, turning to Jed, "Are you

134

quite sure Jed, that you didn't leave James for even a moment yesterday?"

Jed straightened more to attention. "It's as I told you, your grace. 'E was never out of my sight, and 'e didn't speak to anyone either, not lest I did too. Why, we even visited the convenience together. . . ." He blushed mightily at the indelicacy of this statement, and subsided.

Barrington seemed to come to a decision.

"Well, if that is true, then we can acquit James of carrying the paper to an accomplice. I think we should have some food now, Mrs. Griffen. Albert will escort the servants to the kitchen, and remain with you. Prepare enough for yourselves as well as the guests, and return here. This afternoon, we will begin to search the baggage."

He looked politely at Mrs. Orvis-Ryder, who was bridling and red with anger, but although he paused to allow her time to speak, she thought better of it and closed her mouth with a snap.

There was little conversation when the servants left the room. The twins murmured to each other, Letty stayed by her mother's side, and Beth did not respond to her father's speculations until he asked her how she did.

"Oh, I feel much better, Father, truly I do! My headache is gone, and the ankle is much stronger for the rest it has had. I do not remember, however, ever being so angry in my life! How dare he suspect us?"

She sent an angry look toward the duke, seated now before the fire, his pistol still very much in evidence. Mr. Cummings remonstrated with her.

"Beth, Beth! 'Return not evil for evil,' my dear! How can the duke in good conscience exclude us? 'Twould be most unfair! It is very worrying, however—where could the paper have gone?"

He continued to muse on the subject until the servants returned with large trays of food for themselves and the guests. The meal was most uncomfortable, and at its close, the duke stood up and said, "We will search the gentlemen's rooms first. Host, you will assist me, while Albert remains here."

They were gone some time, and in the many silences that fell, they could be heard first in the twins' room, and then in Mr. Cummings', moving the furniture and opening the baggage. Neither the twins nor Mr. Cummings looked at all concerned or frightened; Tony shuffled the cards and beckoned Dolph to the seat opposite him, saying, "It appears this will take quite a while, twin!" Mr. Cummings composedly read a book. Henry eventually reappeared and apologetically asked the ladies to retire to their own rooms while the gentlemen's persons were being searched. Beth rose and, leaning on her father's arm, went to the door. Albert saw she could manage the stairs and let her pass, followed by a frightened Letty, who scuttled past him as if he were about to leap upon her, knife drawn. A vastly angry Mrs. Orvis-Ryder was close behind.

Beth went into her bedroom and took the wing chair near the fire, her thoughts chaotic. A knock on the door admitted Barrington, with an anxious Bessie and Henry behind him.

"My apologies, Miss Cummings," he said formally. "I will try not to disarrange your things any more than I must."

Beth made no answer, merely nodding her head frigidly and giving him a level, considering glance. The duke asked Bessie to go through the contents of the dresser, and then requested Henry to remove the drawers so that he could look behind them. The clothespress was emptied and searched; he even moved it away from the wall to be sure there was nothing concealed there. Pictures were taken from the walls, the rug was rolled up, and even the pocket of her cloak was investigated. The bed was stripped of its blankets and sheets, and the mattress turned. When everything had been completed, even to subjecting her

136

books to a careful page by page perusal, he turned to Beth, although he had been careful not to glance at her before, and said, "If you would be so kind as to stand away from the chair?"

Beth rose, leaning on Bessie, who hastened to help her. The duke turned out the cushions and felt them carefully before restoring them in the proper position. He hesitated for a moment, his lips tightening, then asked Henry to wait outside, saying to Bessie, "I must ask you to search Miss Cummings now, Mrs. Griffen. I cannot leave the room, but I shall turn my back," and suiting his actions to his word, he turned away. Beth drew a deep breath and was about to object to the invasion of her privacy when she realized it was useless.

"Oh, Miss Cummings," Bessie wailed helplessly, "please forgive me! I don't like to do this at all!"

She looked so upset and horrified that Beth spoke to her kindly in spite of her anger. "It is quite all right, Mrs. Griffen! Please do as he asks. If you do not search me, I am sure the duke will do it himself, and that indignity I agree for once with Mrs. Orvis-Ryder would be strenuously objected to!"

She saw the back of the duke's neck redden at this remark, as Bessie patted her gown halfheartedly. She raised her skirts so Bessie could see she had nothing concealed in her stockings, and sat down to remove her Roman boots.

"I am sure that is not necessary, Miss," Bessie protested.

But Beth answered with composure, "Yes, it is! A shoe is a very good place for a folded paper."

She gave them to Bessie, who was soon able to assure the duke that Miss Cummings did not have the paper on her person. He turned to find Beth putting on her boots, her face as white as his was red.

"I did not expect to find anything, of course," he began, but he was firmly interrupted, the apology dying on his lips.

"If you are quite through, your grace, I would appreciate your leaving my room as quickly as possible!" Beth snapped, her gray eyes dark with anger. Barrington stared at her and bowed formally. At the door he turned to her again.

"I must ask you to remain in your room until either I or Albert comes to get you."

"Of course," Beth said. "Would you care to lock me in, your grace?"

Barrington made a frustrated gesture. "I shall assume that is unnecessary, unless you prove me wrong. A maid will be up shortly to put your things back in order."

He left abruptly, trailed by Bessie, and Beth could hear him knocking on the Orvis-Ryder door a moment later. She put her hands up to her flushed face as she stared at her belongings strewn on the bed and tables. She had a large lump in her throat and felt that at any moment she would burst into tears. She had never been so miserable in her life! A timid knock at the door brought Jill to help her restore order, her eyes large with excitement and fear. There was little conversation after a shriek was heard from the Orvis-Ryder room when the personal search was begun, followed by a torrent of speech delivered in Mrs. Orvis-Ryder's piercing tones.

Beth dismissed the maid as soon as possible and lay down on the bed to rest and to think. Her headache had returned, and her ankle was throbbing, so although she meant to study what she must do, she soon fell into an exhausted nap.

When she awoke it was dark, and Abby was making up the fire and lighting a lamp.

"If you please, Miss," she said, "his grace has asked all the guests to repair to the coffeeroom for dinner, and 'e sent me to 'elp you change."

"Thank you, Abby," Beth said, sitting up. "Just bring some hot water, please for I shall not change for dinner tonight."

138

The maid left the room, and Beth went to the dressing table to brush her tangled hair. Her eyes looked heavy and wretched still, but she put her chin up. What did it matter how she looked? No one had come to her door, so she supposed the paper had not been found. What was next? When she finally opened her door it was to find Albert stationed, complete with pistol, at the top of the stairs. He gestured her to go down, and she was aware of his eyes staring at her back with every step. It was almost a relief to open the coffeeroom door and limp inside. Barrington stood before the fire in what by now seemed to be his customary position. Beth allowed herself one quick glance at him; his face seemed strained and tired, and he wore a ferocious frown, his dark brows almost meeting over his narrowed eyes. He bowed to her slightly, as did the twins, rising from chairs a short distance from the hearth. Tony smiled at her encouragingly and went to help her to a chair.

"Miss Cummings," he said, "how is your ankle this evening? I see that you still limp somewhat."

Beth was grateful for this return to normalcy. "Thank you, m'lord! As you see, it is much better! I hope by tomorrow to be able to put all my weight on it, for I rested it all afternoon." She looked around. "Where is my father, does anyone know? And the Orvis-Ryders," she amended hastily.

The duke answered her harshly. "Your father will soon join us, and the Orvis-Ryders too, although they preferred to dine in their room. It could not be allowed."

Beth stared at him. "I see the servants are absent. Does that mean that they have been acquitted of suspicion?"

"By no means," Barrington said. "Jed is watching them, and even Willy must stay in the kitchen until all the guests are here in the coffeeroom. I suppose it would be more accurate to say they are all watching each other, at the present moment," he added.

139

Dolph spoke up. "So the paper was not found, your grace?"

Barrington frowned again as the door opened and the Orvis-Ryders and Mr. Cummings joined the group. "No," he said briefly, "the paper was not found. Since we are now all assembled once again, let me tell you what I propose to do next. Tomorrow morning I shall send Albert with a message to the commander of the garrison at Wolverton. Until the troops arrive you must submit to being together here, or locked in your rooms. I apologize again to all of you who are innocent, but the spy must be found, and the paper returned."

Mrs. Orvis-Ryder sniffed and took a seat without a word. Letty, still in her traveling gown, remained close to her mother as Mr. Cummings came to ask Beth how she did, and Albert appeared at the door, holding it open for Henry and Bessie to carry in the dinner trays.

When they summoned the guests to the table, there was none of the fussing about seating that had occurred previously. Mrs. Orvis-Ryder directed her daughter to sit at Mr. Cummings' right, and aggressively took the seat next to her, still without uttering a word. Beth found herself between the twins on the opposite side, and the duke took the foot. There was an awkward silence, and then Mr. Cummings spoke up mildly.

"If you will permit me," he said, "I feel it would be appropriate to begin our repast with a prayer this evening." Barrington nodded, and all bowed their heads.

Mr. Cummings spoke softly. He asked the Lord to bless them, and to be with them in this time of trial, giving them patience and forbearance, and he closed his prayer with a plea that the paper soon be found.

For a few moments there was nothing but the sound of silverware against the soup bowls. Then Barrington suddenly put down his spoon and spoke. "If you please! I realize the awkwardness of this dinner, but I feel it would be better for everyone's digestion if normal conversation could be carried on." He looked at Mr. Cummings, who nodded in agreement.

Tony spoke up bravely. "Has anyone checked on the weather? If the paper is found, we could all be on our way tomorrow, unless it comes on to snow again."

"God forbid!" Mr. Cummings said in horrified but not unpious accents.

"Jed told me the fair spell is holding," Dolph contributed, "though it is still very cold. I wish we *could* get on tomorrow!"

He blushed as all eyes turned to him, with the exception of Letty, who seemed mesmerized by the onions floating in her soup. Mrs. Orvis-Ryder dropped her spoon with a clatter and turned to Bessie at the sideboard.

"This soup," she said in her positive way, "is terrible! One certainly does not expect cooking of *cordon bleu* quality in such a place as *this,* but one does expect cooking that is at least edible! Do not eat it, Letty, I pray you! It appears fit only for peasants!"

Bessie twisted her apron and looked as if she were about to burst into tears. "Your pardon, ma'am," she finally got out. "We have all been so upset, I don't know 'ow I got dinner ready!"

Beth suddenly championed her. "Nonsense! The soup is fine, Mrs. Griffen, and I for one wonder how you were able to cook anything at all so good with such horrible suspicions and alarums going on! When I think how very long you have had to feed us without replenishing your larder I am amazed, and thank you for the excellent meals we have had." She smiled at Bessie and then gave Mrs. Orvis-Ryder a haughty stare. Barrington had the irrelevant thought that she looked very much a duchess as she did so.

Mrs. Orvis-Ryder bridled and ostentatiously refused to touch her soup. Her full bowl was carried away with the others, and a joint and vegetables were presented. The duke asked the twins about the London

141

theater, and who was being lionized now, and they were soon regaling everyone with accounts of plays they had seen the past season. Dolph especially seemed almost carefree, although he was careful neither to direct a remark or even a glance at the Orvis-Ryders. Beth ate her dinner and contributed little more, and as carefully as Dolph, she avoided glancing at the duke, so she was startled when he asked her a direct question about Lord Liverpool's administration, formed the previous June when he had been abroad.

Beth buttered a roll, her eyes downcast. "I believe Viscount Castlereagh is the foreign secretary now, your grace," she replied, and then turned abruptly away. "Father," she said, "be so good as to let me borrow a book this evening. I have almost finished mine, and would like something to read after dinner."

Mr. Cummings frowned slightly at her abruptness in terminating the conversation with the duke, but agreed. As soon as the covers were removed, Beth asked to be excused. The duke had not spoken directly to her again, and since Letty did not open her mouth except to eat, and Mrs. Orvis-Ryder's comments were a few more complaints about the dinner, it was an awkward meal even without the strain of suspicion they were all under. The twins and Mr. Cummings tried valiantly to keep up a flow of inconsequentialities, but it was with a sense of relief felt by all that they finally rose from the table. Mr. Cummings asked the duke if it would be all right if he went up with his daughter to fetch her the book she had asked for, and the duke agreed to it, and then added, as they made to depart, "Albert will spend the night in the stables guarding the horses. It is the only way I can be sure that no one will be able to leave before tomorrow— that, and, of course, locked bedroom doors."

Mr. Cummings bowed, but Beth merely looked at Barrington distantly before dropping a small curtsy to everyone and leaving the room. She was followed shortly by the Orvis-Ryders, but not until that lady had favored the duke with a withering speech.

"I shall retire, with my daughter," she began, "for I am not at all *well*. If, as I suspect, my *health* has been permanently damaged by the insults and outrages I have been subjected to, I shall know at whose door the fault lies, and I shall *take steps*." Here Dolph looked very upset, thinking she was referring to him, until he saw the venomous look she gave Barrington.

"Furthermore, I fully intend to write the secretary for war and the Colonies to apprise him of the indignities I have suffered at the hands of one of his couriers. As an Orvis-Ryder I have every expectation of being closely attended too, and you, duke, will soon find out the seriousness of your behavior to one of *my station*. Come, Letty!"

Without a bow or a word to the others, she swept from the room, followed by her daughter, who was too frightened to even remonstrate with her favorite phrase.

As the door closed, Barrington took up his position in front of the fire, seemingly unconcerned by her dire threat. Tony looked at him curiously.

"Your grace," he said, "if the paper is not found, what then?"

Barrington stared into the flames before answering, and when he did, it was with such quiet intensity that Tony was startled.

"The paper *must* be found! It is too important to the crown—indeed, to all of us—not to be! It *will* be found!"

CHAPTER VII

To everyone's relief, the weather held through the following morning. It was gray, gloomy, and overcast, but no new snow fell, and the temperature had risen above freezing again. If only the paper could be found there was no further bar to their hastening on their separate ways without additional delay.

When Beth finally opened her eyes, it was quite late. She had spent a restless night, tossing and turning and feeling miserable, which she put down to the injuries to her head and ankle, firmly dismissing the more logical conclusion that the duke might have had an influence on her sleeplessness. One of the maids had been in to make up the fire, and there was warm water for her to wash with, so she rose and dressed slowly, thinking as she glanced out the window that the weather exactly suited her mood. When she had brushed her hair and smoothed it into an extremely severe coil on her neck, she made her way to the coffeeroom.

She was the last to arrive. Letty was alone at the breakfast table; her mother was seated before the fire sewing, and looking as if she wished she had the duke's neck between her needle and embroidery, so tightly did she pull her thread. Mr. Cummings was glancing through a book, the twins were halfheartedly playing cards, and Barrington was staring out the window. Of Albert and the rest of the servants there was no sign. Beth went to her father and kissed him good morning. As she was turning to join Letty at the table, the duke spoke.

"I will call for some breakfast for you, Miss Cummings," he said, without the trace of a smile. Beth nodded distantly and turned to Letty to ask how she did. She and her mother were dressed for traveling once again, and Letty looked completely cowed and frightened; but whether this was due to the duke, Dolph, or her mother's obvious rage it was hard to tell.

Bessie soon brought Beth her breakfast and smiled at her kindly. She thought the young lady didn't look at all well, and asked if her ankle was paining her. Beth tried to smile and assured her it was much better. As she ate her breakfast, Barrington wandered over to watch the twins' card game, upsetting Dolph so much he promptly lost a promising hand.

Unable to feel any appetite, Beth finished her coffee, rose from the table, and went to the window. She leaned her head against the frame and stared into the yard, wishing she might go out and get some fresh air at the very least. The sculpture party seemed an age ago! Behind her, the duke addressed the party.

"Your attention, please! I think you will all agree that everything that could be attempted to find and restore the paper to me has been done. Therefore I have no other recourse but to summon troops and have you all transported to the nearest garrison for further questioning. That is what I propose to do now, unless whoever took the paper will return it to me immediately." He paused, but there was no response, so he resumed in a crisper tone.

"Very well, we will do it the hard way. I shall ask Albert to leave at once!"

He went to the door and called his man. Beth did not turn around, but continued looking out the window. Idly she checked to see if the snow-Jed was still intact, and noticed the right arm had slipped again. Even the telescope had not been enough of a brace, she thought. And then abruptly she straightened up and put her hands to her suddenly burning cheeks.

"Oh no!" she exclaimed aloud. Everyone turned to her, startled by her cry, and Barrington's eyebrows rose at her obvious agitation. She turned to the company, and looking straight at Barrington, said, "There is no need to send for troops, your grace. I know where the paper is. I . . . I took it!"

For a moment there was a hushed silence, and then everyone began to speak at once. Mr. Cummings hurried to her side, asking what on earth she was talking about; the twins expressed disbelief in fervent tones; and Mrs. Orvis-Ryder, her strident voice rising in satisfaction above the others, said she had suspected it all along, and it was no surprise to her that Beth was a common spy, and personally she hoped she would hang for it!

Barrington cut in abruptly, ordering everyone to be quiet, and accompanying this with such a violent frown at Mrs. Orvis-Ryder that she swallowed her next comment and subsided.

He strode quickly to Beth's side. "What is this, Miss Cummings? *You* took the paper? Be so good as to explain immediately!"

Beth leaned against her father for a moment, and then straightened and looked up into the duke's stormy eyes. Her resolution faltered a little as she read the anger there, but then she put up her chin and spoke to him directly, ignoring the rest.

"I took it, as I said. I did not do it deliberately;
147

indeed I was not even aware what it was. If you will allow me to go as far as the gate, it will quickly be restored to you."

Barrington looked out the window, much puzzled, but he gave his assent, ordering Albert to accompany her. Beth did not know if she felt more annoyance at her clumsiness in forgetting the paper she had used for the telescope, or anger at the duke for insisting she be guarded on such a short journey. She took up her shawl, patting her father's arm in passing, for he looked so very upset, and then she left the room, closely followed by the Indian, pistol in hand. Marching to the gate, she reached up and removed the frozen telescope, causing the sculpture to lose its right arm as it fell unsupported into the snow. She turned to see everyone staring at her from the window, Tony's face especially horrified as he realized where the paper had been all this time. She tried to brush the snow away, but soon perceived that this would probably destroy the writing inside, so she carried it carefully back into the coffeeroom and presented it to Barrington wordlessly. He stared at her, his eyes still angry and remote, so she turned to the rest to explain, feeling more despairing than ever.

"I must apologize to you all, but I had no idea the paper was important, and had in fact forgotten its very existence until just now. While Lord Anthony and I were making the snow sculpture we saw we would need to brace the arm, and I came into the inn to find something we could use. I dropped my mitten, and as I was picking it up, noticed a paper under the settle. Thinking it had been discarded, I rolled it up and got some string from Bessie in the kitchen. Then I molded some snow around it until it froze and we could use it for our snow-Jed." She paused, as murmurs began amongst the others.

"Well!" exclaimed Mrs. Orvis-Ryder. "I find that a very flimsy explanation, and one that is hard to credit! She must have copied it before she used it!"

Tony frowned at the lady and hastened to say kindly to Beth, "My dear Miss Cummings! If only I had had my wits about me and remembered the paper before this! I am much at fault!"

"No, m'lord, do not blame yourself!" Beth said, impulsively putting out her hands to him. "The fault is mine alone." She turned reluctantly to the duke, who was carefully blotting away the snow as it melted in the warmth of the room. "I am afraid it will be unreadable, sir, for I wet it most thoroughly."

"That is unimportant," Barrington said absently. "I can reconstruct the résumé from my notes, if this is indeed the paper." Beth watched him as he carefully unrolled it and spread it out on a napkin on the table.

"Ah yes, I recognize a few words; the rest are blurred." He straightened up and looked at them all, although it seemed to Beth that he avoided looking at her directly.

"Allow me to apologize to you all for the treatment you have been subjected to. Through my carelessness, the paper was lost, and I am aware the fault is mine."

Dolph broke in. "No harm done, your grace, no harm done! But if you could write another anyway, why was it necessary?" His handsome face was puckered in incomprehension.

"It was necessary because the information must not be relayed to the enemy, m'lord. As long as I did not have the paper in hand I could not be sure it would remain confidential."

"And how do you know it will be now?" Mrs. Orvis-Ryder demanded. "I think you should still summon troops and look into this most thoroughly! She could have memorized the contents to use later if she hasn't already copied them!" She glared at Beth, who was aware she had never disliked anyone so much in her entire life. "When I think what I have gone through! The insults! The indignity of having *my person searched!* Well! I demand that she be arrested at once!"

149

Mr. Cummings spoke up in dismay, as Letty breathed, "Oh, Mama!" in the background.

"I trust that will not be necessary, sir! I am sure my daughter had no intention of relaying any information, and although I realize that my vouching for her loyalty is no guarantee, I beg you to allow us to proceed to town, where there are many people who would speak in her behalf!"

Barrington gestured abruptly, and Mr. Cummings stopped.

"That will not be required. I saw enough of the sculpture party from my window to be sure the information was not memorized, copied, or relayed in any way. Why, I had been abovestairs only a few moments after collecting my papers that afternoon when I observed Miss Cummings with the roll of paper in the yard." Her father looked much happier, but Beth was now as white as she had been red a minute before, and she stammered slightly as she spoke, trying to order her confused and angry thoughts.

"I must apologize again. I can only assure you all that I did not so much as glance at the contents, for if I had I would have immediately returned it to the duke. No one has ever questioned either my or my father's loyalty to the crown before this!"

She stared challengingly at Mrs. Orvis-Ryder, who snorted in disbelief, but Tony took her hand and held it for a moment as he said, "Do not be distressed, my dear Miss Cummings! All's well that ends well, you know!"

Beth tried to smile at him, but inwardly she felt it had not ended well at all, and could not remember ever being so distressed. Her misery of the morning seemed a small thing now she was aware of what she had done, albeit inadvertently, and the look on the duke's face when she had confessed she was the "thief" she would never forget, as long as she lived. Mrs. Orvis-Ryder's malice, while it made her extremely angry, was nothing in comparison. Dolph broke into her thoughts as he chimed in eagerly, "Yes, Miss Cummings! Just think what an exciting time we have had of it! Wait till I tell them in town that I was suspected of being a spy! Fore gad! Adolphus Allensworth ... not much in the cockloft, y'know ... a spy! Who would have thought it!"

Barrington spoke harshly. "You will not speak of it to anyone, m'lord! This incident is best forgotten as speedily as may be. Besides the obvious secrecy in which the report should be kept, think of Miss Cummings' reputation! It can only cause her much distress to have her name bandied about in such a connection!"

Much struck by this, Dolph chivalrously agreed, and immediately swore an oath of reticence. "My lips are sealed! Do not fear for your reputation on *my* account!" He raised his right hand solemnly. At another time Beth would have laughed at his seriousness, but now it was all she could do to force a thank you past the large lump in her throat.

Mrs. Orvis-Ryder rose ponderously to her feet, and beckoning to Letty, said sarcastically to the duke, "I assume it is permitted that we take our departure, your grace, now there is no need to suspect *us* of treason? The sooner my daughter and I are quit of such company and such surroundings the better!"

Barrington nodded, his expression grim. "You may leave immediately, ma'am. In fact, I strongly suggest you do so, before I completely lose my temper and let you know exactly what I think of you!"

Mrs. Orvis-Ryder opened her mouth to reply, but something in Barrington's scornful glance caused her to think better of it, and she hastened from the room, closely followed by Letty. The twins announced they were for the road too, and hurried away calling to Willy to saddle their horses. Barrington sent Albert to fetch the Griffens, and when they bustled in, gave them an explanation which did much to relieve the stress, for Bessie kept saying, "Who'd o' thought it?

And I 'elped tie it up tightly! Why, why, I'm an accomplist as they say!" Beth wished fervently she could retire, and glancing at her father, who was smiling at Bessie, beckoned with an indication of her head that she would like to go upstairs. The duke intercepted the glance and spoke up firmly, above Bessie's exclamations.

"If you please, Miss Cummings! I beg a word with you in private! If the rest of you would be so good, and with your permission, Mr. Cummings . . ."

That good man looked puzzled and somewhat alarmed, so the duke continued, "There is no question of your daughter being detained, man! I just wish the indulgence of a moment alone."

Still puzzled but no longer uneasy, he began to leave the room, informing Beth he would ask a maid to begin her packing so they could leave as soon as they could. Beth felt suddenly breathless, and wished with all her heart that she had been allowed to leave as well, as the duke shut the door firmly behind Henry and Bessie, but she stood quietly, her hands folded before her to still their trembling. After the trouble she had caused, she was in no position to make any demands, so she waited as patiently as she could to hear what the duke had to say.

He did not speak at once, but took a turn or two around the room. Finally he stopped in front of her and glared at her.

"You little fool!" he said harshly. "What evil demon ever possessed you to pick up that paper, and not even looking at it, take it away and cover it with snow? And having done so, why could you not have remembered the incident? Look at the trouble we have all been put to, besides having to endure that ghastly woman for two whole extra days!" He saw her stricken face and his voice changed. "Ah, Beth, my dear, it's no use! One moment I want to shake you and rip up at you for your improvident rashness, but when I look at

152

you, I forget it all in a moment and just want to take you in my arms and kiss you!"

He made as if to do just that, but Beth moved hastily away, all her apologies forgotten as rage swept over her.

"How dare you! Do not touch me! It was not my fault you were so careless as to lose the paper! I worry for the future of the commonwealth if such as *you* are entrusted with state secrets!"

She saw by his suddenly white face that she had scored a hit, and felt bleakly exultant as she raced on. "And how dare you suspect me of being a spy, and my dear gentle father too! And searching my room . . . and . . . and me as well!"

Barrington stretched out a restraining hand. "Beth, do consider what you say! You know I had to suspect everyone to be fair! I never really thought 'twas you, I swear it!"

"No?" Beth riposted in scorn. "And yet, just a few minutes ago, you looked at me in such a way . . ." She put her hands to her face and dashed away an angry tear that threatened to fall. "You did suspect me! You know you did!"

The duke tried hotly to deny this, but Beth was having none of his explanations. She calmed her breathing with a visible effort.

"I beg to be excused, your grace," she said coldly. "If, as Lord Anthony says, all's well that ends well, let us both be glad the ending has been reached. May I say that if there was an evil demon involved, he was first present when he allowed you to put up here at this inn, destroying everyone's peace! I only hope that I never have to see you again, as long as I live!"

She swept past him, deliberately neglecting to curtsy as custom demanded. The duke made one move to stop her, but seeing her angry face and flashing eyes, dropped his hand to his side in defeat. He noticed she closed the door quietly and sourly wished she had slammed it. He had not even had the opportunity to tell her that he loved her, and now she was gone. He sat down for a moment by the fire, his face bleak. Surely he had handled it very ill, for all his age and experience!

Barrington had learned years ago about women, or at least he thought he had. He had assumed his title before he reached the age of twenty, and had been so much sought after and pursued for it and his wealth that it had made him cynical. Mrs. Orvis-Ryder's pushing Letty at him had come as no surprise; too many anxious mamas had tried to engage his affection for their daughters, no matter whether the girl took him in repugnance or no. He had had a few mistresses but had never felt the slightest desire to marry until now, and he had not considered that being in love would make any difference in his handling of the situation, for he had never been rebuffed.

He had a natural scholarly bent and had soon found that the life of a London Corinthian did not appeal to him any more than being toad-eaten did. The duke had been of some service to the crown before this, and enjoyed it more than he did being on the strut, gambling away his inheritance, drinking blue ruin till dawn, or racing his horses with the other blades. He was supremely unconcerned with the cut of his coat, the elaborateness of his cravat, or the beauty of the latest Incomparable. It was really not at all surprising that he had fallen so desperately in love with a woman who shared his interests; what was surprising was that she did not appear to share his sentiments as well. If he had thought about it at all, he would have assumed from some of her smiles and expressions that she was not completely indifferent to him.

Damn the paper! And damn the report! It had brought him nothing but misery, and all through his own carelessness. And that was her fault too! He had brought the papers down to the coffeeroom because he hoped to see her and talk to her, and look where it had led! Women! He groaned and put his head in his hands.

Albert found him like this a few minutes later and was surprised when the duke, who had been so eager to be on his way, decided to remain at the Bird and Bottle for another night. Barrington felt that the least he could do was to give the Cummingses a chance to travel ahead of him without danger of putting up where he might be staying on the road to London. To Albert's query, he refused any food or drink, and went up to his room. He paused briefly on the landing, considering whether knocking on her door and demanding to be heard would help his cause. Since she had been so adamant about never wishing to see him again, he realized no good could come of such an impetuous move, and went into his own room, where he planned to remain until all the others should have left the inn.

Mrs. Orvis-Ryder was the first to do so, but not until several minutes had been spent bickering over her bill, which she claimed was monstrous high for the quality of the food and lodging obtained. The loss of a private parlor was mentioned, and the fact that she and her daughter had shared a room for the past two days, instead of occupying two, and even the fact that she had not eaten the full dinner the evening before was aired, until Henry, in despair, lowered the amount owed in order to get rid of her. James, standing behind her holding her cloak, sent the landlord a commiserating glance, as Mrs. Orvis-Ryder triumphantly paid her shot and made ready to depart. Letty, her cheeks red with embarrassment, scuttled out of the inn before her and allowed Jed to help her into the rented chaise, without bidding anyone goodbye, she was so mortified. Her mother wore a smile of victory as the chaise tooled away down the road.

The twins were not long behind them. Tony went to Mr. Cummings to say his graceful farewells, seconded by his twin, but when he asked for Beth, was told that she was busy packing and could not be disturbed. Mr.

Cummings assured the Allensworths that he would relay their compliments to his daughter, and their wishes that they might meet again in town, and they all shook hands in good spirits before the twins clattered off, after bestowing handsome *douceurs* on all the servants. The cheerfulness with which they paid their bill made Henry feel a good deal better.

Mr. Cummings sent some food and hot tea to his daughter's room, and she managed to swallow a few mouthfuls before her appetite deserted her completely. When he had paid their bill, he went and knocked gently on her door, and found her ready to travel, her cloak over her arm and her color high. She hurried down the stairs to find both Bessie and Henry in attendance, and shaking the landlord's hand, apologized once again for the trouble she had caused. Bessie was so moved by her unhappy face that she quite forgot herself, and putting her ample arms around her, gave her a hug.

"There, miss! Do not fret! 'Twill all come right, you'll see!" she said, which caused Mr. Cummings to wonder what on earth the good woman was talking about. Beth had no such doubts, and rested her head on Bessie's shoulder for a moment, completely shaken. Then she gave her head a little shake, to rid it of the tears that threatened to fall, and kissed Bessie heartily.

"Thank you, Mrs. Griffen! And thank you all for your good care of us," she said, and went out to the carriage, where she shook Jed's hand and warmly said goodbye. The baggage was strapped on the back, and Jed wrapped her in the warm carriage robe as her father gained his seat and took up the reins. Beth stared stonily ahead as they left the yard, and after one glance at her face, Mr. Cummings did not try to question her.

At the window of the second-best bedroom, the curtains fell, and the duke moved back to the table, where he had been trying to rewrite his resume, much dispirited. He called Albert to bring some ale, and putting her firmly from his mind, made himself set to work again.

The inn seemed empty with just Barrington in residence, and as he had asked for a simple meal to be served in his room with only Albert in attendance, the residents of the inn relaxed over their supper for the first time in days. Willy was almost boisterous in his relief when he learned that the duke and the Indian were leaving early in the morning. Bessie shushed him as she put the laden plates on the table.

" 'Ere, Willy! Wot's all this? Sit down and be quiet!" She brought a pitcher of ale and a platter of bread and then settled herself thankfully in her chair, with a deep sigh.

"Aye," Jed said, looking at his sister kindly, "you be tired, don't ye, m'dear? Well, and no wonder!" He turned to his brother-in-law. "Henry! Can you ever remember such a time as we 'ave just 'ad?"

Henry gave it some thought. "Well, there was the time the gypsies came to the village and the squire's barn burned down and ... but no, can't say I ever remember such a dust-up! What with the blizzard, the nobility, and an Indian from the Americas ..."

"And the likes o' Mrs. 'Igh and Mighty!" Bessie added darkly, without her usual kindness.

Henry raised his fork and pointed it at her. "If you please, m'dear, I'm eating! 'Twill surely ruin my appetite if I have to think about 'er—and the amount I 'ad to take off 'er bill! Argh! Penny-pinching old termagant!"

"Not to mention we was all thought spies!" Jed added.

Abby shuddered. "Aye, I was some feared! The look on the duke's face when 'e said it! I'll never forget it!"

"Pass the salt, girl," Henry said absently, then added, "I must admit it was most uncomfortable. Thank the Lord Miss Cummings remembered she 'ad taken it. I 'ad no wish to go to a prison, and I can guarantee you

157

we all would 'ave 'ad to, if it 'adn't been found."

"Poor lady," Bessie said. " 'E fair ripped up at 'er, didn't 'e? And all the time I thought . . ."

"Thought wot?" asked Willy, helping himself to more of the joint.

"None o' your perkiness, young 'un!" Jed admonished him, smiling at his sister as he did so. "Don't fret, Bess, it may all work out after all, if so it should be."

Jill broke off a piece of bread and said dreamily, "That James was nice though, wasn't 'e, Abby? It's a shame 'e has to be in *'er* service!"

"Let's 'ope we never see 'er again, that's what *I* say!" Henry said sternly. "And by the way, Willy my boy, first thing in the morning build up the taproom fire. I expect to see some o' our regulars any time now, now that the roads are clear."

"Wot a shame the duke's leavin' in the mornin'," Jed remarked thoughtfully.

"Why is it a shame?" Willy demanded to know, remembering Albert and another night on the kitchen floor in store for him.

"Why," Jed explained, "think 'ow good 'twould be for custom if we 'ad an Indian from the Americas here. They'd all be out like a shot for their pints if they knew!"

Henry and Bessie laughed with him, but Willy looked distinctly alarmed, as if he thought there was a possibility that Jed might talk the duke and his manservant into staying, thereby prolonging his exile from his own comfortable pallet in the barn.

"I liked his Lordship, though," Bessie said. "Lord Tony, I mean. 'E was a nice young man, and I'm sure I don't envy 'im 'aving to look after that brother of 'is! Coo! Wot a devil!"

Abby and Jill agreed fervently.

"So good looking, the two o' them!" Bessie continued. "And that Miss Letty! But there! She probably wants to escape from 'er mother as soon as ever could be, and who could blame 'er? Pretty young thing that she is to be saddled with such a one!"

"Miss Cummings was the best, though," Jed added. "She's very pretty too, although you wouldn't notice it with Miss Letty shinin' 'er down," he added fairly. "But she's quality, and not too puffed up in her own importance to be friendly and kind. The reverend too—a good man!"

The servants finished their meal, and as the two maids began to clear the table and do the dishes, Henry went up to the duke to see if there was anything he required before bedtime. Barrington assured him there was not, except for the small matter of a bottle of brandy and some more wood for the fire. Albert, engaged in removing the dinner tray, looked at him carefully, and told Henry he would serve him.

Long after the other lights went out in the Bird and Bottle that night, a light still burned in the second-best bedchamber on the second floor. The duke had finished rewriting his résumé some time earlier, and Albert had observed him first moving to burn the water-stained "telescope" in the fire, and then thoughtfully smoothing it and folding it into a small square, which he placed carefully in his pocketcase. Now he sat in a brown study before the dying fire, the brandy bottle by his side, and mused about the events of the past week. He would never be the same, he knew, and wondered if it *had* been an "evil demon" who had determined that he should find his way here. Fate had a funny way of taking charge, no matter how a man might think he ordered his life. He wondered what would happen next. He knew he had to see her again for he had to try and change her mind.

A dozen random thoughts and plans whirled in his mind, and it was very late before he blew out his candles and went to bed, and the Bird and Bottle was again quiet and sleeping in the cold January night. Since no better arrangement came to mind, he had decided to follow his original plan and hurry to London to deliver the report; then he would seek out the Cummingses at Woltan. Perhaps time would be on his side, giving her anger a chance to cool so that she would at the very least allow him a chance to plead his case.

By the time Willy rose the next morning at Jed's call, the duke and Albert had gone, slipping away at dawn after bidding farewell to Henry Griffen in the cold coffeeroom. Albert had harnessed the horses and carried down the bags while Barrington paid his shot, declining breakfast. He apologized handsomely once again for the contretemps he had caused, and then he strode from the inn and a moment later was tooling along the road leading to London.

CHAPTER VIII

It was several weeks later before the Cummingses found themselves at last in London. After completing their delayed trip to Oxford, and the business to be settled with the bishop, which took much longer than Mr. Cummings had expected, they had made their way to Woltan only to find that the dowager duchess was not in residence, having removed early to town. Mr. Cummings was dismayed that he had not realized how it would be, knowing his mother as he did. This redoubtable lady professed to be delighted with the country, up through the Christmas festivities with the huge party of house guests assembled to help celebrate; but if the weather turned cold, or if there was a lot of ice and snow and dismal days, she would be sure to start planning an early departure for London, sometimes as soon as the last carriage bearing members of the houseparty bowled down the avenue. Miss Martin, her elderly companion, would wring her hands and exclaim over dear Althea's fitful starts, so unsuitable in a woman of her age and station, but as the dowager never paid any attention to this faded lady, she soon found herself relentlessly whisked back to town.

Last year they had remained at Woltan through Lent, but it had been an open winter, unseasonably warm. Mr. Cummings knew it was not just the lack of amusements that made his elderly mother so restless; she suffered from a form of arthritis that the cold exacerbated and the dower house did nothing to alleviate, in spite of the huge fires kept burning at all times. William, the present duke, chuckled at his brother when he and Beth made their appearance early one afternoon.

"Good Lord, Edward!" he exclaimed as he welcomed them. "You didn't really think Mother would still be here? Off like a shot she was, as soon as the roads were cleared after the blizzard! Not but what we are delighted to welcome you anyway! How are you, my dear Beth? You look a bit peaked! Has all this traveling about worn you down, m'dear?"

Beth kissed her prosy uncle and assured him she did very well, although in truth she had been fighting a mood of depression ever since they had left the Bird and Bottle. As she listened to her gentle father and pedantic uncle catching up with each other's news over a glass of Madeira, she was once again startled. How anyone like her grandmother had ever borne two children so unlike herself was a mystery! The dowager duchess was now in her late seventies, but she was still lively and fun-loving, and with one son in holy orders and intent only on his books and research, and the other content to manage his estates and fuss only about crossbreeding and the best type of drainage ditch, she must often have been bored. Beth did not wonder she had left early for town.

The Cummingses spent a few days with the duke and his wife, and Beth could not remember when she had been so impatient with life at Woltan. Maybe she was more like her grandmother than she had supposed, for no matter how kind her aunt and uncle, or how attentive her cousins, she could not seem to shake off a feeling of despondency. It seemed to rain all the time they were there, for a thaw had set in, and one rainy day succeeded another without pause. Mr. Cummings had told his brother of their enforced stay at the little inn, and most of what had occurred there, and seeing Beth so unlike her usual cheerful self, decided she was probably worn out with traveling. He asked the duke if Beth might remain at Woltan for a long visit, and was assured they would be delighted to have her stay with them. When apprised of this treat, Beth vehemently denied she was tired, and demanded to know how soon they could leave for town, and as her father had no inkling of the real cause of her depression, he accepted her explanation without question when Beth told him she thought the weather was affecting her, and a change of scene and the chance to see her dear Grandmama again were all that she needed.

Accordingly they took coach again and arrived in London early one March evening, to be heartily welcomed by the dowager.

" 'Pon rep, Edward!" this lady said as they advanced into the drawing room, where she was seated awaiting dinner. "You here? And my dear Beth! Come and kiss me, both of you!"

Beth warmly complied after her father had embraced his mother and asked how she did, but when that lady looked at her shrewdly and asked what had happened to put her in such a state, she refused to be drawn.

Taking off her cloak and bonnet, she went to the huge fire and held out her hands to it, trying to smile naturally.

"Why, ma'am!" she said easily, "how unkind of you to say I am not in my best looks! I think it must be the weather; I told Father that if it continues to rain much longer we should consider the advisability of building an ark! I, for one, was not at all surprised to find you had left Woltan and bolted back to town!"

"Beth!" her grandmother exclaimed, successfully drawn off the scent. "I never did! Bolted indeed! At my age! We traveled most decorously, I do assure you!" Then, turning to her son, she said, "I hope this visit means that you will make a long stay with me, Edward. I have not seen you or Beth for such an age!"

Mr. Cummings took a sip of his sherry before he replied.

"Now Mother," he said, "you know I must return to my parish and my studies before too long. A fine thing for a parson to spend his time raking in town! I will be here, however, for a few weeks at least, and Beth may stay and bear you company as long as she likes, of course."

His mother snorted. "Ha! Raking, indeed! I know very well, my son, that your idea of 'raking' is to haunt every library in town. Admit it! 'Tis not just the pleasure of seeing your mother that has drawn you here!"

Mr. Cummings laughed and had to agree. The dowager knew her second son too well. She turned again to Beth.

"And you, my love? Will you stay? I have been feeling so stale since Christmas! Do give me your company for the season, I beg of you! It will be wonderful to have someone to talk to again who enters into all my feelings."

Beth assured her she would be delighted to make a long stay, and then belatedly asked what had happened to her grandmother's companion.

"Oh, Belinda!" she said carelessly, dismissing her with a wave of a much bejeweled hand. "There was a death in her family—some distant cousin I believe—and she is gone into the country for a while to attend this aunt. Not," she added with a wicked twinkle, "that she is so enjoyable to talk to anyway. She proses on just as William does, always telling me that what I want to do is unsuitable! But you and I, my love, have

164

always had a deal to say to each other. It will be famous!" She abruptly changed the subject without warning, as she often did. "Do you wish to change for dinner? I fear it is almost ready, but perhaps I could have Pierre delay it . . ."

She looked so doubtful about the wisdom of disturbing the routine of this paragon of a chef that both Mr. Cummings and Beth laughed at her and told her that if she did not object, they would join her as they were.

Wardwell, the butler, announced dinner shortly thereafter, and Mr. Cummings offered his mother his arm. Entering the dining salon, leaning slightly on her cane, she addressed a further remark to Beth over her shoulder.

"Where had you that horrible traveling gown, my girl? It is positively dowdy! I can see we have a vast amount of shopping to do if you are not to put me to the blush!"

Beth, admiring her grandmother's still-slim figure and erect carriage and her decided air of elegance, agreed she needed some new gowns. She knew the lady had unerring taste and could be depended on to help her select whatever was the most becoming of the new fashions; furthermore, there was nothing she liked better than a morning spent in the better shops, approving this bit of lace or denouncing all those tacky loops of braid.

The following days, the Cummingses went their separate ways—Mr. Cummings to the reference libraries, and the two women on their shopping expeditions. The duchess had had the story of their adventures during the blizzard, but Beth had refused to discuss it any further than to say it had all been very exciting, and did her grandmama think she would look well in rose or would she prefer the violet for her new afternoon dress? The dowager was not sidetracked by this, and although she followed Beth's lead and changed the subject to clothes, her mind was working busily. So! Something had occurred at that little inn, and she would find out what it was, sooner or later. Beth had all the earmarks of a girl in love, from her forced gaiety when someone was looking at her to her sudden silences when she thought she was unobserved.

The dowager had been disappointed when she had sponsored Beth in her first season some years ago. The girl seemed uninterested in society and serenely content to whistle down all her chances at matrimony. When Beth announced at the end of the season that it had all been very interesting but that now she intended to retire to her father's parish to assist him in his work, the dowager had accepted the inevitable and washed her hands of trying to find Beth a husband who came up to her impossible standards. She decided Beth was too much like her father after all, and blamed her son for educating Beth as he had, putting all kinds of notions and knowledge in the girl's head that were not a particle of use that she could see. But now, with Beth agreeing to spend the season, and actually interested in her appearance, things looked a great deal more promising. She determined to find out more.

Coming into the library one afternoon when Beth had run upstairs to fetch her a forgotten shawl, and finding her son immersed in his books, she demanded his attention.

"About this inn, Edward," she began abruptly. "Just who was it who stayed there when you and Beth did?"

Mr. Cummings patiently put a finger in his book to keep his place as he replied. "Why, let me see. A Mrs. and Miss Orvis-Ryder, the two Allensworth twins—you know the family, Mama—and the Duke of Barrington."

The old lady nodded her head thoughtfully. "I see. Thank you, Edward, how very interesting!" She went away then, a speculative expression on her face.

A few days later, as she and her granddaughter were about to step into their carriage on Bond Street after visiting Madame Celeste's establishment to choose a new ball gown for Beth, they were hailed by two handsome young men. The dowager's eyes narrowed

166

as Beth presented the Allensworth twins. They were dressed with great modishness for town, and although they favored different tailors, one could see at a glance how alike they were. Dolph's shirt points might be higher, his cravat tied more elaborately than his brother's, his person might be tricked out with all manner of fobs and jewelry, but that was all the difference.

The dowager was gracious, and when Tony begged permission to call on both ladies, she smilingly agreed. She stole a glance at Beth as they drove away. Her granddaughter looked very handsome this afternoon too, she thought, in her new dress of blue superfine trimmed with velvet braid, which exactly fitted her admirable figure. Her now fashionably styled brown curls were topped by a tassled bonnet, dipping roguishly over one eye. Her complexion was more rosy than usual, which could easily be attributed to the cold north wind, but somehow her grandmother did not feel this was the cause. She settled back in the carriage, a small smile on her wrinkled face. More and more interesting! Now which twin was it?

She did not realize that Beth had been embarrassed by the meeting and the memories it conjured up. She was trying very hard, though not with much success, to forget the whole interlude, especially as it pertained to the duke. She could not help wondering now and then, however, what had happened to him and where he was at present. For all she knew, he had delivered the report and gone back to America, and since she had told him she never wanted to see him again, why did this thought make her feel so miserable? She shook her head mentally to rid it of such unproductive musings, and set herself to be extremely vivacious at Lady Gordon's, where they had been invited to tea.

Unbeknownst to Beth, the duke, far from traveling to America, was even then leaving the vicinity of Woltan. He had managed to gain an invitation to visit an old friend whose estate was only some six miles distant, only to discover within the hour of his arrival that Mr. Cummings, his daughter, and his mother, the dowager duchess, were in London. To say the duke was annoyed was putting it mildly, for he had been in the capital himself just the week before, and might have been straightening out the tangle even now; instead he was forced, by courtesy, to spend at least a couple of weeks visiting and being entertained by his friend. Bleakly he realized that they had gone their separate ways since they had both been up at Oxford together in more ways than one, and wondered that he had not remembered how much of a bore Lord Moulton was. He was forced to endure many long hours before the fire or in the billiard parlor when the weather turned inclement and there was no hunting or riding to be had, the attentions of Lord Moulton's niece, whose mama was determined to capture this unexpected prize, and several country evenings complete with all the local gentry, their simpering wives, and tedious offspring. Never the most courteous of men, he was often hard put to control his temper.

He met the currant Duke of Woltan, and although he saw the family resemblance to Mr. Cummings he realized that his brother had none of the minister's intelligence and learning, and wondered how Beth came to have such a dull relation. He thought the duchess infinitely worse. He took to riding out with Albert whenever he could escape, and after one especially horrendous evening spent listening to Miss Moulton sing and accompany herself on the pianoforte, soulfully addressing melting glances to him alone, was pleased to find a letter for him in the morning post. It was only a short note from Viscount Castlereagh complimenting him on his report, but he sought out his host without delay and without even a twinge of a guilty conscience announced that state business called him immediately back to town.

The twins appeared at the Cummings town house within days of their reunion with Beth. They stayed only the permitted half hour, and Beth soon forgot her diffidence in laughing and joking with them. Tony begged her to go driving with them in the park the following afternoon, and she agreed cheerfully. As Dolph was assuring her he drove to an inch—top of the trees m'lady!—and was a great gun with the ribbons in his high perch phaeton, her grandmother was sure it was Tony Beth preferred, for she stigmatized Dolph as a silly fop with more buttons than brains. Beth felt much better by the time they took their departure, but by then her grandmother was not equally enthused. It had not taken that lady thirty minutes to realize that Beth treated them both as younger brothers, so she had not been in love after all.

But stay! There was another gentleman at the inn, she remembered. Could it be the duke of Barrington that Beth favored? She had initially dismissed him from consideration as being too old, but now she thought of it, he could not be above five and thirty. What a splendid match that would be! Speculatively she looked at her granddaughter, now seated at the escritoire writing some cards.

It was not possible that she had been mistaken in the symptoms, she thought. Certainly Beth had never been so interested in fashion or in the various parties now being planned as society returned to town for the season. Well she remembered Beth's begging her to make her excuses for a ball, a soiré, or a Venetian breakfast, the year of her comeout. And to try to get her into anything resembling a smart ensemble had taken all her coaxing. Yet here she was, several years older, much concerned with the cut of her gowns, the curls her hair was dressed in, and the invitations delivered every day at the door.

Even as her granddaughter did, she wondered where the duke was at the moment. He had not been seen in town for two seasons; surely he would put in an appearance this year, now he was returned from his travels. She thought of asking her son for more information, and quickly dismissed the idea. Edward was a dear man, but she knew he would be absolutely astounded at her reasoning. He had seen nothing unusual when he had them both in his eye, or he would have told her. Men she thought, were absolutely of no help at all when there was something like this in the wind!

Beth drove out with the twins and enjoyed herself thoroughly, as she did when she met them thereafter at evening parties. If Tony was engaged with another group, Dolph would be sure to hurry up to her to chat or beg for a dance. It was extremely comfortable to know they were there, so attentive, and introducing her to several of their friends as well. Beth might not be swamped with admirers, but she never lacked a partner in the dance or a gentleman to exchange witticisms with, and soon gained quite a reputation as a scintillating conversationalist who was ever ready with *jeux d'esprit* to enliven the evening. Many of the dowager's cronies commented on how much dear Beth had come on since her first season, and the duchess smiled to herself and was delighted with the twins for being so useful. Beth herself was amazed at how easy it suddenly was. She had been very shy and retiring her first season, for she had lived such a simple scholarly life with her father. Now it seemed easy to flirt, chatter gaily on any subject, and make the gentlemen laugh with no effort in the world. If she wished the duke could see her with her new popularity, she kept it to herself.

One evening she was surprised to see Letty Orvis-Ryder across the room at an evening reception. Letty was accompanied by a middle-aged lady of kindly aspect, and as Mrs. Orvis-Ryder was nowhere in sight, Beth was encouraged to make her way to them and greet her. Letty turned quite pink, but when she saw that Beth had no intention of reminding her of her bad behavior with Dolph, she became more at ease. She introduced Beth to her aunt, Lady Rogers, who bowed and smiled and suggested the two girls walk in the park some morning soon, for she was delighted to further Letty's acquaintance with the duke of Woltan's niece. Beth agreed, and a date was set before she returned to her grandmother.

She told the Dowager about Letty the following day, describing her mother in such vivid terms that her grandmother was stricken with a fit of laughing and finally begged Beth to stop.

"Fore gad, Beth," she said when she had caught her breath, "draw line! I am sure you are making her up, for no one could be that puffed up with her own consequence or that vulgar! By the way, who are the Orvis-Ryders?"

Beth chuckled. "No one seems to know except the lady herself, ma'am! Letty was at the party last evening with her aunt, Katherine Rogers."

"Oh yes, Lady Rogers; I know her a little. Unexceptional. Do you join the girl if you like."

When Beth and Letty met to stroll in the park, she asked, out of courtesy, for Mrs. Orvis-Ryder, and Letty blushed bright pink.

"Mama went back to Durham," she said, and then added in a rush, "Oh, Miss Cummings—Beth—it was just awful! The scene with my aunt you cannot imagine! I thought I would sink when Aunt Katherine said the only way she would sponsor me in London for the season was if Mama removed herself. The things she said! And then Mama had one of *her spells,* you know, and . . . and . . . well, it was too terribly lowering!"

Beth tried hard to control her dimple and quivering mouth, and pretended to be absorbed in tightening a button on her glove.

"Do you like your aunt, Letty?" she asked.

"Oh my, yes," Letty said fervently. "It is so comfortable, for she knows just how to go on, and there are never any scenes, and she has bought me the prettiest new clothes, much more in keeping with my age, she says, than what I had before," she added naively. They strolled for a few steps before she added as a

171

postscript, "Of course I miss Mama, but Aunt is right I'm sure."

Beth looked at her inquiringly.

"Well, she told me that Mama's health would be better in the county, and that on no account could she bear the racketing of town life if she is stricken by *her spells* so easily. I am sure she is right."

Beth agreed privately that Letty would do better in town too, without her mama, and when she observed the beaux she soon collected knew she would be married before the season was over. It would come as quite a shock to the lucky man when he met Mrs. Orvis-Ryder for the first time, but Beth was sure Lady Rogers would make sure the betrothal was announced before she allowed that to happen. The fact that the Allensworth twins were not among her admirers was not remarked.

The dowager duchess told Beth for her own good to stop seeing Letty after she had observed how beautiful the girl was, for, as she said bluntly, Beth could not hope to compete with such perfection. Beth laughingly agreed. "I know why you say so, ma'am, but indeed I have no desire to make Letty a bosom bow, and not for the reason that she shines me down, either. For all she is an Incomparable, she is just too stupid!"

Several evenings later, Beth accompanied her grandmother to the first large ball of the new season, given by Lord and Lady Jervis. The dowager thought she looked exceedingly handsome in a dark-gray satin gown trimmed with dove gray lace—a gown much too sophisticated for a miss in her first season. It had a deep V neckline banded in the lace, which barely touched Beth's shoulders before sweeping to an even deeper V in back. Her hair was dressed high on her head in a smooth elegant style, with only two curls allowed to dangle over her white shoulder. She wore her mother's pearls, and the duchess thought her in quite her best looks.

Tony hastened to greet the ladies as they entered the ballroom and immediately begged a dance, and the dowager took a seat with some friends and prepared to enjoy the evening. As the dance ended, she glanced at her granddaughter, now chatting gaily with Tony as a tall dark gentleman approached and bowed to them both. Idly wondering who this could be, for she prided herself on her knowledge of the ton, she was shocked to see Beth turning hurriedly away, as pale as she had ever been. She left the ballroom abruptly, even as the dowager was beckoning to her, leaving a bewildered Tony with the stranger, whose face was flushed with anger. The two men left the dance floor together, and when she saw them exchange bows, she crooked an imperious finger at Tony, motioning him to her side. He bowed and smiled, but he looked very uneasy.

"Please be seated, m'lord," she said, and waited until he obeyed. "Who was that man that you and Beth were talking to just now? And why is my granddaughter so upset?"

Tony hesitated a bit, but he knew the fierce old lady would get it out of him eventually, so he replied as casually as he could, "Why, your grace, 'tis the Duke of Barrington! We met at that country inn during the blizzard, you remember. I am sure Beth has told you all about it." Tony himself had been shocked by Beth's behavior. When the duke appeared and bowed, she had exclaimed, *"You! You here? I beg to be excused!"* and flounced off before either he or the duke could stop her.

The dowager nodded, her thoughts busy. "And why was Beth so upset at the encounter?" she demanded.

Tony tried to smile. "Well, madam, there was some talk of a missing report of Barrington's; he had dropped it in the coffeeroom and Beth inadvertently picked it up. The duke thought it had been stolen by a spy—but it all came right in the end. I do not know why Miss Cummings is so upset, however, for the duke assured her he knew she was not at fault." He paused as the musicians began to play. "You must excuse me, madam. I am engaged for the next dance."

The dowager dismissed him carelessly, her mind elsewhere. When Beth finally returned to the ballroom and made her way to her side, she made no mention of the duke or what Tony had told her. Time enough for that when she had Beth alone, where they would not be interrupted as they were about to be now by the Earl of Brixton, come to claim his waltz. Beth smiled at him, her color restored, and the rest of the evening passed uneventfully. The duke did not appear again in the ballroom, although the dowager spotted him in the card room on her way to supper. She wondered at Beth; he was certainly not a bit handsome with his swarthy complexion and carelessly worn evening dress, but perhaps if he were to stop frowning he might have more countenance.

Beth slept late the following morning, and the dowager was just finishing breakfast with her son when Wardwell brought in a salver with a card on it and presented it to Mr. Cummings.

" 'Pon rep, Edward! Callers this early?" his mother inquired, pouring herself another cup of coffee.

Her son frowned briefly over the engraved inscription, and then his face brightened.

"Why, 'tis the Duke of Barrington! I did not know he was in London still!" He turned to the waiting butler. "Take the duke to the library and tell him I will attend him shortly."

As the butler left the room and closed the door, he said to his mother, "I wonder what he can want? A most fascinating man, Mother! His travels in the Americas, his education—I can assure you he made an otherwise tedious stay at that inn bearable."

His mother was deep in thought. "You know, Edward, I think I shall cancel my morning appointments. If you should wish to see me, I will be in the morning room."

Mr. Cummings looked bemused, but he nodded as he excused himself and went to the library. His mother drank her coffee and waited as patiently as she could, wishing she had had a chance to speak to Beth before this particular visitor had arrived.

In the library, Mr. Cummings shook the duke's hand heartily and begged him to be seated.

"I am delighted to see you again, your grace," he said. "Did the report go well? I do hope nothing has occurred . . . I mean, my daughter's actions with the résumé . . ." He floundered to a halt, and the duke hastened to reassure him.

" 'Tis nothing to do with the report, sir, but it does concern Miss Cummings. I have come to ask your permission to pay my addresses to your daughter."

Mr. Cummings was dumbfounded. He sat down abruptly in the nearest chair, completely surprised.

"My daughter? Beth?" he asked, bewildered.

Barrington smiled at him. "Have you another daughter, sir? I must tell you I have wanted to marry her ever since we became acquainted at the inn, but I must also tell you that I do not feel your daughter is in charity with me; we met last night at the Jervises ball, and she all but cut me!"

"And you still wish for her hand?" Mr. Cummings asked, more bewildered than ever.

"Yes, I do! I think she loves me too, or at least is not completely indifferent to me, you see, but she is still angry about what happened at the inn. I handled it very ill, sir, very ill indeed, when I spoke to her before you left." He paused a moment, a flush staining his high cheekbones, and then he added, "If I could be assured that you have no objection to my suit, I would like to try again."

Mr. Cummings looked out of his depth, but he said, "As to that, sir, I have no objections at all, although it is not my decision, after all, for I have educated Beth to make up her own mind."

The duke looked ruefully at him. "Yes, I thought

you might have. I could almost wish we lived in an earlier time when these things were arranged for young ladies by their elders, for I foresee a difficult time of it for myself!"

Mr. Cummings looked thoughtful. "Let me speak to my mother. She might know Beth's feelings better than I do on such a matter."

The duke looked a little happier. "Thank you, sir. I am sure you are right, for I must admit I am at a loss as to how to continue; I do not see how any courtship can prosper if one of the participants refuses to have anything to do with the other! Maybe the duchess can advise me, for ladies often know what the right step to take would be!"

He rose, refusing a glass of wine, which Mr. Cummings belatedly remembered to offer him.

"I thank you for your permission to try to win Beth, sir. You may be assured that I love her very much."

His color rose again when Mr. Cummings patted him on the back as they walked to the door. "My boy, I am sure you do. I will seek my mother's advice and communicate with you as soon as possible. Until then," he added with a twinkle, "perhaps you had better avoid my daughter, unless you feel that would be cowardly! My, this is most unlike her! She is generally the gentlest of women!" He shook his head and bid the duke good morning.

When he rejoined his mother in the morning room, that lady looked at him expectantly.

"Well, Edward? What did the duke want?"

He took a seat and said, "Why, Mother, I was never so surprised! He came to ask my permission for leave to pay his addresses to Beth!"

The dowager chuckled. "Well, Edward, I am not surprised at all! It has been perfectly obvious that something was afoot from the way Beth has been behaving!"

"It was?" Mr. Cummings asked. "I never noticed anything!"

"Of course not, dear," his mother said brightly. "Gentlemen do not, I believe. And did you give your permission?"

"Oh yes, of course! In the eyes of the world, a brilliant match for Beth. But I did not agree for that reason! He is perfect for her; his intellect, his knowledge and understanding—everything I could wish for her! There is only one problem, though—"

Lady Cummings interrupted. "Yes, I know. Beth will have none of him, am I correct?"

This was too much for even the mild-mannered pastor. With something very close to exasperation in his voice, he demanded, "Will you be so good as to tell me, Mother, why women always seem to 'know' these things that are so unintelligible to men? And yet the majority of them cannot generally either balance accounts, understand Greek, or be at all logical in their thinking!"

The dowager laughed out loud. "Why, Edward," she exclaimed, "I believe we are blessed with something that has been left out of the masculine makeup—a sense of intuition! Or perhaps it is because we consider romance more important than Greek or logic! But come, what is to be done?"

Mr. Cummings looked at her earnestly. "I thought perhaps you would know what is best, ma'am, and I told the duke I would ask for your opinion. However, I must tell you firmly that if Beth does not welcome this liaison, she shall not be forced into it, brilliant match or no!"

His mother replied soothingly. "I am sure she does wish it, Edward. In fact, I think she is as much in love as the duke is, but now, clutching the shreds of her pride and her anger, she has backed herself into an impossible corner. Perhaps you had better tell me again everything that happened during that blizzard— especially the part dealing with the missing paper!"

Mr. Cummings was agreeable, and starting with finding the overturned coach, told her the whole, not without several interruptions as his mother sought clarification on some point she considered important. As he had not observed anything of a personal nature between his daughter and the duke, his tale was a factual accounting of events, but the dowager had no difficulty at all in filling in the gaps. When he ended his story, she sighed in satisfaction.

"Now, Edward," she began, with a great air of resolution, "this is all going to have to be managed with the greatest discretion. You are not to mention the duke or his request to Beth at all; that is of the first importance!"

Mr. Cummings sighed. "Proverbs Six, Mother, Proverbs Six! 'The Lord hates a lying tongue'!"

Lady Cummings replied tartly, "You have gone to the wrong chapter, my son! I give you Proverbs eleven! 'A man of understanding remains silent. He who goes about as a talebearer reveals secrets, but he who is trustworthy in spirit keeps a thing hidden.'"

Mr. Cummings appeared much struck by this, and she continued smoothly, "You must write to the duke, Edward, and ask him to call on me tomorrow—in the morning, I think, about eleven. Beth will be walking with that tiresome Orvis-Ryder chit who begged for a meeting. Ha! Probably wants Beth to tell her which of sixteen proposals she should accept! That is by the way; what is important is that Beth will be out of the house."

Mr. Cummings agreed, and faithfully promised to write the note *before* he began his research that day.

The old lady found her granddaughter idly turning over the cards of invitation in the hall. She gave her a happy smile and did not ask why she looked so sad, but only what her plans were for the day. Beth sighed. She had spent the better part of the night thinking, and tossing, and turning, and did not feel like doing anything she had planned. She shrugged. "I have a luncheon engagement, Grandmama, with the Everlys; were you not invited too? And then this afternoon
178

Tony and Dolph are to take me driving in the park."

"Capital, m'dear! Yes, I will join you at the Everlys', and then go on to my shopping, since you will not need the carriage. Do you wear the peach muslin that arrived yesterday—quite one of your prettiest dresses, I think!"

Beth agreed, and went away to dress wishing she had never come to London, wishing she were back at the inn, wishing she had never met the difficult duke, and then wondering if he would care for her in peach.

When the Allensworths arrived later that afternoon, she tried very hard to match their high spirits. Dolph bubbled over about some horse he had backed at Newmarket that went by the inprobable name of Kiss in a Corner.

"Assure you, miss, impossible for him to lose! Saw it in a moment! Such shoulders and legs! Well, I put my blunt on him and he led the field all the way. Very plump in the pockets, very plump!"

"Until the next race," Tony said cynically. "Or is it this evening you are engaged to play macao at Brook's?"

"No, no, Tony!" Dolph exclaimed, "Havin' a winning streak, don't you know? Impossible to lose! Often that way!"

Tony sighed. "I do hope your winning streak does not extend to a certain little redhead of our acquaintance!"

Beth, seated between them on the seat of the high-perch phaeton, had to laugh at them both, and it was then that she caught sight of the duke cantering toward them. He had almost reached the carriage, and she caught her breath sharply, but before she could turn away, he touched his hat and gave them a small indifferent bow without even slowing his horse.

Beth clenched her hands into fists as Dolph asked brightly, "I say, wasn't that Barrington? Like his horse!"

"Yes, better than his manners!" Beth snapped, as Tony gave her a sideways glance. The lady's eyes were flashing, and he did not miss the fists or her high color. 'Ere, wot's to do, guv? he thought, remembering her reception of the duke at the ball and now this meeting, but he did not pursue it, and turned the conversation easily.

"Do you go to the Markhams' masquerade? I have been trying to find a pair of historical twins for us to emulate; perhaps your father could help me out. There must be someone in Greek mythology who is not too awful."

Dolph agreed firmly. "Don't want to go as a Bad Man!"

Beth steadied her breathing and said she would inquire. When Dolph asked her about her costume, she said it was a secret.

"Should be an entertaining evening," Tony continued. "Are you acquainted with the Markhams, Miss Cummings? Always everything of the finest, the best music, champagne, and decorations. It should be one of the season's largest crushes!"

Beth agreed she was looking forward to it, and when the twins drove her home, she promised again to inquire of her father for a set of famous twins.

The next morning, the dowager duchess bid Beth a cheerful farewell as she left to walk with Letty in the park. It seemed to Beth that the more depressed she became, the happier her grandmother seemed to be. But then, she did not have to endure Letty's chattering inanities, she thought, somewhat spitefully.

The dowager directed her butler to bring the Duke of Barrington to the morning room as soon as he arrived, and settled down with her needlework, her mind busy with possible plans. The duke was punctual. He had a slight frown on his face as he entered and bowed, and the dowager thought again that he was not at all a handsome man. He was dressed with propriety for a morning call, but he would never be mistaken for a dandy; his coat was much too loose, his shirt points only moderately high, and his only jewelry was a heavy signet ring. The dowager bade him be seated, and they chatted casually until Wardwell served the Madeira and bowed himself out, although he was extremely interested in the caller and his business. As he reluctantly shut the door, the dowager got right down to it.

"Now, Barrington," she said, "I understand from my son that you are desirous of marrying my granddaughter, but that things are not going at all well. I have had the tale from Edward, but dear man though he is, he did not notice anything at all relating to either your or Beth's feelings in the matter. Perhaps it would be best if you told me your version."

The duke frowned again and turned his glass absently in his hands, at a seeming loss for words.

"Just start at the beginning, man! No need to pull your punches with me!" She then added encouragingly, "Perhaps you will feel a deal better if I tell you that I suspect Beth to be as much in love as you are yourself! She has been very unhappy since the Jervis ball, although she says she is just 'tired.' Ha! It will take some managing, but once we find a way to circumvent her silly pride and anger I am sure all will end happily." She looked up at the duke and saw he was smiling at her in relief. Ah, she thought, now I know what Beth sees in him! What an attractive smile he has, and the light in his eyes is pure deviltry!

The duke put down his glass as he came to a decision. He told the dowager all the things that her son had not even suspected, and assured her he had not thought Beth was the spy, and could not understand why she had been so angry, although he did admit he had ripped up at her at the end.

"You called her a 'little fool'?" the dowager asked. "How very unfortunate, to be sure! Beth has been raised to pride herself on her intelligence, so of course she ripped right back at you, did she not? And probably said she never wanted to see you again in her life, I'd wager!"

The duke looked at her respectfully. "Her exact words, your grace. How did you guess?"

181

"Oh, it went without saying! If she loved you and you showed her how angry you were, and how upset with her, of course she would have to say that. She didn't mean a word of it, you know! Now, what happened at the ball? I saw her rush away very pale, after you approached."

The duke sighed. "Yes, I guess it startled her, my appearing without warning like that. She only said, 'You here? I beg to be excused!' Not very promising!"

"Only because she was not expecting to see you, I do assure you. It is too bad that she could not have been warned."

She seemed deep in thought, and the duke added, "I must also tell you that I saw her yesterday in the park, but Mr. Cummings told me I must not approach her again until I had spoken to you, so I gave her only the most distant of bows."

The dowager was exasperated. "Oh dear, Edward, why . . . ? *Men!*" she added darkly. "So that was why she was so languid and miserable last night and refused to attend the opera! A headache indeed! Well, it cannot be mended now, but perhaps you had better give me a list of your engagements for the next few days. Any more of these impromptu meetings, with first Beth cutting you and then you cutting Beth, and even I will not be able to make all right!"

The duke meekly complied, and it turned out that the next time they were due to meet was at Viscount Castlereagh's for dinner in three day's time. The dowager frowned.

"Oh dear, I turned down that invitation, thinking it would be one of those tiresome political evenings that Edward could just as well escort Beth to, for I knew they would both enjoy it! Perhaps . . . no, we will have to hope for the best."

With a great deal of resolution, she rose and began to pace the floor. "Now, Barrington, the first thing you do is to send Beth a note, accompanied by some flowers. I am sure I can leave the exact wording to you, but be sure you apologize yet again, and beg for a meeting. You won't get it, but ask anyway! And be sure you mention your love for her. I am positive you know what to say!"

The duke agreed, his eyes crinkling in amusement, that he was capable of writing a love letter.

"Now," the old lady continued, ignoring this sally, "additional flowers every morning if you please, but just enclose your card. That will put her in a more receptive frame of mind. On no account are you to seek her out for a serious conversation at Castlereagh's. You might try to be placed across from her at dinner, and a few melting glances might be in order, but do not attempt to settle this in a crowded drawing room!"

"Of course not, madam!" the duke agreed in a hurry.

"Yes, yes, you say that now, but I know you men! So impetuous! The next day you can again call on Edward, and he can then tell Beth you have asked for her hand, and then, in the privacy of the library, you can plead your case. That should do it! I will, of course, be helping all I can when the flowers start arriving."

The duke grinned at her wickedly. "I shall trust you implicitly, madam! If you would like me to draw up a list of my credentials—my family connections, my good character, my education, etcetera—I would be happy to do so!"

The dowager laughed and tapped his hand with her tambour frame. "That will be quite unnecessary, Alistair. I have no intention of touting off your good qualities in the slightest, but you may trust me to handle it. Away with you now—you have a fervent letter to write, remember!"

The duke bowed, kissed her hand, and took his leave. Wardwell was moved to remark to the second footman that something was afoot, of that he was sure, for not only had the duke been smiling broadly as he left the house, so also had her ladyship when she left the morning room.

CHAPTER IX

The Duke of Barrington was even more precipitous than the Dowager Duchess of Woltan had suggested, and when Beth returned late that afternoon with her grandmother, she found Wardwell directing one of the footmen to carry an extremely lavish bouquet of roses to her room, and bowing to her, he presented her with the envelope that had accompanied the flowers.

Beth was pink as she turned it over and saw the crest it was sealed with. Her grandmother pretended to be arranging her hair.

"Why, what beautiful flowers, my love!" she said. "Who are they from?"

Beth looked up blindly, still clutching the unopened envelope. "Why, I do not know, Grandmother. If . . . if you will excuse me!" She turned and ran lightly up the stairs, causing Wardwell to allow a very uncharacteristic expression of puzzlement to cross his generally imperturbable features at her rudeness. His employer smiled at him, completely undismayed.

Upstairs, Beth dismissed her maid, and still holding the envelope, bent to examine the flowers. She sat down slowly at her desk and carefully opened the letter and read it quickly, a small oh of astonishment on her lips, and then she read it more carefully, her cheeks growing very pink as she did so.

It had taken the duke a long while to write the note to his satisfaction, for he had seldom in his life had to humble himself or beg pardon of anyone. He had ruined several sheets of hand pressed paper and uttered many oaths before he was through; at one point he was tempted to hurl his wineglass at the bricks of the fireplace in frustration. He had paced up and down his library for several minutes and then sat down and dashed off the copy Beth held. He had not been completely satisfied and had felt it would have been easier to translate his entire report into Greek than to get the few lines right, but it said what was in his heart, and it would have to do.

"My Dear Miss Cummings," the note began formally.

> Please accept these flowers as a token of my regard and affection. I do most humbly apologize again for the incident at the inn, and beg you to forgive me! I think you are aware that my sentiments for you remain unchanged; indeed, dear Beth, I will always love you. Please do not be so unkind as to deny me an interview. I am sure it will be easier to tell you what is in my heart when we are together.
>
> Yours, etc.,
Alistair St. Clare

Beth traced the bold black signature with one finger and then carefully folded the note, a small frown on her face. He really was arrogant, this Duke of Barrington, to think he had only to ask her to grant him a meeting and she would fall into his arms without delay! Well, he would see that she was not to be had by a snap of his fingers! She was smiling a wicked little smile as she sat down to write her reply, in the third person and her very best penmanship.

Miss Elizabeth Cummings regrets she is unable to grant the Duke of Barrington an interview, for although the roses are lovely, they do not soften her heart to one who has behaved toward her with such arrogance and distrust.

She paused, biting the end of her quill thoughtfully, and then signed her note with a flourish,

Not yours, etc.
Elizabeth Cummings

She sanded her note, a smile of satisfaction on her face, and summoning her maid, directed her to have the note delivered to the Duke of Barrington immediately.

That evening she was in excellent spirits, and even told her grandmother gaily about the flowers without any prompting. The dowager frowned a little.

"Barrington? Oh yes, that swarthy gentleman who has been in the Americas! I wonder he dares to approach you, my love, even if you were thrown together during the blizzard!"

Beth looked confused. "Why, Grandmother, what do you mean? Why should he not?"

The dowager smoothed a flounce on her dress and replied, carefully not looking at her granddaughter, "Well, he is quite old, is he not, my dear? Besides being so very ugly!"

Beth was startled. "Ugly? I do not think him ugly precisely, ma'am. And he is only in his thirties; that is not old!"

Her grandmother laughed lightly. "Oh, compared to the Allensworths or the earl of Brixton, my dear Beth, he is quite outside the pale! I hope you have rebuffed him for his temerity!"

187

Beth answered slowly, "Well, yes, I did, but surely his lineage is impeccable, ma'am. I do not understand you at all!"

"My dear Beth, since you have denied him, what more is there to say? I do so wish you to have a happy marriage, and someone like that . . . well! He would probably drag you all over the world on his diplomatic missions, not caring at all for your comfort, besides boring you to death at dinner with tedious discussions of politics and Parliament. And do regard that he has never married, and at his age that is surely suspicious! So careless in his dress, too! Not at all a pretty suitor! No, you do very well to dismiss him, my love."

She turned the subject neatly as Wardwell came in to announce dinner. The two ladies were dining alone before joining a party of friends at the theater to see Kemble act. The dowager had the satisfaction of seeing Beth lost in thought several times that evening, and decided it would only be wicked to ask her what she thought of the play, since she was willing to wager her diamond brooch that Beth had heard very little of the great actor's histrionics.

Beth was confused, for she had not expected her grandmother to take exception to the duke, and when she thought of being dragged all over the world by him could only admit to herself that she would like it above all things! And she could not imagine ever being bored in his company.

When they left their carriage and Wardwell admitted them to the house, she was startled to see he was presenting her with another note. Ignoring the interested servants and her even more interested grandmother, she opened it immediately.

It was unfortunate that the duke had lost his temper again when he had received her reply. The insulting way she had signed it had sent him hotfoot to his desk, furious at her rejection. This time he wasted no paper or thought, and, ripping off a few words, sent a footman back with his reply without pausing to think. Beth stared at his brief inscription.

You will be!
Barrington

She looked up, her eyes dark with anger. How did he dare! Seeing herself the center of everyone's attention, she put her chin up and remarked haughtily to her grandmother, "From Barrington! You were quite right, ma'am, in your assessment!"

With that she swept up the stairs, leaving the dowager to wonder why she had ever thought she could bring this hot-headed, tiresome couple together in the first place. What had the silly man written now, she wondered, and how seriously had he impaired his chances? When she saw that Beth would not even accept the floral offerings that were delivered the following days, her heart sank.

The duke, after a restless night, had realized that perhaps he had exceeded the dowager's instructions with his second, angry note, and was trying once again to make amends. The flowers were returned to him, and the notes he spent so much time writing were not even opened. He arrived at Viscount Castlereagh's for the dinner party in something very like dismay.

Beth and her father were among the last guests to arrive, for Lady Cummings had been most insistent that Beth have her hair redressed. "It does not look at all well that way, my dear," she exclaimed. "Do you dress it a little looser, girl, for I cannot like those tight bands at all!"

As the maid hastened to take out the pins, Beth frowned.

"What difference does it make, ma'am? 'Tis only a dinner party, and the gentlemen will all be involved with politics or the war!"

She stood impatiently as her grandmother checked her gown. It was becoming, but she wished Beth's expression were not so forbidding. "Who will be attending, I wonder?" she asked after Beth had collected her reticule and wrap and they strolled down the stairs together, Beth supporting her arm.

"Perhaps Barrington will be there," she said casually. "He is a friend of the Castlereagh's, I believe."

Beth stiffened but made no reply, and the dowager watched her join her father without being able to add anything more.

Beth stayed close beside her father when she entered the drawing room and saw Barrington before the fire, his eyes intent on her. She turned to greet her hostess and moved away from the danger. Barrington frowned as he saw her avoiding him, but he made no move to seek her out, remembering the dowager's advice. Perhaps after dinner . . .

He took in Lady Versley and was not pleased to see that Beth was placed at quite the opposite end of the long dining table. There were twenty-four guests, and unless he stood on his chair he did not see how he would be able to direct anything remotely like a "melting glance" at the lady. Fate seemed to be conspiring against him! Although the company was brilliant and the conversation stimulating, both he and Beth felt they had never attended such a long tiresome party.

Lady Versley was a stunning woman of his own age who had a great reputation as a flirt. The duke realized she was also much in command of double-entendre, and at another time he would have enjoyed exchanging witticisms with her. When she occasionally turned away, he found himself gazing into the limpid blue eyes of Mrs. Berkley, whose fragility was misleading, for she demanded a complete account of his American adventures, especially the more gruesome stories of battles, wounds, and torture. It did not go very well with either the pheasant or the baron of beef.

Beth, on the other hand, was seated between Lord Barton, an elderly gentleman who was extremely hard

190

of hearing but refused to admit it, and Mr. McCauley, a friend of her father's whom she had dearly loved from childhood. She found it difficult to respond to his teasing and compliments. He thought dear Beth very subdued, and wondered at it, for he was used to conversations with her that fairly rattled along from one person to the next full of excitement, and in which she generally participated with vigor.

Course succeeded course without pause, but it was much later before the signal for the ladies to rise and leave the gentlemen to their port was given. Barrington looked wistfully after Beth as she left the room, but then Castlereagh asked him a direct question, and he was forced to put her from his mind.

Beth took a seat in the drawing room, seething at Lady Versley, who besides wearing a gown cut much too low had a tinkling laugh that Beth stigmatized as insipid, although Barrington had seemed to enjoy it. She wished she could leave, claiming a headache. Indeed, she did have the headache, she realized, even as she smiled and chatted with the ladies.

When the gentlemen rejoined them, Barrington made his way purposefully straight to her side, and since she was at that moment quite alone, he did not have to maneuver an interested female away from their conversation. "Miss Cummings," he said, bowing to her. She nodded her head slightly, and he took the seat beside her.

"I always seem to be apologizing to you, do I not?"

Beth looked at his smiling face bent toward her, and her heart turned over.

He continued, "May I ask you to disregard my second note which was written in anger, and believe the first one to be the accurate account of my feelings? Although I do so very much want you to be 'mine, etcetera'!" He paused, and Beth looked wildly around for her father. She saw him completely absorbed in a conversation on the other side of the room, so there was no help there.

191

Barrington waited, so she drew a deep breath, and not looking at him, replied, "How dare you bring this up now, in a crowded drawing room where I cannot escape you? However, if you insist on it, let me tell you that you may consider my *one* note to be accurate, sir. I will *not* grant you an interview, I will *not* accept your flowers and notes, and I must ask you to stop badgering me!"

The duke made as if to speak, but she rushed on.

"I must also tell you that it is all quite useless, for I am about to become betrothed to another." Horrified at what she had said, she stopped and stole a glance at the duke. Barrington was very pale, his narrowed eyes intent on her face.

"And who is the lucky man that I must wish happy?" He paused, unable to continue, but Beth could still feel his piercing eyes. She wished with all her heart that she could recall her words! Why had she said something so untruthful and so foolish? She thought for one desperate moment of confessing the lie, but if she did, he would think her mad, not understanding that she had spoken heedlessly, breathless from being so close to him. She thought that quite the most dreadful part of this conversation was that it was conducted in smiling whispers, with occasional nods to the other guests who glanced their way.

The duke spoke again, his voice rough with anger. "Is it a secret, Miss Cummings, this gallant suitor of yours? You need not fear I mean to harm him; if you prefer him there is nothing more to be said!"

If Beth had been attending she would have heard the rough emotion in his voice and seen the bleak look in his eyes, but she was casting desperately about in her mind for a scapegoat.

"Oh, as to that, your grace," she said airily, "I am sure it will not be a secret much longer! It is Allensworth, of course!" Dear God, she thought, now what have I done? I only hope Tony will understand why I had to use his name!

Barrington rose and bowed to her. "One can only hope that it was Anthony Allensworth you chose; Dolph would be sure to drive you mad in a month! Of course it is unfortunate that you will have the second son!" he added sarcastically, deeply hurt.

Beth looked up at him furiously. "How dare you!" she hissed. "As if being the second son made any difference to me! And let me tell you, sir, that even Adolphus Allensworth would be preferable to you!"

Barrington bowed again, and left her to enjoy an extremely hollow victory. She sat quietly for a moment, regaining her composure, and then she joined her father by the fireplace, trying to appear unconcerned. She chatted with Nicholas Vansittart, chancellor of the Exchequer, and asked a few questions of Lord Eldon, but her heart was across the room with the duke, gaily conversing with the ladies Versley and Richardson.

At last she was able to persuade her father to leave, and retired to her room as soon as they reached home. She was thankful that her grandmother was nowhere in sight, and that Mr. Cummings had not mentioned the duke as they drove home, to her great relief. Now all she had to do was write to Tony, asking him to call on her before the duke got to him first. She shuddered at the thought.

The next morning, the dowager duchess was surprised to receive a letter from Barrington at the breakfast table. Her son was deep in some papers, but he finally looked up as his mother murmured, "Good heavens! The man's not fit to be let out without a keeper! I told him not in a crowded drawing room! And as for your precious Beth, sir!"

She was easily persuaded to explain, and she read him the letter which detailed everything that had gone on since the duke's visit to her. When she reached the part where Beth had informed Barrington of her coming engagement to Tony Allensworth,

Mr. Cummings exclaimed, "There! You see you were wrong, mother! She did not love him after all!"

Lady Cummings snorted in disbelief. "If Anthony Allensworth knows anything about this, I will eat my best bonnet! This is all a fairy tale, but I could shake the girl! And now the duke has retired to his estates, and says he will give her up! I do not know when I have been so angry with all of you!" She rose from the table and swept from the room, leaving her bewildered son to wonder what he had had to do with it.

In reply to Beth's urgent note, Tony arrived that afternoon to take her driving, without Dolph as she had requested. She had told her grandmother of the expedition, and that lady had stared at her and said only, "Very well, if that is what you want, girl!"—in such a gruff tone that Beth was sure her arthritis was bothering her. When they had completed a circuit of the park, and Beth had not seen the duke anywhere, she leaned back, and stealing a sideways glance at Tony's handsome profile, drew a deep breath and began to speak.

"I have a confession to make, Tony," she said. Tony turned and smiled down at her. "I am afraid you will be very angry, and indeed I do not know what made me use your name, but . . ."

She paused, and Tony asked lightly, "Now how could I be angry, Beth? You know you have only to command me!"

Beth twisted her gloves in agitation. "Yes, but I don't think one can command in a situation like this! You see, I have told the duke of Barrington that we are betrothed!"

Tony nearly dropped the reins, causing his grays to skitter nervously.

"You what?" he asked incredulously.

"I . . . I told him we were to be married!"

"And why did you do that, may I ask?"

194

Beth did not dare to look at him again. "Well, he was bothering me to marry him, you see!"

"No, I *don't* see!" Tony exclaimed. "In that case, your reply should have been, 'Thank you very much for the honor you have bestowed on me, your grace, but I find myself unable to accept, for we should not suit,' or something of that nature. You do not refuse a man by claiming to be engaged to another!"

"Well," said Beth, determined to be honest at last, "I could not do that, for we *should* suit, and I would like it above all things!"

"You would? Then why did you refuse him? I shall never understand women!" he added darkly, bowing to Lady Jersey.

"It is not easy to explain. Oh, Tony, what am I to do now? He made me so angry, and I wanted to punish him, and now I have lost him forever!"

Tony took one look at the anguish in her face and swallowed his retort that he appeared to be punished himself as well.

"There now, Beth, perhaps all is not lost! If we don't become engaged he may try again, and you can tell him you were mistaken in my character or something. After Dolph's behavior at the inn I'm sure he will find it easy to believe we are both loose-screws! To tell you the truth, although I would be willing to render almost any service to you, I do not wish to marry!" Feeling this had hardly been complimentary to the lady, he added hastily, "Not that I wouldn't like to marry you, of course, if matrimony were in my immediate plans!"

Beth had to chuckle a little at this, and then she fiercely blew her nose. "Please do not fear entrapment, my dear Tony! But oh dear, what if he does not try? I have really been horrid to him!"

Tony did not think the haughty duke would ever have anything to do with her again, but he had no intention of stating that opinion. Suddenly she grasped his arm. "I know! Tony, could not you see him and explain?"

"*Me?* And what do you think his reaction would be if your supposedly successful suitor went to him and told him we had decided to call the whole thing off? Lord, I'd not make such a cake of myself! Besides, he'd probably shoot me for insulting you—devilish fine shot, the duke!"

They drove in silence for a while, Beth racking her brains for a solution, and Tony picturing a misty dawn and pistols for two. He shuddered.

"If I were you, my girl, I would tell your grandmother the whole. Up to snuff on every suit, she is. I'm sure she will be able to advise you better than I can!"

Tony became much more cheerful as he contemplated laying this burden on the dowager's elderly shoulders. Beth agreed reluctantly, and changed the subject, trying to chat gaily of the masquerade the following evening. Tony confided that Dolph did not like the idea of a costume, for which Beth was thankful. She had completely forgotten to ask her father for help with the twins' disguises. Tony said she would know them by their scarlet dominos, and then asked if she thought Barrington meant to attend, in a slightly worried way. Beth did not know, but begged him to be attentive to her if he was, so as not to cause the duke to realize she was a liar.

It was a confused Lord Anthony who finally handed her down from the carriage at the end of their outing. Driving off, he wished he had urgent business to attend to in northern Scotland, at the very nearest.

That evening, still unable to find a way to approach her grandmother with what she had done, Beth asked her casually if she thought the Duke of Barrington would be at the Markhams' masquerade, and the dowager replied carelessly, "Oh, he has gone out of town! Now who had I that from?" She frowned in thought.

"No matter, Grandmother," Beth said in relief. If Barrington had indeed left town, she need not fear a quarrel with Tony on her account, but her relief soon turned to sadness when she realized that she would probably never see him again.

CHAPTER X

Meresly Park was not the principal seat of the Duke of Barrington, but it had the advantage of being the closest of all his properties to London, and it was here that the duke retired, after writing his letter to Althea Cummings, the dowager duchess. He would not admit it to himself, but he had hopes that somehow she would be able to straighten out the tangled affair, and he would be summoned back to town.

He was far from optimistic, however, and Albert took to watching him carefully, wondering what was wrong. The duke spent most of his time alone in the library, although he was not occupied with estate matters, for he denied his agent admittance when that man came to present the books. He was also exceedingly curt when addressed, he wore a perpetual frown, and only Albert knew how long he stayed before the fire in the evening, with a bottle of brandy as his only companion. Careful questioning of the servants, including the duke's butler and valet, brought no light on the situation to the Indian.

Barrington was indeed miserable. He had not really believed Beth when she had told him she was about to become betrothed to Tony Allensworth, but when no reply to his letter came from the duchess, he was forced to reexamine the situation. He recalled how attentive Tony had been at the Bird and Bottle; the way he had looked at her and held her hand when they were building the snowman; the times he had taken her driving in the park. Why, even the first time he had seen her in London at the Jervis ball, she had been dancing with Allensworth! Perhaps she did prefer him—he was certainly a handsomer man and much closer to her own age! He groaned as he thought of them together. Perhaps he had been mistaken in his assessment of the lady's feelings, and blinded by his own love into thinking it was returned.

The morning after he had these illuminating but discouraging insights, he told Albert that he was thinking of returning to Canada and would see about passage for them both. Albert was pleased, not only because he was at long last going back to his own people, but also because he felt the duke would do better away from here. Albert had learned a great deal, and his English was much improved, but he still considered the duke's people to be crazy—the way they dressed, and talked, and the houses they lived in! How could any sane man be content to live as they did, he wondered to himself, especially crowded into the filth and noise of London? He remembered the forests and clear streams of his own country, and he thought of his father and mother, and all his tribe, especially a certain dark-eyed girl, and knew it would be a great relief to be back among his own people, where he was not stared at and feared. He had borne the pointing fingers and whispers for the duke's sake, but he had not been content here, although he allowed no sign of it to mar his imperturbability. Surely the duke's poor spirits would disappear when they rode together through the trackless forests of America!

That evening, when he came late to the library to see if there was anything the duke wanted, he surprised him holding the waterstained résumé that Beth had used for her telescope. Unaware of the Indian, Barrington was smoothing it carefully, a look of such misery on his face that Albert was stunned. Could it be that all this uproar was over a silly, worthless woman? If the duke wanted her, why did he not take her? Albert knew that if he had asked for his maiden and been refused, he would have assembled a raiding party and carried her off without delay. Something very like a smile crossed his dark face as he contemplated the inevitable ending to such a raid, but since he knew the girl was willing, he did not have to go to that extreme; indeed he knew she was waiting patiently for his return, for they had been promised to each other a long time ago.

He folded his arms and stared at the duke intently. Barrington had shown himself a brave man many times, once saving Albert from death when an American had fired on them from ambush. If the duke had not thrown him to the ground a second before the shot, he would be dead now. He owed the duke his life, and since it appeared that he was not prepared to settle this affair himself, Albert determined to do it for him. Then they could all three take ship to Canada if there was an uproar over the loss of the woman. He knew he did not know all the English ways, so he assumed it was not from loss of bravery that the duke held back, but he found it hard to believe that any fuss would be made over one girl; there were plenty more around.

As Barrington folded the paper and returned it to his pocketcase, Albert moved forward to add another log to the fire. The duke poured himself some more brandy and tried to smile.

"Go to bed, my friend," he said. "There is no need of both of us losing our sleep!"

Albert nodded, and then spotting some invitation
201

cards strewn on the desk, went to straighten them, causing one to fall to the carpet. The duke frowned down at it.

"Ha! The Markham masquerade! They will have to do without the Duke of Barrington, I'm afraid! I had intended to go dressed as you, brother, in ceremonial robes. What a sensation that would have been, for we are very much alike, my friend, except for the color of our skin, and that could have been remedied." He picked up the card and stared at it. "Tomorrow night! Well, I have no intention of going and watching Allensworth dance attendance on her. Women!"

He dropped the card to the carpet again and resumed staring at the fire. Albert picked it up and turned it over in his large hands, but he did not return it to the pile on the desk.

The next morning he asked Barrington for permission to be away that night, and the duke granted it absently, absorbed in his own thoughts, thinking that perhaps Albert had found a willing maid in the village. The Indian packed a large saddlebag carefully and left that afternoon, dressed in the conventional clothes of a servant. When he reached the duke's town house, he slipped into the stables with his horse and rubbed the animal down carefully. Then he saddled two more horses and left them in their stalls while he went into the house with his saddlebag. It was full dark before he left again, riding one horse and trailing the other. He was wrapped in a voluminous cloak of the duke's, and since the servants had become used to him, no one remarked his appearance or errand. Mrs. Beatty, the housekeeper, had given him directions, and he soon found himself in Eaton Square, where the masquerade was being held. He halted the horses away from the bright flares that lit the doorway and watched the guests arriving. It was early, but from the crowds of carriages, sedan chairs, and people, all London had been summoned to appear. He snorted in disbelief as he saw the costumes, and could barely control a laugh at an obese elderly gentleman dressed as Henry VIII, and his wife in her huge hoops, and powder and patches. Finally he rode on, on the other side of the street, avoiding the links boys and crossing sweepers, and the crowds of curious Londoners come to see the spectacle. At the corner, he turned into the mews behind the houses. It was quieter here, but Albert had no intention of leaving the horses near the Markham stables, where there was a lot of light and activity. He found a house farther away that was in complete darkness, and slipped from the horse's back to reconnoiter. The shutters were up, and there was no sign of life, so he led the horses into the yard and tethered them to a convenient post.

Quietly, he crossed the yards by slipping quickly from one patch of darkness to the next until he gained the side of the Markham townhouse. There were few lights on in this portion of the ground floor, but he could see that the ballroom above was brilliantly lit. He frowned, looking up to the shallow balconies outside the long windows, for he did not like to be trapped in a situation that offered scant chance of a quick retreat. There was no help for it, however, if he wanted to observe the masquerade, so without further delay he went to a drainpipe and tested it to see if it would bear his weight. In a few seconds he was on the balcony, cautiously peering through the undraped window at the fantastic scene inside.

The Dowager Duchess of Woltan and her granddaughter were even then arriving at the front door. Beth had tried many times to speak to her grandmother, but her throat always seemed to close up tight, so she was no nearer a solution to her problem than she had been on her drive with Tony. She knew he would ask her tonight what the dowager had suggested, and she would have to disappoint him. Bleakly Beth thought that it was a good thing that the duke had not returned to town, for she did not want Tony to come to any harm. Lady Cummings was becoming impatient,

203

waiting for Beth to confide in her, and had determined to speak to her tomorrow.

Beth was dressed as a wood nymph. Her grandmother had been unable to arouse in her the slightest interest in her costume, and had finally chosen one for its simplicity and good looks without further consultation. The white gauze of the gown was decorated with gold braid and a knotted belt, and Beth wore a wreath of wild flowers on her head. Golden sandals and a mask completed her costume. The dowager was not in disguise—one of the advantages, as she tartly pointed out to Beth, of advanced age. "Probably one of the few, now I come to think of it, my love, for when you are older you don't have to do the silly things convention demands! No one will be at all surprised that I am not decked out as Lucretia Borgia or Cleopatra! Ha!" She pointed out a man dressed as a devil. "Do you look at that, Beth! If I'm not mistaken, 'tis Staunton-Reed, and someone should have told him his legs are not good enough to carry off that scheme!"

Beth paid the unfortunate Staunton-Reed little attention, for she had spied two scarlet dominos bearing down on her. The dowager frowned.

"Do you be so good as to smile, Beth! Wood nymphs are not supposed to look so miserable, although I am not perfectly sure why they are always pictured as being in transports of delight. I should think it a miserable existence, myself!" Beth inquired why, absently, and her grandmother added, "Well, rain, you know, to say nothing of ants!" This surprised a laugh from Beth, who curtsied to the gentlemen in scarlet.

"Miss Cummings! Your grace! Knew you at once!" one of them exclaimed, bowing to them elegantly.

"And why should you not, you silly man," the dowager exclaimed tartly, "since she is standing right next to me! Go away and dance, Beth, and enjoy yourself. And do not come near me again or everyone will

204

know who you are. The unmasking does not take place till midnight, you know."

Beth curtsied and agreed, and let Dolph lead her away. Tony muttered something about the next dance, and she nodded.

Unfortunately, Albert was not so lucky in guessing her identity, for this exchange had taken place out of his line of sight. Although Beth whirled right by the window he was staring through, he did not recognize her. He frowned, for he had not thought it would be so difficult to identify his quarry, but he had not reckoned with the costumes and the masks. He knew it was only a matter of time before someone looked out the window, or decided to open it for a breath of air, and he was becoming impatient. Originally he had thought he would be able to spirit Beth away, without making more than a brief appearance at the party, but now he saw that such measures would not succeed. He would have to join the merrymakers in the ballroom, and he was not at all certain he would be able to carry off his deception that he was the duke in disguise. He knew now, however, that he would have to try.

Soundlessly, he left the balcony the way he had come. He had found an old mask in the Duke's drawers that afternoon, and now he tied it on, feeling very foolish. He had the card of invitation for he had observed at other parties that he had accompanied the duke to, that these were necessary to gain admittance, but still he lingered under the window wondering if there were not perhaps some other way. Albert was no coward, but the thought of entering that hot crowded room pretending to be Barrington was more unnerving than killing a viper, shooting a mountain lion, or knifing an enemy, none of which he had ever hesitated to do without the slightest qualm.

Meanwhile, Beth had had to admit to Tony that she had not spoken to her grandmother. He looked so glum, that she said rallyingly, "Come, m'lord! Barrington is not here. He has obviously given up his pursuit, for I know he was invited to the party! Perhaps if we just go on as before—"

Tony interrupted her. "Yes, but eventually, you know, he will wonder why he does not see the announcement in the papers, and he may then very well seek me out for an explanation. What am I to say?"

Beth thought about this carefully, and then she sighed. "I guess I must speak to my grandmother after all. I faithfully promise to do so, m'lord, for I would not have you hurt for my sake."

"Lord, no!" Tony agreed fervently. "Not that I would not be glad to be of any service," he added doubtfully.

The masquerade continued, and as Tony had been right about the quality and quantity of the champagne, soon became more boisterous. Beth danced with Julius Caesar, a Pope, and a very bad imitation of Byron which caused her to remember a happier time. It was surely one of the season's most successful parties. She spotted Letty Orvis-Ryder dancing with Mr. Witherall whom she had confided to Beth had made her an offer. The gentleman looked dazed with his good fortune, for he was blessed with neither a title or immense wealth, but Letty had tumbled into love with him over her more prestigious suitors, and with her aunt's approval had accepted his proposal. Beth tried to be happy for her.

Albert, in the meantime, had made up his mind, and he retraced his steps to the horses, where he removed the duke's dark cloak. From the saddlebag, he drew out a feathered headdress and his own robe, which he donned carefully, and then he walked quietly around to the front of the house. Just before he came into the light of the portico, he put on his feathered headdress, and then he strode forward. The footmen came to attention, eyes wide, as he walked up the shallow steps and produced his card of invitation.

"Your grace!" said one, holding open the door with a low bow. Albert nodded carelessly, as he had seen Barrington do, and went inside. He shook his head as

206

another servant attempted to take his cloak, and went to a mirror to adjust his headdress, for he had observed that gentlemen often did this when entering, in order to straighten their cravats.

He looked magnificent, and every guest in the hall and on the stairs stared at him in astonishment. He wore soft doeskin breeches, almost white in color and trimmed lavishly with fringe and beads. Over a matching vest was thrown his long white fur robe, tipped with black mink tails. The feathered headdress made him appear very tall, even in his beaded moccasins, and he had his knife and a beaded pouch belted on his hip. His sinewy arms were bare except for two wide gold bracelets in the shape of serpents. He turned slowly, returning stare for stare, and wished to himself that he was facing an enraged grizzly instead of these English. Suddenly he remembered one other accessory, and drew from the pouch the duke's quizzing glass which he raised haughtily to observe the company. A shout of laughter came from the stairs, and a man in a black domino hurried down to him exlaiming, "Barrington! You cannot fool us, you know, even if you have dyed your skin! 'Pon rep, what a fantastic costume; it must be the real thing! I would have sworn it was your servant. So that is why you have not been among us these past few days!"

Still chattering gaily, the man took Albert's arm and led him up the stairs to the ballroom. Albert nodded to the guests, but he did not speak. The black domino escorted him into the ballroom, and called to several gentlemen nearby. "Look who has come among us, m'lords! 'Tis Barrington—is he not magnificent?"

Beth, who was once again dancing with Tony, turned to stare at the apparition in the doorway and stumbled. Tony appeared to be in shock as he steadied her and whispered, "I thought you said Barrington would not appear, Beth? The fat's in the fire now!"

Beth stared at the Indian as the other guests crowded around him, exclaiming and complimenting him. "Yes, but Tony, I am not perfectly sure that it *is* Barrington!"

Tony did not seem to hear her as he led her forward until they could hear the conversation. A man in pale-blue brocade and a powdered wig was asking the Indian what he had used to get his skin such a perfect shade. "For gad, sir," he simpered, "I fear that the masquerade will go on for many days for you, 'tis so well done!" Albert bowed distantly and replied in his native language. He knew he could not use his limited English here. The gentleman applauded, which he would not have done if he could have translated the highly uncomplimentary remark that Albert had made, and one lady said in a piercing tone, "Why, he is speaking Indian! How perfect!"

Someone presented Albert with a glass of champagne, which he refused, and folding his arms, he proceeded to search the ballroom. His eyes paused at the wood nymph, but he was not sure. The figure and height were right, and the hair the correct color, but he could not be certain. The musicians struck up another dance, and most of the crowd dispersed, to Albert's relief. He studied the guests again, his gaze returning to the lady in the white-and-gold gown. Suddenly he made up his mind, and as the dance ended and Beth curtsied to Tony, he strode purposefully up to her and took her arm. Beth was startled as he bent down and asked, "Miss Cummings?" She nodded without thinking, her eyes fearful, and without another word, Albert swung her up into his arms and stalked to the door.

"I say, sir!" Tony exclaimed, "You can't do that! Put her down!"

Albert paid no heed, and left the room, now an uproar of conjections and conversations. No one moved to intercept him, for such a thing was so unprecedented that the gentlemen were frozen where they stood, and for their sakes it was just as well. Albert came down the stairs and marched to the door, and the footmen hastily opened it for him. The quality had some strange ways, and it was not their position to

208

interfere, thank heavens, for there was a look about the man that held them back decisively. Beth said not a word, but since she was even more shocked than the rest, this was understandable.

Upstairs in the ballroom, an outcry against the duke was taking place, and Tony hurried to the dowager's side, fearing the elderly lady might be in need of his attention. He was surprised to find her sitting bolt upright and trying to look indignant, although he could have sworn there was a smile quivering behind her firm mouth.

"Your grace!" he said. "What should we do? Should we go after them?"

The dowager twinkled up at him and said, "You'll never catch them, m'lord! 'Pon rep, I have not been so entertained in years!"

Her old friend Lady Frances, seated beside her, dropped the salts she had just located in her reticule. Whatever did poor Althea mean? Surely she must be deranged by the incident!

Tony gaped at the lady too, and she rapped his hand smartly with her fan. "On your way, if you intend to save my granddaughter," she said, and added, "but I should warn you that the duke will not be easily persuaded to give up his prize!"

"Althea!" Lady Frances exclaimed. "Whatever do you mean?"

Several guests had crowded around by this time, and the dowager spoke loudly enough for everyone to hear. "Such a novel way of announcing a betrothal, don't you agree? I have known this age, but I did not know that Alistair planned to carry her off the way savages do! So that is why he would have me dress her as a wood nymph! I shall roast him for this, I assure you! I wonder if he means to return to accept congratulations on their engagement?"

The guests turned away in relief, agreeing the duke was certainly an original. Tony stayed beside the lady's chair, and she whispered, "No, it was not planned, Tony, but it could not be better!"

"But, ma'am," Tony whispered back, "I do not think it was Barrington after all. I believe it to be his servant, and what will he do to Beth?"

"Keep that thought to yourself, m'lord, I beg of you! He will take her to Barrington and that is all, and if the duke cannot settle this by himself, I wash my hands of him!" She snorted, and then smiled at her friends nearby.

At the same time, Albert had reached the horses and felt somewhat safer from pursuit. He stood an indignant Beth on her feet, and drawing his knife, showed it to her. "Do not scream, or make any sound at all!" Beth drew a deep breath as she looked into that serious threatening face, and nodded. He took out a leather thong from his pouch and proceeded to tie her hands before her, and then he removed her mask, and, opening the saddlebag wrapped a fur-lined cloak around her shoulders, bringing the hood well forward to hide her face. He removed his headdress and robe and donned the duke's dark cloak again, and after repacking the bag and securing it to the horse, he led Beth to the other mount.

"Wait!" she said, "I cannot ride astride in this!" She looked down at her gauze gown and thin evening slippers, but Albert merely grunted and threw her up on the horse's back. She grasped the saddle to steady herself as he handed her the reins.

"You ride!" he said grimly, and holding the leading rein mounted his own horse, and started them walking to the end of the mews. Beth thought of risking a scream, but there was no one in sight, and she really was frightened of the Indian now—he had looked so savage when he showed her the knife. She did not believe he would hesitate to use it if she gave any trouble, so she remained silent.

When they had left the vicinity of Eaton Square by way of the back streets, he picked up the pace a bit until they were on the outskirts of town. Beth had all she could do to keep her seat, for she was not used to riding astride, and it was difficult to control the horse with her hands tied, even though Albert did not let go the leading rein. There were few people about, for it was nearly midnight, and although once Beth saw the watch in the distance, she did not try to get their attention, for Albert turned and stared at her until her courage failed her. She was glad he had thought of the enveloping cloak; the night air was chilly, but more important, her gown had risen above her knees when he had put her in the saddle, and she had heard it rip for an ominously long time! She hoped he was not taking her far, for she could feel the skin on the inner sides of her legs beginning to chafe.

Once past the cobblestones, Albert urged the horses into a canter, and Beth realized it was to be a long ride after all. She set her chin and determined she would not show him any sign of weakness. On and on they rode for over an hour, until Beth thought she must have a respite or she would not be able to go on. She called to him, hating her frailty. "Albert! Can we not rest?" He slowed the horses, but he did not stop. "Not far, we go on!" he said, and she longed to have that knife for just a moment, especially as he added, "My lord's woman strong!"

Well, she thought indignantly, I'm not! His woman, I mean! And if he is taking me to Barrington, they will both be sorry!

She was not sorry, however, when Albert turned into a drive after several more long minutes of riding, and led her horse up to the front of a large country residence. There was very little light showing and it did not appear as if they were expected. Albert jumped lightly from his horse, and came to her to help her dismount. Beth would have avoided him, but when she tried to stand she was grateful for his support, for her legs were so sore that they would not hold her. Albert let her stagger a few steps, and then he picked her up, and throwing her over his shoulder, strode up the steps and through the door. She could not see much but the floor. She was in an absolute fury now. To be treated so, like a sack of meal! The Indian stopped and knocked on a door. There was a pause, and then a familiar voice called, "Come!" Albert opened the door and walked in.

As he put her down and turned her around, her flashing eyes saw Barrington rising incredulously from a chair beside the fire, spilling a glass of brandy in his astonishment. *"Beth?"* he asked, looking as if he were seeing a ghost.

Albert gave her a push toward the duke, and that was the final straw. She turned and raised her bound hands, and struck him a blow on the chest. "How dare you?" she exclaimed. "Take your hands off me!" Albert stood stoically, merely reaching out and capturing her flailing hands in one big fist before turning her around again to the duke.

"I have brought you your woman, sir," he said in English.

"I am *not* his woman!" Beth spat out in contempt, and Albert gave her a little shake.

"You will be!" he promised, unknowingly repeating Barrington's promise.

The duke by this time appeared to have regained control of himself. When he had first seen her carried in by the Indian, he was sure he had imbibed too much of his excellent brandy, but now he saw it was indeed Elizabeth Cummings in person, and not a drunken reverie. In spite of the voluminous cloak and the ruin of her gown, he was able to see that Beth was dressed for the masquerade, even down to the floral wreath in her hair, now somewhat the worse for wear. She looked like a furious kitten held so easily in Albert's strong grasp, and his mouth quivered appreciably for a moment before he strolled toward them.

"Miss Cummings," he said gravely, bowing to her. "And Albert! So this is why you wished to absent

212

yourself this evening! Am I correct in assuming that you attended the masquerade? Did you go as yourself, or as me? My reputation, Albert, my reputation!"

Albert spoke at length in his own tongue, and the duke laughed out loud. "Of course! The quizzing glass convinced them!" He seemed to recall Beth. "Come, my dear," he said, holding out his hand to her. "Please be seated before the fire, I am sure you must be cold. A glass of wine will soon have you feeling more the thing."

Beth shook herself free of Albert and said coldly, "Undo my bonds, if you please, sir!"

Barrington seemed to consider this carefully. "Do you know, I don't believe I will just yet, for I am afraid you might try to do me some harm, and having more conventional manners than my brother, would not feel able to defend myself!"

Beth stared at him. "I believe you are inebriated!"

"No, no," the duke assured her. "A little shot in the neck perhaps, but by no means pot-valiant! Albert, do you fetch me some bread and cheese, and a cup of coffee! That should do it."

He led Beth to a chair by the fire, and gravely seated her. She reached up her hands to brush a strand of hair away from her face, and managed to tip the wreath over one ear. The duke turned away for a moment, and then said to her, with just the bare suggestion of a laugh in his voice, "If I may be so bold, my dear Miss Cummings, you look in worse case than I! I fear you have had a very rousing time tonight! Was it very good champagne? Shall I procure you some coffee too?"

Beth glared at him and clamped her mouth shut tightly.

"In the sulks, my dear?" he inquired, pouring her out a glass of brandy. "Here, drink this, I was only funning about the champagne! You will soon feel much better."

Beth thought of refusing, but she was thoroughly

213

chilled, and knew the brandy would warm her, so she accepted it in both hands and took a small sip. The duke smiled down at her and then stirred up the fire and threw on another log, before taking the seat across from her.

"I shall be most anxious to hear your version of this evening, Miss Cummings," he said courteously, "when you have stopped being on the fret, you know."

"I have no intention of conversing with you, sir," Beth said distantly. "I am sure it would be a waste of time, for as well as being intoxicated, you appear to have lost all sense of propriety!"

"Very true," the duke agreed amiably. "I wonder that it took me so long to do so! I am exceedingly grateful to Albert for showing me the way!"

The door opened, and the Indian slipped in with a tray. He poured the duke some coffee and handed him the cup before moving to stand again before the door. The duke drank thirstily, and ate some bread and cheese before he spoke again.

"Now, that is more like it! Thank you, brother. Now let us consider what has to be done." He looked at Beth carefully, and then rose and went to his desk, where he wrote a short note. As he sealed it, he said, "I am sorry to have to ask you to return to town, Albert, but it is necessary that this note be delivered as soon as possible."

Albert nodded, and then asked him something in his own tongue which caused both men to burst out laughing.

Insufferable! Beth thought to herself. "Just you wait, my Lord duke!"

After a few more instructions, the Indian left, and Barrington strolled back to the fire. "You must excuse me. Albert merely wanted to be sure I did not require his help in handling such a little wildcat. I was able to reassure him, however! The note is to your father and grandmother, for I would not have them worry about your whereabouts. I have invited them to join us here ... er ... tomorrow!"

"Tomorrow!" Beth exclaimed. "But ... but that will be too late! I must return to my grandmother tonight, for my father is gone out of town!"

The duke looked at her intently. "It is already too late, my dear. I have no intention of returning you to anyone, ever again. I told you you would be mine, and now you see I meant it! It is really too much for you to expect that I will meekly return you to young Allensworth; I am not that altruistic!"

Beth was furious. "You may ruin my reputation, your grace, but nothing on earth will compell me to submit to you, of that you can be sure. So unless you intend to keep me tied up forever, you have lost!"

Barrington came to stand over her, and as he put both hands on the arms of her chair, neatly imprisoning her, she shrank back in alarm. His face was very close to hers, and his eyes were very serious as he said, "If I thought you meant that, ... but somehow I do not! Now I am going to give you up to my housekeeper. You will feel more the thing after a good night's rest."

Beth wondered that he did not touch her or kiss her after all his threats, and was completely confused, but the duke was holding himself on a very tight rein. He would wait until the dowager was in residence before he went any further. He wanted no reluctant bride, nor one that had been forced into marriage by the circumstances. He knew that by right he should order a carriage and restore her to town this very night, but the brandy had made him careless of convention. He rang the bell, and then strolled back to Beth.

"Now, my dear, I am going to untie you. It is entirely up to you whether this goes any further or not. I shall explain to my servants that the dowager has been delayed but will be with you tomorrow morning. If you behave yourself, and stop trying to think of revenging yourself on me, we can carry it off. I have no desire to harm your reputation, after all." He bent and untied the thong from around her wrists, and moved away, watching her carefully, as she chafed them.

"Since my reputation is now in shreds, I do not see how it can be harmed any further," she said furiously. "But do not fear, sir, I have no wish to treat your servants to a hysterical scene!"

"How very wise of you, my dear! You will make a superb duchess, I have always thought so! Althea Cummings will of course let it be known that she traveled down to Meresly Park from the ball this evening, and my servants of course will concur, in the extreme unlikelihood of their being asked about it."

There was a knock on the door, and the duke's housekeeper entered. If this good woman was surprised, she gave no sign of it, just as if, thought Beth, she was used to being summoned in the middle of the night and told to put miss in the blue bedchamber and prepare rooms for the young lady's grandmother every night in the week. The duke bowed to Beth, a devil dancing in his eyes, as she gathered her cloak around her to leave.

"A very good night to you, Miss Elizabeth," he said formally. "Oh, Mrs. Kiley, the lady's baggage has gone astray. Please be so good as to procure her some nightclothes. These highwaymen!"

Mrs. Kiley smiled and nodded, just as if she believed such nonsense, and said, "Come, Miss, you will soon forget them. What a fortunate thing the duke rescued you!"

Beth made no reply as she followed her from the room, her mind in a whirl. She thought she would have trouble sleeping, but when Mrs. Kiley had lit the fire and brought her hot water and slipped a warming pan between the sheets, she was more than grateful to accept the nightgown that had been provided and get into bed with a cup of warm milk. Her last thought was that she would know better what to do in the morning when she felt more the thing.

The dowager duchess was not at all surprised to receive the duke's note when Albert had galloped back to town, for she astounded her butler by saying that she would wait up, as she was expecting a message, and desiring Wardwell to bring some tea to the library. She was just as glad that Edward had gone out of town for a few days, for she knew he would not approve of this situation at all. She herself had had to call on all her wit and experience at the masquerade, as friend after friend had come up and demanded the true version of the engagement, but she had managed to fob them off by saying she had known of it all along. Her one worry now was that Beth would dig in her heels and refuse to marry the duke, no matter what happened to her reputation, but when Albert appeared and was shown into the library by an astounded Wardwell, and she had read his note, she felt better.

"Now Albert . . . is that your name, sir?" she asked the Indian. He nodded respectfully. "Well, you may return here to escort me to Meresly Park at eight. That should be early enough, especially after such jollification as society has indulged in tonight! I do not expect anyone will see us leave, a matter of the first importance!"

Albert nodded, and bowed and took his leave, and the dowager went up to bed after giving her dresser several instructions and telling this austere person to keep her tongue between her teeth over the matter unless she was prepared to immediately lose her position without any hope of a reference. Miss Atkins sniffed. "I wouldn't so demean myself, your grace, as to mention it."

The dowager was ready the next morning in good time, and let Albert hand her and her dresser into the duke's traveling coach, while the coachman secured their baggage. As they were arriving at Meresly some time later, Beth was just waking up, so she missed the gratifying sight of her grandmother being welcomed by the duke. He took her to the breakfast room and poured her a cup of coffee.

"Now, duchess! I cannot tell you how delighted I am to see you again," he said, a positively wicked grin on his face.

"I'll be bound you are, Barrington," the old lady said tartly. "I only hope we can bring her safe out of it. What a stir at the party last night when your Indian swooped her up in his arms and strode from the room!"

"I wish I might have seen it!" Barrington said fervently.

"I, for one, am glad you did not! I have convinced everyone that it was you, you see, and it was your original way of announcing your engagement. No doubt they think you have picked up some unusual habits among the savages, but I felt no compunction at all in sacrificing your name! I am sure that between us, our credit is good enough to carry it off. What did you say to Beth? Is it settled?" She leaned forward eagerly, but he shook his head.

"I may have ragtail manners that even include abduction, but even I know better than to press her when she is so helpless. Besides, if I had proposed last night, she would have created a scene that would have awakened the dead! You have no idea how angry she was. Whew!"

The dowager laughed. "I can imagine it! Under that meek exterior there lurks quite a temper, all unbeknownst to her father. But, if I may, Barrington?" She paused until he nodded.

"I think the time for apologizing and formality is over. It has not stood you in very good case up to now, I am sure you will agree." She stopped again, and looked at him consideringly, and the duke's eyebrows

218

rose. "You are still of the same mind? She has not angered you to the point? . . ."

Barrington interrupted. "No, no, ma'am! In fact, I am more determined to have her than ever! But Allensworth . . . she told me . . ."

"Pooh!" Lady Cummings said grandly. "Pay it no mind! That was just a red herring to draw you off the scent, but I am afraid she will refuse you again, if you let her!"

The duke rose and said, "I have no intention of giving her the chance!"

"Good!" the dowager agreed with a smile. "And now perhaps I could see this tiresome granddaughter of mine? I have a few things to say to her that might be helpful. I will send her to you presently."

The duke had his butler escort the lady to Beth's room, and waited impatiently in the library. It seemed a very long time before the butler knocked and announced, "Miss Elizabeth Cummings, your grace."

The dowager had found Beth still in bed, sipping her chocolate, and rung a grand peal over her before she had a chance to tell her own indignant story. Beth stopped trying to interrupt her after the lady said tartly, "Now Beth, *you* know you love him; *I* know you love him! What good purpose will it serve to continue to be so stupidly obstinate? Let me tell you, my girl, pride makes a very cold bedfellow! Do you really care so little for Alistair that you will whistle him down the wind for a stupid whim or sense of injury? Why, he has been so miserable since you told him of your approaching nuptials with young Allensworth that even the Indian noticed it and resolved to help him! And if I may say so, miss, I never expected the daughter of a minister to be so blatantly untruthful! Think carefully, and then tell me if you can that you do not love the man . . . and mind, no tall stories to me, if you please!"

Beth blushed, and tears started up in her eyes. "Of

219

course I love him, Grandmama, but . . . Oh dear! It is all so dreadful!"

The dowager begged her to wipe her eyes and not be such a wet goose as she rang the bell for her dresser.

"Now I will leave you, my love. Do you wear the peach muslin, and let Atkins do your hair becomingly. When you are dressed, the butler will take you to Barrington."

"Can you not come too?" Beth whispered, and the dowager laughed as she turned to leave the room.

"I cannot conceive of what use I would be at such a scene! Or why you would both not be wishing me at the devil after a very few minutes! Do not be silly!"

Beth allowed herself to be dressed in the peach muslin, and all too soon found herself going meekly downstairs to the butler. Her heart was pounding so hard as he announced her that she was sure both men heard it, but she curtsied to the duke and kept her eyes lowered. She heard the butler shut the door behind him as he left, and then heard the duke's footsteps as he came to stand before her, but she did not raise her eyes.

"Beth? Will you not look at me, my love?" she heard, in accents so unlike the duke's usual tones that she looked up startled. He was very close to her, and her eyes widened at what she saw in his dark face. Before she could speak, he reached out for her and clasped her in his arms. He held her very close, and she was sure he heard her heart beating now, even as she felt his. For a long moment he searched her face, and then he bent his head and kissed her. She tried to put up her hands to hold him away, but he was too strong for her and had no intention of letting her go.

Whatever she had imagined an embrace to be, she was completely unprepared for the tide of emotion that welled up in her breast, and before she knew what she was doing she put her arms around his neck, and stopped trying to get away from him. His mouth was warm and insistent on hers, and she kissed him

220

back eagerly. After a long moment he raised his head and smiled at her.

"My love!" he said huskily, and then he gave her a little shake. "You will not marry Allensworth! You will marry me, do you understand? You will never leave me again!"

Beth laughed unevenly as his hands tightened possessively on her shoulders. "If you continue to hold me so tightly, I do not see how I will be able to do so!" she said, and immediately he dropped his hands and moved away slightly.

"Do you want me to, my dear?" he asked softly.

Beth hesitated, and then she raised her chin, and smiling at him, came back into his arms. "Now I will be honest at last and tell you I do not! I have been such a fool, for I have loved you for such a long time!" She buried her head on his coat in sudden embarrassment at her boldness.

The duke held her close and showered kisses on her hair, her cheeks, and her throat, and Beth closed her eyes in delight as he found her mouth again. This kiss surpassed even the first, and they were both breathless when they broke apart.

" 'She walks in beauty like the night,' " the duke murmured, and finished the quote. This called for further kisses, and it was some time before he took her arm and led her to the French doors overlooking the terrace. Opening them with the other hand, he drew her out into the sunlight. She looked at him shyly, and he smiled down at her fondly.

"I think we had better stroll up and down here, m'love, for I am about to propose to you without further delay, and if we remain in the library I may forget to do so! Just a formality, of course, but since I am known for my impeccable behavior . . ."

Beth laughed at him. "*And* your gentle manners, *and* your obsequious servants!" she agreed cordially.

He grinned. "I'll have no sarcasm from you, my girl!" he warned her. "I know what is due to one of my

221

exalted station! Persons of *my quality* have to be treated well, or *steps will be taken!*"

Beth laughed out loud at his imitation of Mrs. Orvis-Ryder, but then she stopped as he took both her hands in his and looked at her seriously.

"I always meant it, my dear, you know, for I have loved you more dearly than I had ever thought possible, even before the misadventure of the missing paper." Beth started to speak, but he put his fingers gently over her lips. "No, do not interrupt me, love! I have the honor to ask you to be my duchess, and the only thing you had better say is 'yes,' for I have not only your grandmother's but your Father's consent as well!"

Beth withdrew her hands and swept him a grand curtsy. "If you please, your grace," she said, "Elizabeth Cummings will be honored to be 'yours, etcetera,' and wishes it above all things!"

The duke drew her up and clasped her in his arms again, to the delight of an undergardener engaged in trimming the rose trees, an upstairs maid who was shaking a duster out one of the bedroom windows, and a dowager duchess who now stood at the library window. "Thank heavens!" that elderly lady exclaimed, and went out into the sunshine to join them.

A touch of romance... from Cordia Byers